atable and bitingly funny, *Dragging Mason County* is a
of friendship, self-acceptance, and the importance of
uring."

RISTOPHER SNIPES, author of *Milo and Marcos at the End*

d with big heels, big laughs, and a big heart. *Dragging*
ty reminds us about the importance of community, the
bility—regardless of where you live—and the courage it
ourself."

NCIS, author of *Fruit*

ry single page is overflowing with hilariously sharp, sassy,
g prose—making the amount of times I found myself gig-
unatic, screaming 'Oh my GOD' impossible to count. Make
son County part of your self-care routine."

UAL BONANNO, writer and performer of Aunty Donna

son County is like a good drag show: fun, messy, celebra-
r much too soon. Peter and the queens of The House of
ss show us how much a positive queer space means to
cially young people."

ON, author of *The Year Shakespeare Ruined My Life*

nd full of heart . . . Come for the snappy dialogue and an
o cutting it's almost lethal—stay for the surprisingly com-
der heart underneath."

A MAE JONES, author of *The Queen of Junk Island*

son County feels like the teenage love child of David Sedaris
ters. Smart, funny, relevant, and ultimately touching."

cIVOR, award-winning playwright and performer

startlingly timely story about drag's ability to transform
son, but a community."

OLIVEIRA, GLAAD Media Award–winning author

PRAISE FOR
DRAGGING M

"Hold on to your wigs! *Dragging
heartwarming story of acceptance
sickening cast of characters with
talent to spare."
—**ERIK J. BROWN,** author of *Lose
in the World*

"With biting humor and big perso
serves up enough memorable on
RuPaul's Drag Race. But at its shi
emotionally tender story about lea
are . . . and celebrate it as well."
—**BRIAN D. KENNEDY,** author of *A*

"*Dragging Mason County* is a timely
with its humanity. This gem of a r
and hairspray. A worthy and import
—**BONNIE-SUE HITCHCOCK,** autho
Houses and *Everyone Dies Famous*

"I loved Peter's personal journey of
lenges of prejudice and intolerance
show his county has ever seen. *Drag
ing young adult novel that celebrates
advocacy in a digital age, and the tra
—**BOMBAE,** from *Canada's Drag Ra*

"A hilarious romp through small tow
all sequins and glitter, but behind t
messy, fraught friendship and self-d
—**TANYA BOTEJU,** author of *Kings, Qu*

"Painfully r
timely tale
proper con
—**KEVIN CH**
of the Wor

"A book fil
Mason Co
need for v
takes to b
—**BRIAN F**

"Literally e
and shock
gling like
Dragging
—**MARK S**

"*Dragging*
tory, and
Rural Rea
people, e
—**DANI JA**

"Fast, witt
acerbic w
plex and
—**ALEXAN**

"*Dragging*
and John
—**DANIEL**

"A sharp
not just a
—**ANTHO**

CURTIS CAMPBELL

DRAGGING MASON COUNTY

annick
press
toronto • berkeley

Cover art by Jenn Woodall, designed by Sam Tse

Interior design and typesetting by Rachel Nam

Edited by Khary Mathurin

Copy edited by Mary Ann Blair

Proofread by Anne Fullerton

Annick Press Ltd.

We acknowledge the support of the Canada Council for the Arts and the Ontario Arts Council, and the participation of the Government of Canada/la participation du gouvernement du Canada for our publishing activities.

 ONTARIO ARTS COUNCIL
CONSEIL DES ARTS DE L'ONTARIO
an Ontario government agency
un organisme du gouvernement de l'Ontario

Library and Archives Canada Cataloguing in Publication

Title: Dragging Mason County / Curtis Campbell.
Names: Campbell, Curtis (Author of Dragging Mason County), author.
Identifiers: Canadiana (print) 20230169120 | Canadiana (ebook) 20230169260 | ISBN 9781773217871
(hardcover) | ISBN 9781773217888 (softcover) | ISBN 9781773217895 (HTML) | ISBN 9781773217901 (PDF)
Classification: LCC PS8605.A54295 D73 2023 | DDC jC813/.6—dc23

Published in the U.S.A. by Annick Press (U.S.) Ltd.
Distributed in Canada by University of Toronto Press.
Distributed in the U.S.A. by Publishers Group West.

Printed in Canada
annickpress.com

Also available as an e-book. Please visit annickpress.com/ebooks for more details.

FOR SCARLETT.

CHAPTER ONE
MIDDLE-AGED MAN-BABY

"This was a terrible idea," I inform Alan. "You know how I feel about mixing with the locals."

The parking lot of the Dairy Freeze is radiating heat, and we're caged in on either side by souped-up pickup trucks. Alan Goode and I don't fit the *quaint small-town life* profile on a good day, but in his short-shorts and coiffed hair, Alan sticks out like a gay thumb. It's drawing the attention of the girl sitting in the truck bed of her lofty war machine of a vehicle. The scrutinizing glare of Chrissy McPhee, wealthiest member of Mason Central Secondary's ruling class, is as familiar as it is unwanted. I'm sure that plenty of guys in Mason County would love to be ogled by a girl with the keys to her own all-terrain vehicle, but I just want to bat her attention away with my notably limp wrists.

"Look, I've always been *very* fashion forward, Peter," Alan replies. "And if people can't handle it, then that's between them and their god."

"Fashion requires wearing clothing," I say, wiping sweat from my eyes. "Your short-shorts barely count as fabric."

I try not to look at Chrissy, knowing that she's got more than a few opinions on the way that Alan's nipples are nearly busting out of the T-shirt he recently whittled into a stringy tank top. Chrissy is tiny, even from the top of her mecha-truck, but she has the legs of a volleyball player, so it always feels like she's about to kick a hole through your chest. Her blonde hair is chemically rigid, and her pinched face always seems to be scanning you for structural weaknesses. Which is exactly what I can feel it doing right now.

From the corner of my eye I catch a second head bobbing out from behind Chrissy. The line moves forward a touch and I pray that Brison Dallas, gay best friend to Chrissy McPhee, remains silent on the topic of our physical appearances for once in his life. Alan and I look like gay kids in a gritty indie movie about plucky rural queers winning a poetry competition. Brison Dallas, on the other hand, looks like a model kick-starting his acting career in a movie about a teen werewolf hunter.

Alan's skin may be clear and porcelain, given his meticulous nighttime skincare routine, but mine is an oozing mess. My face is a perpetual *before* picture in those late-night skin-treatment commercials. Alan, on the other hand, is fat. He says this proudly, never shying away from the word in a crusade to *destigmatize rotundness*. Alan is also the kind of tall that involves ducking through doorways and shopping at specialty stores. My own drooping belly sits below a set of wibbly T-Rex arms and what Alan often describes (in a froggy French accent) as my *li'l floppy tiddies*. At which point he flips both of them like a hamburger and makes a satisfied sizzling sound. Alan has a swooping mane of hair, while my hairline has already begun to consider retirement. My round face gives me the features of an old baby and my terrible posture makes me look like an old man. Think of me as a middle-aged man-baby. I know I do. All of this is to say that Alan and I are not the six-packed gays you see selling supplements while you're scrolling through Poster.

"Oh!" Alan says, lighting up and waving. "Hi, Chrissy, hi, Brison!"

I look toward the truck only to discover that, yes, Brison does have a single eyebrow raised in a galling exhibition of his typical smuggery.

Chrissy waves with an icy titter.

"I hate them," I hiss.

"I know, baby," Alan tuts with motherly concern. He lays his hand between my shoulder blades before realizing his mistake and wiping the sweat off his hand using what little bit of surface area his shorts can afford him. The line ahead of us moves, and it's a relief to disappear from view behind the comically oversized tires of the Mad Max truck to my left.

"And I don't get why you're so nice to them," I continue.

"I'm not *nice*," Alan explains. "I'm just cordial."

"They're not nice to *you*, Alan. You don't need to be nice to them."

I remind him of this despite knowing exactly why Alan continues to offer them a good-natured smile. Alan changes the subject with as much subtlety as his short-shorts.

"I have big news, Peter," Alan announces grandly. "Please don't let your silly little schoolyard grumbles spoil my day."

"I resent that characterization. And, what, did you finally get that piece of popcorn out of your teeth?"

"No," he sighs. "But I have named her Poppy and made my peace with her. I will have you know that you are looking at someone who has recently had a post liked by drag royalty."

I say nothing and scan the menu board.

"Drag royalty, Peter!" Alan presses.

I search for something to say but come up empty. It's not that I hate drag. I just have no opinion on the matter. I consider myself dragnostic. Alan not only loves drag but loves *doing* drag. But to me, drag is a lot like playing the cello or doing the math with all the triangles. I can respect the amount of skill, craft, and determination that goes into it without getting any joy from the result. Not to mention the fact that doing drag just paints another target on your back. This target just happens to be painted with eyeliner.

"Fine," I comply. "What internet drag superstar has descended from the heavens to heart your offerings?"

"None other," Alan announces, "than Tess Tosterone!"

"Who?"

Alan slaps me on the arm, which to him is playful and to anyone on the receiving end is bruise inducing.

"Tess Tosterone is only the winner of *Dragathon* 2017, Peter. Largely considered one of the best seasons of the show, if not *the* best season by many notable media critics."

Dragathon is the Super Bowl for people dressing in wigs and heels. It's a competition show where drag queens from across the globe are selected to compete against one another in weekly performances before someone gets eliminated by the judges. Whoever is left standing at the very end is given a big golden crown and wins a bunch of money and sponsorship deals. *Dragathon* is massively popular, and weekly screenings at drag venues have become standing appointments for queers the world over. Unless you live in the middle of nowhere, like Mason, in the heart of Mason County. Alan is always showing me videos of drag brunch screenings, where queens in massive wigs and drawn-on eyebrows screen the show over eggs Benedict and mimosas while pouring pitchers of water over their fake boobs. Then Alan will sigh longingly and wish aloud that he could go to an event like that.

Because there is nowhere in Mason to actually perform. Alan performs on video and uploads it to YouTube. He's even pretty good at what he does. By the time Alan is done doing his makeup, wig, nails, and accoutrements, he has transformed into a statuesque woman named Aggie Culture. She even has a decent following on Poster.

Alan and, by extension, Aggie Culture, loves country music. While I spend most of my time online trying to find music and movies that bring a little bit of the real world into the hick-state dystopia that is Mason, Alan can't get enough of the local musical cuisine. His first Poster video was a mashup of "You Shook Me All Night Long" and "Ring of Fire." Somehow Alan manages to be from a different planet while still being the perfect product of the Mason County cultural slop bucket. Don't let anyone tell you that Alan Goode doesn't contain multitudes.

Alan grabs my arm in shock. "Oh my god. Who is *that*?"

We draw closer to the window as the line thins, revealing a teenage boy behind the counter who looks to be around our age. His dark, wavy hair is squashed beneath a black Dairy Freeze cap. His smile, delivered to the family in front of us, is slanted to the side. A tiny spattering of acne dots half of his sharp jawline. His eyes are a particularly fetching kind of blue, and when they land on mine, my chest pangs with an electrical lurch. Attractive men are a rarity in Mason, so it's not like I'm used to this kind of thing. Most of the boys at Mason Central Secondary are off the table by merit of their compulsory heterosexuality, to say nothing of their bootcut jeans, military buzz cuts, and their widely held belief that guns are actually kind of interesting.

Seeing a fresh, attractive face in Mason is what I imagine it's like to see a rare species of gazelle out in the wild. You want nothing more than to stare at their dainty little legs and curly horns, but you don't want to spook them in the process.

"The guy in the window?" I ask.

"Obviously," Alan replies, voice lowered conspiratorially. "Are you getting, like . . . *vibes* from him?"

"Vibes?"

"Yes, Peter. Vibes."

"Gay energies? LGBTQ v-i-b-e-s?"

"Vibes of the homosexually inclined, Peter, yes. Or at least some chaotic bisexual energies."

"How can you even tell?"

"Vibes are not predicated by talking alone," Alan pontificates. "There's also outfit, jewelry, hair, and how they pronounce the word *quinoa*. Have I taught you nothing?"

"Leave the poor guy alone. He doesn't need a pair of creeps breathing down his neck."

"I'd do more than just breathe down it."

The family in front of us clears and the Soft-Serve Guy waves us over. Alan places our order with a laugh in his voice while I avoid eye contact, looking at the sun-bleached seating and the spill residue covered in flies. As Soft-Serve Guy makes our chocolate and vanilla swirl dips, Alan plays it cool by scrolling Poster through the cracked screen on his phone.

"Oh my sweet baby god, Peter. She commented." Alan's eyes grow wide as his free hand clamps around his mouth.

"She commented?"

"Tess Tosterone *commented*!" Alan squeals while nearby customers scowl at our audible flouncy-ness.

"Did you just say Tess Tosterone?" asks a voice from behind the counter. Soft-Serve Guy is back, holding two ice-cream cones dipped in chocolate. His adorable face has lit up brighter, his smile becoming somehow even more lopsided.

"Yes!" says Alan. "You like Tess Tosterone?"

We drop our coins on the counter and he looks at us like we've asked if the sky is blue. "She's only the most talented queen to come out of *Dragathon*."

"This is so, so wild!" Alan howls. "We love *Dragathon*. Not a lot of people around here watch it."

Technically only *Alan* loves *Dragathon*, but right now I don't mind being lumped into the equation.

"I'm actually from suburbia-land," he says, shrugging. "I'm just visiting, so maybe I don't count. I still don't see much drag, but I did get to see a few shows at Pride this year before I came to work for my uncle. It's so important to get out there and support local drag artists, right?"

"Okay, you're going to love my page," Alan swears. From a little slip at the back of his phone case, Alan produces a white business card embossed with Aggie's trademark green wig. The two chat excitedly and I say nothing as a feeling of urgency settles over me. Alan has launched into a full song and dance while I can't even muster a quick hello to the only boy in the history of Mason County who can string together a complete sentence. For the first time in a very long time, silence feels like the wrong move entirely.

"I'm Lorne," says Soft-Serve Guy.

"I'm Alan, and this is my BFF, Peter."

I wave, knowing for certain that Lorne can only see my half-moon boob sweat.

Alan smiles widely at Lorne. "Well, let's talk drag sometime soon!"

Lorne waves the card and smiles back. We're halfway across the parking lot, our cones already melting, before it even occurs to me that my last chance to speak has come and gone. I know that I should just be glad I made it out without saying something humiliating, but for some reason I'm not.

"The vibes have been confirmed," Alan decrees, his delight only throwing my self-loathing into starker contrast. He makes for the shady stretch of grass and trees next to the parking lot.

"What, because he likes drag?"

"No, because he *loves* drag."

"Plenty of straight guys like drag, I bet. The bar for being a progressive straight dude has got to be *super* low, right?" I reason. "For all we know, he could just like the attention, like the time you deleted all your social media accounts for the weekend just to see if anyone would notice."

"It's called *Swift-ing*, Peter, and it is a perfectly acceptable means of gauging one's social standing."

"No," I contend, shaking my head. "You're doing what you always do."

"*Excuse* me? I don't *always* do anything. I'm an enigma, a mystery, like the Phantom of the Opera, or the guy who works at the dollar store who has a dancer's body."

"You always get your heart set on some guy who turns out to be, shockingly, heterosexual. Like the guy who works at the dollar store who has a dancer's body."

"Sorry if I prefer a tragic backstory. You know I'm an empath."

I lick chocolate goo off my knuckles, girding myself for yet another episode of *Why Can't He Just Like Me Back, Peter?* It's not a great show, but it's been on for, like, a million seasons.

"But this is a great day, Peter," Alan continues. "It's just like Tess Tosterone herself said when she commented on *my* Poster post."

"What did she comment, anyway?" I ask.

"She commented, and I quote, 'You love to see the magic of a pair of cowboy boots.' And isn't that, like, my entire brand?" Alan drops with a flourish beneath a tree and raises the cone to his lips before doing something rather unladylike with it.

"There is nothing magical about what you're doing with your mouth right now," I tell him.

"The magic of gay love!" Alan exclaims. "Soft-Serve Guy Lorne is going to follow my channel, and then he will fall in love with me."

I sit next to him and consider my options before I just let it go. I don't have the heart to point out that neither of us stands a chance with a guy like that, even if he is gay. Sometimes I wonder if Alan really does see the world as nothing but flapping bluebirds and a sun wearing sunglasses while waving a Pride flag. Do I tell him that pining after someone he's barely made eye contact with is going to end in heartbreak? Or do I let him play it out while keeping myself clear of the social carnage?

Alan regards me with a discerning eye. "And what about you?"

I blink. "What about me?"

"I have an open heart, Peter. Some could even say that I wear it on my sleeve. But I've known you forever and not once have I seen you take a stab at romance."

"See, that's your problem. Stabbing and romance do not mix."

"Oh, okay." He hunches his shoulders and folds his arms tight. "I'm Peter," he says in a grumpy-faced imitation of me. "I'd much rather make every single interaction a joke instead of knowing what it's like to feel true love." He's not wrong. I may be a constant companion to Alan's romantic misfires, but never once have I tried for romance of my own. I risk a glance back at the window, where the Soft-Serve Guy is leaning out and making small talk with a pair of camo-clad locals. Maybe Alan isn't totally off the mark. Closed off and guarded is *my* entire brand. But Soft-Serve Guy is handsome. I am not. Asking him on a date would do nothing but land me knee-deep in the kind of humiliation I've only received secondhand so far. It would also be a direct violation of my cardinal rule: I will avoid being notable, significant, or otherwise remarkable in any way. Being gay in Mason County is enough of a spotlight, which is why I do my best to keep my head down and avoid the mockery that is built into the gay-teen-in-a-small-town experience. From the casual use of the f-word (not the fun f-word) on the part of my classmates, cold french fries being thrown at my head, and even one instance of that classic locker graffiti thing you see in movies, the students at my high school have a way of reminding you that you are gay and, therefore, a joke. I try to coast through without being the center of attention and avoid the many perils that come along with it.

This does raise the question: *Why would you be friends with the walking Pride parade that is your best friend Alan Goode?* Alan is a black hole when it comes to attention. Alan has always had a compulsive need to be the center *of* attention. It's impossible to stand out if you're standing next to him. So, in a lot of ways, I'm simply hiding behind the big gay quantum anomaly that is Alan Goode.

***

"This is one of my favorite local spots," says a voice from behind us. "It also happens to be owned by my father, so I may be a little biased."

Chrissy and Brison are on the grass now, mugging into a video, as I stand to leave and wipe chocolate droppings off the pocket of my shorts. That's when Chrissy catches sight of us.

"Oh," she says with a yawn. "I guess I'll just do that one again. I'm not filming my fashion nightmares video until next week.

"You're a vlogger now, Chrissy?" I call. "Don't you have to have a person-ality to do that kind of thing?"

Chrissy turns and appraises us sourly. Alan slaps my knee.

"Hi, Chrissy!" he waves. "Your outfit looks super cute today."

Brison and I pretend not to notice each other. Tuning him out is something I got pretty good at this year, after what Alan has dubbed his Cumulative Pride Flag era. Each day, to my pronounced chagrin, Alan dressed entirely in a different color of the Pride rainbow. To his credit, it must be said that Alan contemplated the general mockery of the issue for an entire half-second before declaring: *We are agents of change, are we not? Being an agent of change means painting a target on your back sometimes and hoping that what lands is social advancement.*

Alan always speaks as if he's just stepped delicately behind a podium.

The widespread looks of bewilderment we received in the hallways were nothing I couldn't handle. When Alan Goode claims you as his best friend on the third day of ninth grade, these looks are something you acclimatize to. It wasn't the booing, or the deeply stinging groans, that only heterosex-ual teen boys seem to be able to deliver. No, it was none of that. What really sucked was the commentary from Brison freaking Dallas.

"It's so brave of you to shop at the Salvation Army, Alan," Brison had declared on the first day. "I can't do it, you know. I just hate smelling like the bathroom floor of a Walmart."

"I had no idea Big Bird had a gay cousin," Brison had said on the sec-ond day.

The taunts continued, evolving as Alan's outfits did.

"You're supposed to be *on* a Pride float, Alan. Not the float itself."

"Are they letting blimps into the Pride parade this year?"

Each day would find me winding up to lob something back, and each day found Alan pulling me along with a shush. He would laugh nervously, desperate for the Mason Central student body to think that he was in on the joke.

"Any press is good press, Peter," Alan told me on the fourth day. He adjusted the only green top that he could find, a *Kiss Me, I'm Irish* T-shirt.

"Am I missing something?" I asked sharply as I dropped a history text-book into my locker. I knocked mud off my shoes, now being tracked in by the kids who drive four-wheelers and dirt bikes to school. "Since when do you let people talk to you like that?

"He's going through a lot right now," Alan reminded me. "Have some compassion."

The sudden passing of Brison's father had kept the school rumor mill running for months by that point. Suicide was the commonly accepted cause of death, though the facts remained publicly unconfirmed.

"Poor little rich boy. If this is how he grieves, I have notes. Don't they have staff for him to take this out on?"

"He's just having a laugh." Alan shrugged, the plaster of his smile crack-ing for a moment. "We joke about each other's fashion choices—it's our thing."

"I didn't hear *you* making any jokes."

"Well, it *will* be our thing."

I slammed my locker. "Oh my god, Alan. You can't be serious."

"What?" Alan asked absently, avoiding eye contact.

"You actually want to be friends with them?"

"Chrissy has a huge following on Poster, Peter," Alan protested. "Aggie Culture needs a bump, all right? A video collab, maybe even a monthly guest spot!"

And so I remained silent as Alan laughed along in a vain attempt to pre-tend that The Brison Squad was laughing with him and not at him. My abil-ity to hold on to my carefully cultivated invisibility had begun to crumble. Every insult that Alan welcomed with the open arms of his monochromatic eyesores only made it worse. Now, on the lawn beside the Dairy Freeze, my need to become entirely see-through is breaking at the seams. I hate Brison Dallas. I hate Chrissy. I hate the fact that neither of them needs to have an after-school job but that they both always seem so tired. I hate how clear Brison's skin is. And I hate that both of them never get tired of using Alan as their rainbow-hued punching bag.

"It's nice to see you, Chrissy!" Alan tries. "We really should get together some time."

Brison, looking carelessly strapping in his silvery athleisure gear, raises a derisive eyebrow.

Alan smiles. "Well, guys, we should head out. See you!"

Alan pulls me to my feet while they titter behind us. My face flushes red and I feel my heart rate tapping double time as a cold rage clouds my vision. They have everything. Looks, money, giant houses. And now they're adding Alan's dignity to the list.

"Don't leave on our account," Brison calls out. "It looks like you two were having a really nice date."

The words, when they finally arrive, bubble up from some deep pit at the bottom of my stomach. A dark wellspring of hate that cracks open when I'm not looking. Most of the time I'm able to keep a handle on it. This is not one of those times. I've turned and planted my feet, staring into Brison's movie-poster baby blues. The words burn cleanly on the way out, clicking along perfectly like a long line of dominos falling in perfect formation. They feel really fucking good.

"I get that things suck for you since your dad blew his brains out, or whatever. But for the amount of good you're doing the world, Brison, you might as well do the same."

Alan gasps and so does Chrissy. I think I might even gasp at what has just left my lips. Brison, terrifyingly, retains his composure.

The babble of the Dairy Freeze, bustling in the August heat, fills the silence.

The self-satisfied grin slips from Brison's face, replaced with something scarier. Something that exudes a calm-before-the-storm energy. He's going to pounce on me. Brison Dallas is going to leap forward and punch my pimply face into a pulp with his fit, TV-ready fists.

But instead he just turns and walks away.

"We should go, Peter," Alan says behind me.

Brison strides back to the truck, but Chrissy remains in place, her phone held in front of her chest. She's recorded the whole thing.

CHAPTER TWO

PARTY KILLER

"You know," my father opines, "when I was your age we had to actually talk to our parents at dinner." He rubs the graying stubble on his cheek the way he does when he's about to preach from his mountaintop at the head of the table.

"When you were my age you were all dying of polio and eating mercury for breakfast."

I'm scrolling my Poster profile. No mentions or messages are popping up in my mailbox. Maybe Chrissy hasn't posted the video. Maybe she's never going to. Maybe she dropped her phone while jumping into her giant pool of gold coins.

"Peter, the phone, away," my father demands.

I slip it into my pocket, pursing my lips in annoyance. A dust mote drifts through the sunbeam lighting our table. A couple pulls a pair of children along in a rumbling red wagon on the street outside. KCNM's *News at Six* is now the only sound over the scraping of knives and forks, and I'm almost glad for the heartstring-puller story about some kid building a tree-house for a pig.

"Now how in the hell is that pig getting up there?" Dad wonders.

Brison Dallas could have caved my face in without breaking a sweat. In another version of today, maybe he even did. I know that he didn't, but that other version of today is beginning to seem more real than the one I'm sitting in. I'd all but fled the scene with Alan, my mind occupied with finding new curse words to describe Brison's particular brand of foul-ness. But with my mental thesaurus exhausted, a new feeling is invading. It's hot and itchy and nowhere near pleasant. Maybe I had gone too far. Maybe I deserve to have Chrissy post that video. But this is Brison Dallas. Am I really feeling guilty about him? I must be in shock because clearly my thought process is busted.

"Did you and Alan have a nice time today?" Mom asks from across the table. My father observes the TV screen over his plate, and I refrain from glancing at my phone again. Should I delete all my social media accounts? Should I legally change my name? Does the witness protection program accept applications?

I shrug. "Yeah, it was fine."

"Well," she says, cutting another piece of cold chicken. She laughs a little, and rolls her eyes in the universal sign for *maybe I'm just a mom, so what do I know?* "I don't know how Alan feels comfortable walking around in an outfit like that. But it *does* take all kinds, doesn't it?"

I think I miss the buffer that my sister offered. If Jess was home, I'd be able to stew on my impending internet apocalypse in peace. She has always been good at taking the brunt of my parents' attention. Jess's high school career was filled with sports, high grades, and a string of polite boyfriends. Easily digestible options from the prix-fixe menu of life.

"What?" asks my father, his eyes finally leaving the same ad for The Shoe Barn that has been playing since the beginning of time. The jingle plays tinnily. "What's Alan wearing now?"

"Nothing, Dad—"

"Nothing is a good way of putting it," Mom answers brushing the newly cut mom-bangs from her face.

"It's boiling out there, Mother," I say lifelessly. "Your parents' generation broke the environment, and you all seem fine with it, but just because the ice caps are melting doesn't mean that we need to."

"But Alan likes to, ya know, make a fashion statement," says Dad.

"Oh my god, Dad—"

"And I think that's fine!" he insists, smiling wanly with infuriating nonchalance. "What was he wearing, then?"

"Shorts. Shorts and a tank top. What is wrong with you people?"

"Well, I just think that a little modesty never hurt anyone," Mom asserts. "People love to talk around here."

"Not that you'd know anything about it," I remind her.

"And I just think that sometimes it's better to give them nothing to talk about in the first place."

Dad is playing cool, but he's still looking at me the way he does when this type of thing comes up, like he's not sure who let me into the house in the first place.

"Trust me," I tell them. "That was one of Alan's more reserved ensembles."

I've never mentioned Aggie Culture to my parents. They are terrified of being notable for anything but upstanding citizenry. They're losing their minds over the notion of short-shorts, so it isn't hard to imagine how they'd feel about Alan's tiger-striped miniskirt.

It's not like I'm a drag queen. But being adjacent to one would be enough for my father to fall silent for a month and my mother to laugh nervously until she burst into flames. It was easy to keep myself off the conversational lineup before Jess moved. Her latest volleyball game or math test could keep my parents occupied for an entire week, which allowed me to slip under the radar. This is exactly the kind of parental scrutiny I've worked hard (by which I mean done nothing) to avoid.

"Alan is a good kid," my dad begins. "But he does like to be at the center of attention, doesn't he."

It's not a question.

"As much as anyone else, I guess." That's a lie.

Dad sighs and scrapes his plate. "Good for him, I guess. Kids like that wouldn't have lasted five minutes around here when I was young." He says this as if it's not dripping with the kind of condescension that his generation practically invented.

"Kids like *that*?" I ask.

Dad's face flattens to transmit a look of *I didn't mean it like that, Peter. Don't be difficult.*

I clear my father's plate along with mine and he looks around my shoulder to catch the last of the news. News correspondent Trey MacLachlan signs off in his canned cadence, and I wonder what my parents would be like if I was more like Brison. Then I drop the thought entirely, wondering what my parents would be like if I was more like Alan.

***

Alan debuted Ms. Aggie Culture in his basement, which is a shrine to the very notion of homosexuality. The cement floor is a patchwork of clashingly colored area rugs that give the casual viewer a plunging sense of vertigo. The walls are speckled in fairy lights, and the room is filled with shelves covered in tchotchkes, contradictory fabrics, and posters from every version of *A Star Is Born*. An orangey-brown couch from the turn of the century sits squarely in the middle of the musty room, serving as the audience seating for Alan's downstairs drag depot.

Aggie Culture went live last summer, right before eleventh grade. Alan had been hinting at something dramatic for nearly a month, insisting that he needed just a little more time. This wasn't anything new. In the summer after ninth grade, he'd spent nearly two months teasing what ended up being his experimental art film, *Alan, Alanny, Alanis*, in which he speaks to an off-screen character exclusively via the lyrics of Alanis Morissette.

It is not a good movie, but it is a *great* movie.

So this time around Tilly and I weren't sure what to expect.

Tilly is our friend from St. Beatrice Catholic Secondary, which is down the street from our school. She and Alan attended Mason Christian together in elementary school before Alan opted for a public school education and Tilly's grandmother insisted she continue her religious one. Alan introduced us in ninth grade, and the two haven't let me go since.

I love my gay sons and I don't care who knows it! Tilly often shouts, unprompted.

Alan disappeared after sitting us down on the couch for a screening of the Lady Gaga documentary, which he told us was important preshow viewing. By the time the credits rolled, Alan was still nowhere to be seen. Then the TV was muted by an unseen remote, and Gaga was replaced by Cher's "If I Could Turn Back Time." When the curtain (an old Star Wars bedsheet) at the back of the room finally opened, it wasn't Alan who emerged. It was Aggie Culture. Her green wig was piled high in a thematically potent beehive. Alan's boy-brows were gone, replaced with arching black ones that rose high on Aggie's forehead. Her eyes were painted impossibly large in deep shades of blue. Chest hair poked out atop a mustard yellow dress that had been paired with a set of neon green opera gloves. She was bright, she was as sparkly as the glitter contouring her cheekbones, and she was impossible to take your eyes off. Aggie Culture was a beautiful man and a handsome woman all at once.

Tilly screamed and collapsed in laughter as Aggie's dress billowed in the stale breeze of a box fan. Aggie took center stage in front of the television as I sat frozen, unsure what to do with myself at a regular drag show, let alone one for an audience of two. Tilly, on the other hand, was enraptured. Standing almost as tall as Alan (I look like their child whenever the three of us actually leave the basement), Tilly has frizzy brown hair and wears dramatic eye makeup that almost makes her look like a drag queen herself. She watched hungrily and pushed me over when I didn't match her level of squealed enthusiasm. Aggie worked the room, twirling her dress and kicking her cowboy boots in a feminine display of country charm. I simply watched with a mounting tension. When you're friends with Alan, you get used to sitting through his performances. Like the time he workshopped a monologue from his latest piece of fan fiction: *Call Me By Your Name, But Don't Call Me Late to Dinner.*

Cher faded out and Tilly gave a rousing standing ovation while Alan introduced us to Ms. Culture. Tilly pulled her back beyond the Star Wars partition and the two sunk into hysterics as Alan taught her his newfound makeup routine. I watched from the couch and smiled thinly, knowing that I was going to be the dark spot on an otherwise transformative night for my best friend. Still, I couldn't rouse the same enthusiasm Tilly found so easily. There's something about such an overt display that has always made me turn to stone. It feels as if everyone involved could stop at any time and reveal that they'd been doing it sarcastically and then laugh at me for not catching on sooner. It's better to keep a distance and not commit one way or the other.

Later that night, another queen appeared. Tilly's face was angled with contour and blush, her eyes somehow even bigger than before. Her Amazonian frame was covered in a red gingham dress that fit her perfectly while she performed a rousing rendition of Dolly Parton's "Here You Come Again."

"Of course women can be drag queens," Alan informed me afterward. "The whole point is that you're performing a larger-than-life femininity, right? It's not like you're playing a woman. You're playing a big *celebration* of women! Besides," he continued, "drag is an art form all about gender expression. There are drag kings, drag burlesque, drag creatures—"

"I feel amazing," Tilly marvelled as she flopped onto the couch. "Obviously you're next, Pete."

"Oh, no," I said lowly, trying too hard to sound casual. "Not really my thing."

"It wasn't my thing either, until right now!"

"I'll be gentle," Alan promised.

"It's just not my thing," I repeated.

"What's wrong?" Tilly said in a baby voice. "Scared you're going to love it?"

"Scared you're going to look so stunning you'll never want to de-drag?"

"No," I pushed back, probably a touch too forcefully. "It's just not for me."

An awkward silence cut their frivolity short. I knew they were just trying to bring me in on their fun, but for some reason I couldn't let them. The worst part is that I knew I was being a party killer, but I couldn't grasp at another option.

"Okay," Alan said distantly. "We're not going to, like, force you."

As if on cue, Tilly brightened. She sprung forward on the couch and clutched both our hands.

"Can we please focus on what's really important? My drag name, obviously. She'll need to be Aggie's sister."

"Yes," Alan confirmed, their sisterhood an inarguable fact. "Two corn-fed queens looking to take over the world."

"Tilda Soil."

"Kate Spade."

Tilly screamed and grabbed us both by the shoulder. "Rita Rustique," she whispered. Alan cackled, and I started to feel like a Peter-shaped rock.

"From The House of Rural Realness!" Alan cried, and the two dissolved into elated drag jabber.

"There have got to be other queens, or at least queen-curious people, in Mason," Tilly mused. "We should get the word out. See who wants to join."

I laughed but stopped when both queens regarded me with mild scorn. It seemed that the idea of forming a rural teen-queen super squad was no laughing matter.

"I mean, yeah. That's a great idea."

The House of Rural Realness, or THORR, was born then and there.

***

When I'm finally able to close the door to my bedroom, I drop to the floorboards and immediately open Poster. Tags of my own profile are the first thing I see.

@MissEMissY CW: suicide, self-harm, trauma, homophobia. Not sure who needs to see this, but it's time to call out @ptkns1358 for making light of @brisondallaz and his family's trauma. Seems like internalized homophobia to me.

The video is devoid of any external context and has been edited down entirely to my choice words for Brison earlier this afternoon. I stand there, my gut practically spilling from the bottom of my shirt, with my hip popped and my nasal voice blaring like a storm siren.

@KlarisssaBTon this is so messed up. Is Brison okay?

@Corriner145 not shocked. he is so quiet but when he opens his mouth its always something super gross and twisted. that guy sucks

@andruestein um hey @ptkns1358 waiting on ur apology???

Alarm, and something like carsickness, tumbles through my system. Did I really think that Chrissy would miss the chance to rack up some likes on this one? The opportunity to gain a few followers by basking in the drama of it all?

I move from the carpet to my bed. It's an old single mattress that likes to creak below me in an altogether pointed way, as if it's calling me fat. My bedside table, which is really just a wooden crate, is currently calling me poor. And my secondhand desk, cluttered with last year's schoolwork and the books I've failed to read this summer, is calling me a mess.

But Chrissy is the mess. She's so desperate. She barely has two thoughts to rub together. She has nothing to offer the world, so she has to insert herself into something stupid and petty and pointless. Speaking of stupid, petty, and pointless things, I can just picture Brison leaning over her shoulder while Chrissy edited the video. They probably pressed the post button in tandem, his index finger laid lovingly atop hers.

When I get really anxious, I stare at my poster for the American Film Institute's Top 100 Movies and list their directors. *Citizen Kane* was directed by Orson Welles. *Casablanca* was directed by Michael Curtiz. *The Godfather* was directed by Francis Ford Coppola.

I should tell Chrissy how stupid and petty she is. I should say *exactly that* right in the comments. I should make it clear what happened. What *actually* happened.

Some Like It Hot was directed by Billy Wilder. *Star Wars* was directed by George Lucas. *All About Eve* was directed by Joseph L. Mankiewicz.

But wouldn't posting that about Chrissy be as good as an admission of guilt? And what would I say, exactly? That Brison's continual jabs at me and Alan are worse than the thing I'd said? That he'd deserved it?

My thumbs hover over the phone. *Doctor Zhivago* was directed by David Lean.

CHAPTER THREE
PIMPLY THIRD WHEEL

"Do you know how many strings I had to pull to get the details for tonight?" Alan huffs. He picks up speed, his neck bobbing like a swan running late for a business meeting. A truck rushes past us on the bridge, the passengers calling out into the night as they speed off toward the park below.

"Oh, sure," says Tilly. "Who did you have to blow to get the carefully guarded secret to an event literally happening in a public park?"

Alan rounds on us, the gravel path crunching in a way he's sure to find pleasingly dramatic. "Nobody was *blown*, Tildra. But I did have to kiss up and act all nicey-nice to Anna Towner, at great personal sacrifice. I don't know if you're aware, but last year she—"

"Didn't book you at the Winter Coffee House even though you're much more talented than the tone-deprived friends she did book," Tilly and I recite in monotonous unison.

We turn down the lane to Lion's Park and Alan's only response is to become a faster, tardier swan.

Tonight is the night of the Picnic Purge. One evening every August, students at Mason Central Secondary meet up in Lion's Park on the north edge of town after stealing any and all local picnic tables they can get their hands on. Then, under the cover of darkness, they get drunk and make a huge wooden pyramid out of them while trying to avoid splinters and falling ninth-graders. Mason County lore, if you believe that sort of thing, says that the Picnic Purge started as a senior prank back in the nineties. But Mason loves its traditions, like the spring Chicken Fest, or how the little scooter that Santa Clause drives in the Christmas Parade always catches fire.

After two years of opting out of attendance (which is another way of saying that nobody told us when it was going to happen), Alan has worked his people-pleasing magic to secure the date. This, despite my attempts to stay home and firmly out of the public eye. We turn into the darkened parking lot, and I begin, not for the first time tonight, to convince myself that I'm overthinking this. It could be totally fine. Maybe no one cared about the video in the first place. The internet is always moving on to the next scandal that drops into the feed. Like the time Maria De Smet melted her own hair off while filming a self-bleaching tutorial but uploaded the video anyhow. I bet whoever did the dumbest thing *before* Maria breathed a huge sigh of relief as they watched Maria's hair turn green and drop out of frame.

"I'm not saying that you're going to regret dragging me along to this—" I start.

"Nobody *dragged* you, Peter," Alan yells over his shoulder.

"You literally showed up at my door, came into my bedroom, and begged me to come."

"If I didn't beg, you'd never leave the house."

"How do I factor in here, anyway?" I ask. "Aren't I socially radioactive right now?"

"It's simple public relations," Alan explains. "Chrissy may have swung at us, but we're out here to show that she missed."

"Who is this *we?*"

"I'm in the video, too, Peter."

"Not like I am," I level back. Of course Alan is making this about himself.

"Imagine if we didn't show up."

"I'm imagining it right now."

"Our absence would be noted," Alan reasons.

"We never show up to these things."

"Precisely my point! And to do so again would be to admit defeat."

It occurs to me that Alan can't take the fall for the video if the guy who actually said the thing is taking the conversational bullets for him. This was a setup.

"Alan. I'm serious, what's the game plan?"

Alan waves to someone who I'm pretty sure doesn't exist before he forges ahead into the swell of the night, the area already swarming with scantily clad teens looking to show off their talent for minor public disturbances.

"It's a party, Peter," Tilly says, laughing. She casts a glance around the park, which is currently a grassy version of the Mason Central Secondary's hallways. "You're allowed to have fun."

She shakes me by the shoulders while I grumble. Tilly has more experience with these things than I do. She has a double life: she's a Catholic school student, but she's always trying to bring me and Alan along to their decidedly unsaintly pit parties. Alan is all too happy to join her most of the time. But after twice having to wash the results of Catholic school binge drinking off my shoes, I decided that they're not for me.

"I should just go home," I tell her.

"Are you really worried about what some people said on Poster?" Tilly asks earnestly, stepping to the side as a picnic table is hauled past us.

"No. I'm worried about what they'll say when they see me in three dimensions."

"But you're so cute in three dimensions!" she coos.

I slap her hand away as she pinches my cheek. "Alan only brought me here to take any possible heat, you know."

Tilly's eyebrows jut skyward. Clearly, she sees that I have a point.

"Alan just wants you to have some fun, okay? And so does Mother Tilly. You'll do fine," she assures me. "How does my hair look?"

"It looks great," I say. "But you already knew that."

"I know!" she says with a swat. "I'm gorgeous."

The park teems with people darting through the floodlights, laughing, shoving, and drinking neon colored liquor and cheap beer. Empty cans of Bud Light already dot the grass. Scanning the park, I try to land on someone I can stand to talk to for more than a minute at a time. But already I'm being met with questioning and dumbfounded looks from more than a few faces in the crowd. I pass behind the junior basketball team as they hoist picnic tables over their heads in a display that could only be described as *just a bit much*. A party buzzes in the gazebo, the long, open-air structure currently being emptied of its lines of picnic tables. Wood scrapes the stone floor as bottles of peach schnapps make their way from hand to hand, apparently supplied by a small army of older siblings. Tilly and Alan make their way into the gazebo while I wait at the edge of the party, feeling little else but the urge to turn and walk home.

"Hey Petey," someone calls from behind me.

I turn to find Luke Degraph pushing a mop of red curls out of his face with one hand and holding a can of Pabst with the other. Mouse-faced Luke Anderson snickers beside him, and I wonder if I've ever seen either of these pale creeps on their own.

"Your boyfriend's here, Petey," Anderson says through a smirk.

"Really?" I ask. "I thought I told your dad to stop bothering me."

Anderson's face clouds into a glower while Degraph finishes his can, tossing it into the nearest set of bushes.

"Brison Dallas, idiot," says Degraph, through a jagged belch. "It's pretty baller that you told him to kill himself right on camera."

My face flushes hot while Anderson continues to laugh like a cartoon rat. Instead of letting them see my face crack, I opt for an ironic grin before turning and leaving the Lukes without another word. They call after me, their voices mixing with the sounds of the Purge as I walk into the heart of it.

Picnic tables are being hefted and dropped while I try to find Tilly and Alan in the teenage clutter. I search the gazebo, and that's when I lock eyes with Brison Dallas. He's leaning against a wooden pillar, sipping something bright red from a plastic bottle, his tank top cropped just high enough to show off his abs. As if to say, *Oh, these? Yeah, I guess I do have abs, now that you mention it.*

It's only been a few days since our last encounter, but I could have sworn that it's been at least a week of habitually checking my phone for a new round of outraged comments and reposts. Brison frowns appraisingly, maybe thinking the same thing.

No, that's insane. There is no way Brison has given nearly the same amount of thought to the issue. What do rich people do instead of agonizing over something dumb they said? Travel? Race small dogs? Eat endangered animals covered in gold flakes?

Brison breaks eye contact and turns back to his friends, scandal written across his computer-rendered features. He hasn't always been surrounded by an entourage. We went to Mason Public Elementary together, but we were never friends. While I tended to drift from one pod of kids to another without landing anywhere, Brison had been in with the sports kids. The same ones who had made it abundantly clear to me that the only round, pasty-white thing with a place in their circle was a soccer ball. This was until maybe fifth or sixth grade, when voices dropped and Brison's homo-tendencies began to stick out in contrast. The sports kids weren't so stoked on hanging out with him after that. Brison floated off into isolation. You'd think that two socially isolated, possibly gay kids would join forces, but the damage had already been done.

On top of whatever sport was in season, Brison's friends had had a habit of tossing stones at me at recess. They'd also enjoyed using the word *fag-got* rather than the abbreviated, and more casual, *fag*. They had wanted me to know that I got both syllables of their disdain. Maybe after landing on the other side of their ire, Brison was hesitant to throw in with someone who would bring even more attention to the reason he'd been exiled from Athlete Island in the first place. Brison drew into himself, but something changed when we hit ninth grade. It might have had something to do with the abs. Suddenly, an entire mob of girls, made up mostly of bused-in students coming from Ridgely, claimed him as their own. And at the head of this mob was a Christian school convert named Chrissy McPhee. Not only was she huge on Poster, but she was the envy of every girl in Mason Central. When she chose Brison as her resident gay, the same way you'd choose a handbag or a chunky bracelet, his esteem rocketed high in the school hallways. Sure, he's gay. But Chrissy McPhee's family owns half of Mason, and the Dallas family might just own the other half.

"Hey," someone calls from the playground. Steven Partridge waves while the boys behind watch on with blank faces. "Do Monica next."

From the swing set, Monica Whitehead casts a scathing eye in my direction before aiming it at Steven. She glares at him from behind the bangs of her chemically flattened hair.

"What?" I ask, already regretting it.

"You know," Steven says through a suppressed giggle. "Tell her to kill herself, or whatever you do."

Monica lobs one of her flip-flops at him, which limply smacks off his shoulder.

"That's not funny, Steven." She avoids my gaze while Olivia Hoggart retrieves her shoe, now held aloft in a tipsy game of keep away. "Technically what Peter did was a hate crime."

"I don't know, Monica," I begin. "The only hate crime I'm seeing is your makeup. Does a three-year-old do your face, or do you *like* looking like you fell over in the discount bin at a drugstore?"

The girls scowl while Steven's friends break into donkey wails of laughter, their schoolyard taunting reaching a fever pitch as I make my way toward the parking lot. I was right. This is a setup. Alan may love drama, but this is pushing it. He'll text me about it all day tomorrow, maybe even show up at my front door. I'll make him sweat, I decide, right before I really lay into him. He must think I'm one of those shivery little dogs that always seem to be balding prematurely. You know, the kind that people keep in a purse and sneak into the movies. You'd almost feel bad for them if they didn't make your skin crawl. That's me. I am that dog.

At the edge of the park, I pull out my phone and stare into the screen for a moment, calculating the perfect text. It'll have to be unbothered but scathing.

"You're not leaving already, are you?"

Lorne the Soft-Serve Guy is observing me from the tree he's leaning against, his jaw set in a wry smile. Something in my chest turns over like a rusting engine.

"Oh," I fumble. "Hey."

"I'm just messing with you." Lorne laughs.

It's like I'm embarrassed that he found me thinking my own thoughts. Like he could read every one of them while my back was turned. I nod, my mouth sandy and dry. Even in the dark I can tell that he's dressed better than any of the boys at the party. In jeans and a ratty black T-shirt, he projects an aura of casual style that I know would look strained and boxy were I to attempt it. I'm certain that I'm bloated and getting fatter by the second, like the blueberry girl in *Charlie and the Chocolate Factory*. I'm certain that my face is erupting in acne before Lorne's very eyes and that my head is going to explode like a hormonal Vesuvius. He must have seen the video. He must think I'm trash on legs. He must be coming over to tell me exactly that.

"Yeah," I say. "It's good to see you." As if Lorne has said the same.

Is my brain melting?

"I'm glad you came to the party tonight," he says amiably, gesturing to the whole thing as if he comes here all the time.

"Yeah, well," I slowly mumble, "Alan made sure of it."

"People are making a big deal out of that video, right?"

My chest unclenches in relief.

"Yes!" I exhale. "Right?"

"It's so *not* a big deal."

"Oh my god. Thank you."

Lorne shakes his head and shrugs, casting his eyes back toward the gazebo.

"People love this kind of drama," he elaborates. "But there are so many bigger things to worry about right now."

"Totally."

"Besides," Lorne concludes, "you're *going* to apologize, obviously."

The engine in my chest sputters, halts, and spews smoke.

"Sorry," I try. "What?"

"Oh. My. God!" someone screeches.

Alan appears and smacks Lorne's shoulder. Lorne, unlike most people, is gracious enough not to wince. "Oh *my* god!" Lorne calls back. "It's Aggie Culture!" Alan's face flushes while he tries to play it cool, as if he gets noticed on the street every day. "I watched your videos, Ms. Culture. You're amazing."

"I know, I know," Alan laughs. "But I put on my cowboy boots one at a time, *just* like everyone else."

I smile knowingly, making it clear that I'm in on the joke, too. Alan hasn't even looked my way. His eyes are locked on Lorne, and I'm beginning to feel like conversational wallpaper.

"I didn't expect to meet a drag performer out here," Lorne marvels. "But I guess I needed to check my preconceived notions. The way that Chrissy talks about this place makes it sound like it's a bit of a—"

"A hillbilly factory?" I offer.

"Something like that, yeah." Lorne laughs, sounding a little taken aback. "I can't imagine what it must be like for other 2SLGBTQIA+ youth out here, you know?"

He looks at me knowingly, sympathetically, as if I've limped into the party in a full-body cast covered in rainbows.

"You'd be surprised," Alan enlightens him. "The House of Rural Realness has sister queens all over Mason County. There's Cora Copia, Bailey Hayes, Nifoal Dressage—"

"Oh my god, shut up!" Lorne screams in delight, slapping Alan in an appropriately playful manner that I'm sure doesn't hurt one bit.

"It's true," Alan says proudly, shrugging like he'd done the whole thing in his sleep. "Once Rita Rustique and I got started, it all just took off."

I stare at them, my jealousy building. It's true: they might not have done anything as a team yet, but The House of Rural Realness is still more than I have to show for myself. The lineup hadn't taken long to form after Alan and Tilly put their minds to it. Bailey Hayes and Cora Copia, two of Tilly's friends from St. Beatrice, were already makeup experts. They'd quickly joined the ranks before inviting Cora's one-time fling Nifoal Dressage into the fold. A strange viciousness rises like bile in my throat as Alan and Lorne banter despite the pimply third wheel standing awkwardly beside them.

"So what's your Rural Realness name, then?" Lorne asks me.

"Oh," I say. "I don't actually—"

"Peter doesn't have one," Alan cuts in. "But if he did, maybe something along the lines of *Flora* Culture?"

Lorne screams with laughter and grabs Alan's arm. "You are *too* much, Alan!"

"Yeah," I say. "That's super funny."

Lorne nods while Alan grasps me with showy affection. He is practically twirling in place, dancing beneath the beam of Lorne's undivided attention. If I'm there at all, it's merely as Alan's short gay henchman.

"It's a shame that you're just online." Lorne sighs. "I haven't seen a drag show in person in ages."

"You should come to *our* show!" Alan proclaims. The statement hangs in the air while Lorne stares in disbelief. So do I.

"You have a show coming up?" asks Lorne.

"We do," Alan confirms, nodding vigorously.

My mouth is no longer just dry, it's the Sahara Desert. What?

Alan is lying. If there was a show coming up, it would be the only thing in the world. It would be the center of the entire universe. I would wake up in the morning to find Alan standing over my bed with a to-do list stacked higher than his wig. But then I notice that Lorne's eyes are locked onto mine with polite expectation. I notice something that could even be described as *interest*.

So I lie.

"Yeah, it's gonna be huge."

Lorne crows with excitement. "This is wild! You've gotta send me an invite. This sounds *so* important."

Alan nods aggressively. "It'll be a total experience, our show. Trust me." His eyes lock on mine, both of us speaking across our invisible, best friend mind-to-mind phone line.

What are you doing? my look asks in a panic.

What are you *doing?* Alan's replies.

I'm just playing along, you pathological attention obsessive—

Well, keep it up because I have no idea what I'm doing here.

"Excuse me, Lorne. Can I have a word with you?"

My jaw clenches as Chrissy approaches from the park, pointedly avoiding even looking at me and Alan.

"Hello, darling cousin," Lorne replies breezily.

Of course they're related. Chrissy's father owns the Dairy Freeze, among half the other businesses in Mason. You'd think that unlimited access to deep-fried foods would make Chrissy break out, but I guess that being a spiteful bog witch is good for the skin.

"Brison wants to see you," Chrissy tersely informs him. "He wants you to tell everyone about the time you met Meghan Markle."

Alan gasps, but Lorne just shrugs. "Technically, it was just her relatability coach," he explains.

"Whatever, Lorne!" Chrissy snaps. "Brison wants you." She finally deigns to take us in with a dismissive glance. "Besides. You don't want to be seen talking with these two. Not after what Peter did."

Alan's grip on my arm tightens as he feels me calculating a response.

"They were just telling me about the drag show they have coming up."

Disbelief passes across Chrissy's face, the same one that must have crossed mine.

"You have to come, Chrissy," Alan urges demurely, his face holding a soft look of welcome that seems to anger Chrissy further.

"*You're* throwing a drag show?" Chrissy retorts, her glower locking me in its tractor beam. "With Peter Thompkin? You really think it's a good idea to have Problematic Peter onstage with you?"

"Well—" Alan begins.

"You know what everyone is saying about him, don't you?" she continues, as if I'm not there. "That he's a homophobic gay. Doesn't seem like a ticket-seller, if you ask me."

"Peter won't be performing," Alan offers.

"Because I'll be producing!" I blurt out.

The engine in my chest explodes in a fiery wreck. *What the hell did I just say?*

Chrissy furrows her brow and folds her arms.

"That's fantastic!" Lorne exclaims.

"Totally," agrees Alan. "Totally fantastic."

What was that? Alan asks with a look.

I don't respond, with a look or otherwise. Because I'm not entirely sure myself.

***

With Tilly's curfew looming, the three of us find ourselves approaching the bridge again. The lie Alan and I had bankrolled earlier in the evening sits uneasily between us while he regales Tilly with the story through gasps of laughter.

"I can't wait to hear your excuse for why this magical show of yours falls through," Tilly admonishes him. "What's it going to be? Creative differences? Political differences? Oh, I know: differences of lip liner."

"There aren't going to be any excuses," Alan announces, his chin craning skyward.

"Why? Have we decided that impressing random out-of-town boys isn't a prudent use of our summer? Because I am in full support of that."

"No. Because there *is* going to be a show."

"So you're going to just toss together a drag extravaganza in a few weeks and hope that people actually show up?" Tilly presses. "And what about the performers? Rural Realness has added a few queens, sure. But five hobbyist queens does *not* an extravaganza make."

"I'm an artist, Tilly. It's what I do."

"What, lie to boys you think you might have a chance at kissing?"

"I never said anything about kissing."

"Not out loud, no."

"I'm an artist. I create. I *curate*, don't I?"

"Crap also starts with a *C*."

The two continue their bickering as we pass from the bridge into the outskirts of Mason. The scrapyard outside Mason Tirecraft sits full of hollowed-out car exteriors and hubcap piles. Alan's voice echoes off the garage door.

I'd tossed myself on that conversational hand grenade because Alan needed someone to back up his lie, I reason. But the lie has spilled over and gotten into every other part of my brain, sticking to the rest of my thoughts. I'd lied to impress Lorne. I'd lied to prove to Chrissy, and everyone she will inevitably blab our conversation to, that I'm not some self-hating gay. Maybe I'm the type of person who throws drag shows, who makes a good impression on cute boys from out of town.

"What the hell is going on with you?" Alan asks pointedly.

I look around and wonder what exactly I just missed.

"What?"

"You've been awfully silent this entire time."

"You don't leave much room to be otherwise, Alan."

"You *yes and-ed* the idea back at the park. Now you've got nothing to add?"

"You seemed desperate."

"There are many words to describe me, Peter, and *desperate* is not one of them."

"I can think of a few choice ones right now."

"You said yes. Now's the part with the *and. Yes and* is the foundation of improv comedy for a reason. Sometimes I think you learned nothing from my 'Improving Your Improv-ing' workshop last summer. "

"What?"

"This show is happening," Alan declares to the world at large. "And you just said that you're the guy making it happen."

Tilly pops an eyebrow, waiting for me to blow him off. But I don't. I don't do anything, actually. I stand there, weighing my options. One of the things about living in the middle of nowhere is that awkward silences are often punctuated by actual crickets.

Maybe this is about more than just drag. Maybe the kind of guy who would throw Mason County's first drag extravaganza can't be so bad, after all.

"Yes," I say at last. "*And.*"

CHAPTER FOUR

THE GUY WHO SAID THE VERY BAD THING

"We're meeting him where?"

Alan is driving his mother's car at an aggressively sensible speed. Tall cornfields stretch off on either side of the road as yet another car passes to the left of our law-abiding SUV.

"We're meeting him down Winterhill Drive," Alan explains with a wave of his hand. "Which I think is technically a cow path."

Alan never lets you in on his plan until absolutely necessary because he knows that most of the time you'll say no to whatever fresh hell he's dreamed up. "California Girls" blasts from the speakers as we turn onto Winterhill Drive, an overgrown gravel road, and I become aware that this is one of those times.

"Explain to me why Cora Copia has stipulations about joining the show. She's already a member of Rural Realness, so shouldn't she just be clocking in?"

Alan brushes the hair from his face and dutifully checks his rearview mirror. "Don't make a big deal out of it, okay? When I brought it up at our meeting, the idea might have ruffled some feathers."

"What idea?" I ask, perplexed. "What feathers are there to be ruffled?"

"The idea of Peter Thompkin producing the show," Alan says as plainly as he can manage.

My eyes narrow, and I do my best not to give Alan the dramatic satisfaction he would get at the receiving end of my displeasure. "Right. Of course. They saw the video and now—"

"And now," Alan interjects, "they all just want to be sure that you have their best interests at heart."

"By filming a music video on a cow path?"

"By playing ball, Peter. And by being nice about it while you do."

"I'm very nice."

"You're a producer now. You have a responsibility—"

"Oh god, here we go—"

"A responsibility to represent the queer community here in Mason—"

"Please," I try. "Please don't talk about community and representation and—"

"Representation is everything, Peter! We're not just putting on a show, we're representing—"

"Yes, fine!" I cry out, throwing my arms over my eyes and groaning. "I'll be on my best behavior!"

"The queens said yes," Alan continues, "if we sweeten the deal a little. Well, if *you* sweeten the deal a little. To show that you're a team player."

Sunlight flits in and out through the trees lining the path as the car trundles and bumps along.

"Have they considered that this is hazing?"

"Bailey is calling it *quality control*. We just need to lend a hand on some projects that the girls are working on."

"All of them?"

Alan shrugs. "Tilly let us off the hook. But once Cora made it obvious that her *yes* was coming at the expense of us dragging our asses out to a cow path, the other girls made their terms and conditions perfectly clear."

I decide not to ask what Bailey Hayes and Nifoal Dressage are demanding of me. Despite not drinking a drop at the Picnic Purge, I had woken up the next morning in a daze of regret. I don't know the first thing about producing a show like this—or what a producer even does in the first place. Besides, doesn't it smack of effort? Everyone will be able to tell that the only reason I'm doing this is to run damage control on my public image. Chrissy will probably post a video of her own to demand that nobody support Peter, The Guy Who Said the Very Bad Thing.

The worst part is that I might even agree with her. The memory of our altercation has been hiding behind my mental shrubbery ever since, leaping out when I least expect it in a jump scare of mortification. I should never have given Brison the satisfaction. There's something deeply embarrassing about letting someone know just how much they get under your skin. Especially when you stooped low enough to invoke their recently dead father.

Gravity is momentarily upended as Alan slams the breaks.

"Jesus, Alan!" I yelp.

The dust clouds up around the car while I notice a tall teenage boy with buzzed blonde hair and glue-blocked eyebrows standing on the road. Cora Copia doesn't even flinch at the car that just nearly turned him into a human smoothie. With his eyebrows powdered over and his bulbous blue eyes, Cora looks like an alien escaped from some deep-forest research center. Cora's ancient brown station wagon is parked next to a vine-covered path swarming with gnats in the high summer sun. To most people this is the scene at the beginning of a very low-budget horror movie, but to Alan it is an act of queer solidarity. To me it's something in the middle.

We park on the side of the lane while Cora regards us like a praying mantis watching its dinner.

"Hello, Peter," says Cora, his deep voice lending credence to the general horror vibes as it booms from his twiggy frame. "You're well, I trust."

"Hello, Cora," I reply, attempting to mask the unease in my voice. The few times I've met Cora Copia have left me with the sense that he wouldn't say no to stuffing me full of pink insulation and hanging me from the wall like some *Most Dangerous Game* knockoff. Cora Copia falls somewhere on the darker side of the drag spectrum. She's the kind of queen who smiles to reveal black ooze dripping from her mouth, sports white contact lenses, and wears press-on *claws* instead of nails.

"So good to see you, dollface!" Alan calls, throwing his arms around Cora's bony shoulders. Cora's eyes never leave mine, and I wonder if this was all a ruse to get me somewhere my screams will go unnoticed.

"You'll be recording the video on my phone," Cora informs me. "Unless camera phones are a touchy subject for you right now."

Alan cackles while Cora remains motionless. A creep *and* a comedian. Great.

I toss my hands up in barely contained rage. "Are you *kidding* me? Even the Catholic school kids are going on about that?"

Cora shrugs as Alan slings a duffle bag from the back of the car and over his shoulder.

"Come on, girls. I'm not getting any younger." Alan saunters off down the cow path. The cicadas buzz as the brush rises in thick green patches around us.

"You know, next time you could let me in on the Rural Realness secrets before I get in the car," I call ahead as I swat scratchy fir branches out of my way. "Like the one where you all decided that Peter has to prove himself a worthy gay."

I hop over a stagnant puddle full of nasty-looking crawlies with plump bodies and enormous wings.

"They're not *secrets,* thank you. They're part of my process."

"Fine. Any other parts of the process you feel like letting me in on?"

Alan walks with his head held high, despite the mud caking his pristinely kept white sneakers. "You're so dramatic," he scolds. "Which is annoying, because that's my thing."

"I know this is supposed to be about impressing Lorne—"

"Allegedly," Alan cuts in.

"But are you sure it has nothing to do with Aggie getting more Poster followers?"

Cora keeps pace between us, quietly tracking our exchange.

"It's a complex tapestry of reasons." Alan wipes the sweat beading on his forehead with a vicious flick. Alan's hairline is swampy on a good day, but in the humidity of the brush it's practically oceanic. "But, if you must know, it wouldn't hurt to get the right kind of attention. The kind that a queen needs to get her career started."

From the moment that Aggie burst forth in a shower of hair spray and shapewear, Alan has spent great swaths of time turning over the concept of *getting his career started*. Maybe he'll move to New York City and work the bar scene, or maybe he'll go to LA and catch the eye of some hip young movie producer who really understands what Aggie Culture is all about. Maybe he'll skip it all and get cast on *Dragathon*.

"Look, Alan. You can go to college *and* be a drag queen. People do it all the time."

Alan laughs haughtily, rolling his eyes at my clearly uninformed opinion. It's obvious to him that I'll never understand the greatness he is being called to. "I never said I'm *not* going to college. It's something I'm considering. Besides, some people take a year off before going to school."

"Sure, but those people always end up extending that year into what turns into the rest of their life. Like my cousin Harrison. He took a year off and he's still living in my aunt's basement as a professional online poker player."

"Harrison's a pervert, Peter. Perverts *should* live in their mom's basements and play online poker. It sends a clear message to the rest of us."

"Oh, come on," I chide, flattening a massive mosquito currently making a meal out of my arm. "He has a foot fetish; I'd hardly call that perverted."

"He asked Tilly what size toe ring she wears. As if that's common knowledge."

The path branches off to the right, and we turn into what I quickly realize is the back of a fenced-in horse field. Except, as I look closer, I can see that the cloven-hoofed things trotting about aren't horses.

"Are those alpacas?"

"Mhm," Cora confirms, setting down his bag and retrieving a makeup mirror. He thrusts the mirror into my hands. "Aren't they gorgeous?"

"Is nobody going to tell me how the alpacas fit into all this?"

"They're the drag queens of the barnyard, obviously," Cora mumbles, drawing on an eyebrow. "They've got high heels, luxurious fur, and they'll spit on you if you fuck with them."

"Right," I say. "Of course."

I examine the fence and the dozy, four-legged throw blankets that are munching grass behind it. They flick their ears and eye us with a subdued skepticism that I can easily relate to. The queens build a geared-down version of their drag faces while I slap at gnats and peer about for anybody moving around the farmhouse. I get the feeling that we're not technically allowed back here. There's a flash of green as Alan fixes Aggie's emerald wig atop his head. Cora Copia adjusts a mane of white-blonde hair, her transformation now complete. When I look back to the farmhouse, I'm certain that I spot movement beside the barn.

"Is this private prop—" I begin, but Cora cuts me off by thrusting her phone into my hands.

"Don't go snooping in there," she breathes. "A girl like me has a lot of secrets."

Cora slinks off to join Aggie Culture and I try to stop myself from imagining the bleached animal skeletons that she clearly wants me to discover in her photo reel. At least I hope they're animals.

"We're going for multiple angles," Aggie instructs, connecting her phone to a little tube speaker. "So we'll film a few different takes. And don't worry about getting my good side," she smolders. She reconsiders the green boa draped across her shoulders and decides against it, tossing it over mine instead. "They're *all* good."

I press record. As the two launch into their lip sync, their GarageBand beats give way to a House of Rural Realness original:

She's the green queen and she's gonna make you scream,
Like that movie from the 1990s.
Aggie Culture, coming at you homegrown,
From the corn stalks to the internet throne.
She's a closet queen busting onto the scene,
Making history, not even eighteen.
She's a small town thriller, a bad vibe killer,
Hairier chest than a caterpillar.

Their song may sound like a Weird Al reject throwing up in the mouth of a junior high talent show, but Aggie Culture and Cora Copia are killing it. They're having a good time, feeding eagerly off each other's energies as they twirl, snap, and bounce through their farmland fantasy. For a moment I even wonder if I'm missing out from my place behind the camera. But then I hear dogs barking in the distance.

"Hey, guys?" I call out. The queens turn, scandalized by the interruption until they hear the dogs over the buzz of the music and see the tall grass bending in the distance.

Images of dog teeth and punctured skin tumble through my head as the girls realize the implications of the sound getting closer by the second.

"*Not* this," Cora mutters. "This is not what I was invoking when I tried to summon hellhounds last week."

Cora flings off her heels and bolts, moving with more grace than I'd have given her lanky frame credit for. The dogs draw closer while Aggie scampers to collect her things. A life spent around farms always carries the danger of animal attacks. I'd thought that my preference for staying in town would keep me safe from having my chest kicked in by a horse or my ears torn off by a dog. The movement in the grass grows closer.

"Peter! Let's go!" Aggie whisper-screams. I realize that I've been staring at the field in frozen dread and that maybe she has a point.

Still recording, I tear through the trees and back onto the path as the shouts of the alpaca farmer break through the dogs' sharp yapping. The cow path looks even thinner on my return journey. Its uneven ground has me certain that I'll roll my ankle and be eaten by a slobbering pack of herding dogs driven mad from years of alpaca servitude. Soon the dogs are somewhere to our right, off in the trees, converging on the path itself. We pelt through the overgrowth, costumes and wigs trailing behind the queens and rapidly collecting pine needles. The green boa on my shoulders is snatched away by a branch. In one of the easiest choices of my life, I leave it there.

The path opens again. Aggie fumbles with her keys, scrabbling for them in her press-on-nails.

"Good god, Alan!" I scream, yanking the bag away and fishing them out for myself. "A broken nail or a broken neck, take your pick!"

The door to Cora's station wagon slams shut as she throws herself inside.

"Oh, please!" Aggie hurls back as she unlocks the door. "I could do more in press-on nails than you can in *painted* ones."

We leap into Alan's car just as the farmer and his small army of dogs burst into view from inside the foliage. He's younger than I would have expected, maybe just over thirty. He has blonde hair and a weirdly gym-ready body. Most of the time you picture a farmer as the creepy old man with the pitchfork from that painting, but Mason is filled with boys who want nothing more than to get their Ag-Tech degree before moving home and shoveling pig shit for the rest of their lives. Or alpaca shit, apparently.

Kind-of-hot farmer guy stares at us in astonishment as four dogs pool around his feet, barking their warning cries. Before the farmer can say a word, we're peeling out of the place with Aggie shrieking through a crack in the window. "So sorry to have bothered you, sir!"

As we peel off along the dirt road, I half expect the farmer to at least shake a first in the air and hurl a quick slur our way. Instead, he just stares with increasing perplexity as our motley trio disappears down the lane,

Cora's station wagon leading the way.

"Wow!" I say through gasps for air. "I was really expecting some sort of hate crime back there."

"I know!" Aggie screams in delight. "He's a total ally."

We crumble into hysterics as the car speeds off into the afternoon, our laughter mixing as we roll the windows down and plot Aggie's future with her newfound alpaca-farming husband.

CHAPTER FIVE

AN EFFEMINATE GOPHER

@monicawhlol Not sure who needs to hear this but @ptkns1358 hasn't apologized, and I doubt he will. Focus on the people hes hurt. Like me. He once said I looked like a stain on the ceiling and our teacher just sort of laughed. He's not just anti-gay he is anti-woman.

@brianahmakk lol i go to mason central and i dont even know who this @ptkns1358 guy is hes hilarious tho cuz that guy sux

@KlarisssaBTon radio silence from @ptkns1358? not shocked.

Alan plucks my phone away.

"You goddamn bitch," I snipe, snatching at his hands.

Without consideration, Alan drops my phone down the front of his shirt. I should probably just consider it lost to the sweaty, hairy jungle that is his chest.

"Don't you think calling the drag show *annual* is a bit lofty?" inquires Nifoal Dressage, blending her cheeks at her makeup station.

Alan shakes his head. We're sitting in Nifoal's humid attic bedroom in Port Anders, sweating in the stale August heat. Our twenty-minute drive to the Mason County coastline was a window-down blast of wind and pop music, but without any moving air I'm beginning to wonder why we left Alan's basement in the first place.

Nifoal blots her lips while Alan and I swat at each other.

"It's aspirational," Alan explains, "like when I wear satin finish foundation or when Peter tried to pull off that jean vest."

"You said I should try a new look!" I flick a bent cotton swab at Alan's face.

"The only thing you were trying was my patience," he replies, sighing.

"Give me the phone back."

"No. It lives in my titties now."

"You just wanted an excuse to talk about your titties."

"What?" Alan simpers, doing his standby Marilyn Monroe impression. "Dese widdle tings?" He presses his boobs together through the fabric of his T-shirt and leans over to shake them in my face. I pretend to hurl all over him while Alan squeals with bombshell delight.

Maybe it's a blessing. Someone really should be keeping me from obsessively checking my phone. Mercifully, Nifoal has remained tight-lipped on the controversy following me. Upon our arrival in Port Anders, the three of us had met at Maybelle's, one of the many retro-chic ice-cream windows built to cash in on cottagers and beach-goers.

"Oops," the teenage girl behind the window had said, shrugging after she had upended a cone of raspberry yogurt on my formerly white T-shirt. "Let me get you a new one."

She'd turned back to the yogurt machine with the hint of a satisfied smile.

"Oh my god," Alan had said through a chuckle of incredulity. "She totally did that on purpose."

I wiped fruitlessly at the sticky frozen gloop with a fistful of napkins. When my second raspberry yogurt arrived, I wondered if the sales associate had added any non-menu ingredients. In the steaming heat of Nifoal's bedroom/drag studio, the stain has stuck to my chest. I stare out the window, watching the sun setting over the lake. Nifoal brushes the brunette wig from her eyes while tapping on her phone, at which point Alan catches a glimpse of the screen and squeals in elation.

"Are you on Man Meet, Miss Dressage?"

Nifoal hushes him, her nails raking the air in a display that is somehow both graceful and threatening. "Chill, mama. The little old ladies next door meet for bridge on Wednesdays, and they're bigger gossips than I am." She gestures vaguely to the window, which looks out over the United Church parking lot. If members of the church's bridge club know about that gay dating/hookup app, I would be sincerely impressed. I would also have a few follow-up questions.

Nifoal plucks a rogue chin hair with a pair of tweezers. She lays long fingers against her sharp jaw, turning left to right to admire her artistry. Her high cheekbones and thick black hair make her a catch in either boy *or* girl mode, while some of us can't even pull off one. Nifoal struggles to hide her three-o'clock shadow while I'm trying really hard to push the cheesy stubble out of my upper lip like a human Play-Doh set.

Alan plays it cool but doesn't drop the subject. "Tell me about the man meat you're getting on Man Meet."

Nifoal scoffs and makes a show of checking her nails. "I'm not getting anything. Unless you count DMs from shirtless torsos and pictures of pickup trucks."

"Ew." Alan winces, his mouth puckering in disgust. "Imagine doing anything but running away from a pickup truck. I'm sorry, but you must have confused me with my cousin, Shaylynne. *I'm* not hopping into a pickup with the first guy who shows me his balls. But I *have* requested to sing at their wedding this fall, so at least something good will come out of her teenage pregnancy."

"It's vile, really," Nifoal purrs, fluffing her freshly glued eyelashes. The black wings of her eyes reach skyward. They're the highest and most animalistic eyes of Rural Realness; they look like they could flap and take into the air at any moment. "They're all closet cases, honestly. Married men who want to fuck a teenage boy and then cry about it later. It's like, I'm sorry, Christopher, but ruin your life on your *own* time, darling."

My breath catches for a moment, the dark edges of Nifoal's words sucking the air out of the room. I know that some weird stuff can happen on that app, but I'd never suspected anything like that. The idea of talking to married men, guys who could be twice my age, men who are keeping me a secret, makes me queasy. It's not like the straight kids at Mason Central are having this conversation tonight. It's not like their small-town sexual exploits feel like something out of a true-crime documentary. I watch Nifoal make her final inspections and consider how much older she seems than me. Most of the time, being gay in Mason County feels more *theoretical* than actual. Like I'm more gay by merit of my hetero-deficiency than any literal gay behavior. It's not like I'm out there meeting men the way Nifoal is. The way Brison probably is.

Alan grabs my hands and shakes a bottle of pink nail polish. When I pull back, he just frowns the way he does when someone makes a disparaging comment about Lady Gaga's *Artpop*.

"No nail polish for me, thanks."

Nifoal glances up from her phone and clicks her nails impatiently against the seashell deco case. "It's a unified look, sweetness."

"Girl, it's okay," Alan tells me. "The gender binary can handle some fluids tonight, okay?"

"I just don't like nail polish, all right? It stinks, and the polish remover smells even worse."

"Are you saying you've never done your nails?" Nifoal balks at the idea.

Alan shakes his head in shame. "Peter hasn't even had his toenails painted, Nifoal. But he *is* our producer." He wraps his hand in mine and readies the nail polish. "So tonight it's time to produce, darling."

We take the stairs quietly. Nifoal holds her black heels and chestnut wig rather than walk in them just yet. Her skimpy dress is made of the horse-print fabric your grandmother would make a couch pillow out of, a watery yellow covered in flowers and gently trotting horses. We slip out the back door and through the garden gate while prime-time TV blasts in the living room. Nifoal hasn't made it explicit, but I think her parents are aware of their son's talent as a seamstress and makeup artist. After all, his bedroom is basically a costuming studio littered with errant snips of fabric. Maybe Nifoal is the kind of gay who doesn't require a coming out. Maybe she just kicked the door down and made it abundantly clear to everyone that she's here, she's queer, and she loves sewing her own dresses with patterned fabric. We cut through the church parking lot. To Alan's glee, the evening's bridge tournament has just let out. Church ladies mill about their cars and chat in clucks and titters. Alan waves while they stare in restrained discomfort at the teenage drag queen and her boys dressed entirely in shades of brown. Brown, obviously, because of the rubber horse heads that Alan has in his bag.

"I hadn't figured you for a dancer, Peter," Nifoal observes as we cross the road.

"I'm not a dancer. I'm only doing this because Alan made it perfectly clear that if I don't—"

"You'll never make it to dance regionals?" interjects Alan.

"Perfectly clear," I continue, "that you had your heart set on humiliating me even more than Cora did."

"It's only humiliation if you don't love it." Nifoal shrugs. "And it looks like you're having the time of your life in Cora's video."

Alan has sent me a link to the rough cut, but I couldn't force myself to press play.

"Just one more time," I say. "I'd like to hear your personal assurance that—"

"Yes, Peter!" Alan sighs. "The masks will be staying on. You'll be perfectly anonymous."

It's the third time I've asked, and it's the third time I haven't entirely believed the answer.

***

Port Anders is built around a park, with winding streets that lead down to a cottage-lined beach. At the center of the park is a gazebo where the town stages events, like the Port Anders Spring Fest or the lighting of the Christmas tree. During August it's just an empty gazebo for skateboarders to scrape their knees on. Or, in our case, a place to film a horse-themed drag routine.

Alan drops his duffle bag on a gazebo bench and it lands with an unexpected thud. I give it a second glance while Alan pulls the rubber horse heads from within.

"Are bricks a part of your act now?"

Alan tosses me a flubbery horse head. "A queen never gives away her secrets. It's undignified."

When I pull the horse head over my own, I can't help but recoil at the chemical scent.

"You're right. How dare I besmirch the dignity of all this."

Nifoal attaches a tiny tripod to the bottom of her phone. She places it on the railing opposite us and fixes her hair before turning to take us both in.

"This is going to be a one-shot wonder, boys," she informs us.

Nifoal begins recording. She turns her back to us the way all self-respecting superstars must turn their back to their backup dancers: with dignity, poise, and a mild dose of contempt. The opening vocals to Lady Gaga's "John Wayne" plays tinnily from Alan's phone. Nifoal strikes a pose, her gloved hand pointing skyward while her right leg clomps to the side, allowing her to dip seductively.

I cannot dance. This is not self-depreciation, just an unequivocal fact. The Earth is round, the stars are up, gravity is pushing us down, and I cannot dance. Accordingly, Alan has dumbed down his horsey choreography while insisting that I "channel the energy of the word *gallop*." Inside the horse head I'm dripping sweat and whispering instructions to myself. "Arms out, and pop, and out, and pop, and turn turn turn turn, arms in, and pop."

I turn and find myself running directly into Alan's shoulder. He catches me and props me back up with a laugh. I'm so ready to leap into the bushes that I nearly miss what happens next.

Just as I stand back up, a can lands with a wet *clunk* on the gazebo floor, splashing Nifoal's exposed ankles with a soapy spray of beer.

"Hey!" calls a drunken voice from behind the bushes. "Keep going, we're enjoying the show!"

A stumbling trio slumps their way into the light. The leader, clearly the one who threw the can, is skinhead bald.

"Come on, boys," his friend shouts through adult braces. "Don't let us get in your way."

Another can, empty this time, skitters across the gazebo floor as Adult Braces lets it rip like a skipping stone. The third guy, gaunt and dressed all in black, simply stands behind his friends. He seems impatient, like he's waiting for his friends to get bored with us. Maybe we're keeping them from a planned evening of huffing paint while watching Mark Wahlberg movies.

Nifoal is frozen, her arms held out mid-choreography. We're caught in a fight-or-flight moment. Alan removes his horse head and I follow suit, making the two at the front laugh harder.

"What do you know?" Skinhead calls out. "There are some boys here after all."

Alan slips his mask back into his duffel bag and pretends to be busy.

"Let's just reset," he instructs Nifoal.

Skinhead walks up the steps to the gazebo, his swagger amplified now that he has a stage to perform it on.

"We're talking to you, ya know." He laughs.

"Yeah," replies Alan, still puttering with his bag. "We're just not listening."

Skinhead pushes Alan from behind, but stumbles. His buddies laugh.

Nifoal's phone is in her hands, and she has backed up against the railing, recording it all. Skinhead pushes Alan again, harder this time, with the view of the camera on him. Adult Braces steps into the ring and makes to grab the phone. Without a second thought, I find myself between him and Nifoal, staring daringly into his sunken eyes.

"If you guys wanna be in the video, all you have to do is ask."

There it is. Me finally getting myself killed. Death by a perpetually running mouth. Braces's eyes flare in the kind of rage you only see from men terrified they've been emasculated.

"The fuck did you say to me?" he says. At least I think that's what he says. The whole moment seems to be warbling dangerously out of reality as he steps closer. This isn't the kind of thing that happens to me. It's the kind of thing that happens to the burnout kids who smoke next to the parking lot at school.

"I said you and your friends really are making a big deal out of some boys wearing a bit of makeup. Personally, I think you could use a little blush."

Braces narrows his eyes with clear bloodlust while the Scarecrow in black stands in the grass and waits for their little visit to be over. What the hell is his deal? Braces jolts forward and I stumble back, my foot sliding on something that sends me tumbling onto my ass. Braces is towering over me now, his foot positioned between my splayed legs in a way that could be particularly testicle crushing. My humiliation morphs into something deeper. I wonder how hard you have to kick to break someone's ankle. I wonder if he'll hit his head on the way down and if the blood will blind him long enough for us to get away. If he'll bleed enough for his friends to get the message that they shouldn't have fucked with us in the first place. Under the tumult of thoughts is a single, clear one. There is a part of me that wants to hurt this man even more than he wants to hurt me.

Skinhead pushes Alan harder than before, and Alan whips back to face him. In his hands, he grips a steel baseball bat. With practiced precision he follows through all the way up to Skinhead's skull and pauses there, ready to strike. Behind me, Nifoal gasps. I don't move.

Oh, right, I think with surprising calm. *Alan's dad is really into baseball.*

The bat tickles Mister Clean's stubble while Alan's hands remain cool and steady.

"We're kind of busy, boys," Alan says. "But maybe some other night."

Skinhead backs away quickly, nearly tripping over his own feet. He laughs, his face reddening with embarrassment while he takes us in one more time. He shakes his head like we've spoiled an obvious joke.

"Whatever. Fucking faggots, man."

Skinhead backs down the gazebo steps with Adult Braces following suit. Nifoal pulls me to my feet, surveying my scraped palms.

"You good?" she asks.

I nod, eyes still trained on the three figures receding into the dark. My hands begin to shake.

"Fuck those guys," I mutter.

"Yeah." Nifoal exhales. "Fuck those guys." She brushes the wig out of her face.

We stare at them as the third guy, the one who hadn't left the grass, turns to take us in one last time. Nifoal's eyes meet his for a second before he turns again to trot after his friends.

"You two know each other?" I ask cautiously.

Nifoal laughs despite herself.

"Man Meet," she explains. "Funny, don't you think?"

I search her face for the joke, but I don't find it. I laugh anyway.

Alan drops the bat and wipes the sweat from his forehead. A car ambles along the street on the other side of the park, casually emerging from the beach and taking in the sights of Port Anders at night. The night is very quiet again.

"Well," Alan says, taking a deep breath. "Should we go from the top?"

***

"It's really not a big deal."

My father closes the fridge door and observes my hot-pink fingernails from a distance, as if they're radioactive. In the insanity of Alan almost beheading the locals, we'd neglected the nail polish remover.

"It doesn't bother me none, Peter," Dad insists. "But lots of people around Mason would have a few choice words for you on something like that."

I get the feeling that *none* isn't how much the nail polish is bothering him. I haven't informed him of what really happened tonight, and the thought of proving him right isn't giving me any incentive to do otherwise. I sling off my backpack, and in the dim light I see that he is observing me carefully, the way both my parents have been in the habit of doing lately.

"That sounds like a *them* problem," I tell him, shuffling off my shoes.

"Sure, but you'd be amazed at how quickly people can take a *them* problem and make it a *you* problem."

I hate that he's right. More than that, I hate the way we're even talking about this right now. Shouldn't the kind of person who throws beer cans at kids be expected not to *do* the throwing? Dad waits for me to respond. When I don't, he grunts and disappears into the living room. He sinks into his recliner, hands tossed up in defeat against a world that makes less sense to him by the day. I stand in the doorway feeling like he's dropped a glass of milk and walked off, content to let me clean up the mess. I consider marching into the living room and telling him that he should be directing his passive aggression toward the three stooges in Port Anders who nearly made a news story out of us. He should know that Alan did a better job of protecting me from exactly the kind of assholes my father is warning me about than he ever has. Not only that, but Alan did it with his nails painted bright pink. My hands sting. They begin to shake slightly while my body levels off from the adrenaline I didn't know had been partying its way through my nervous system. I must look like an effeminate gopher, quivering and snapping sibilantly after being plucked from my little hole in the dirt.

The other version of how tonight might have played out isn't far from my thoughts. Something like this is always an option hovering over your small-town gay life. They make movies about it. It's not like Jake Gyllenhaal dies of love and acceptance at the end of *Brokeback Mountain*.

I walk upstairs and flop into bed, tapping expectantly at my phone.

> **@NifoalDressage** Not sure who needs to hear this but @ptkns1358 is a fierce bitch. @MissEMissY, release the full cut.

After a night spent at the business end of a bashing, it's not the worst thing I could have asked for. I follow Nifoal's post to Missy's Poster page, now decked out in pictures of her and her GBF, Brison Dallas. One caption reads:

> This goober. He's been through so much, and still finds time to be the best friend a girl could ask for. Shame that not all of us can see that.

I scroll the comments, hating myself for it while still getting lost in a stream of *yes girlie* and *I don't know WHO you're talking about but he sounds like an asshole*. A simple heart emoji, left by *@lrne4learn,* catches my eye. I tap the profile and find myself face to face with Lorne the Soft-Serve Guy. My chest leaps just a little when confronted with his sideways grin.

This goober. Kill me. That goober has the looks, the money, and probably his pick of guys thanks to the first two things on the list. And then I feel, as I often do, like I'm doing something wrong. The few other gays in town have it all figured out while I'm over here making sure my mentions aren't morphing into death threats. Just once I'd like this gay thing to mean more than a lack of something.

Amadeus was directed by Milos Forman.

Still on Lorne's profile, my thumbs hover over the DM button.

All Quiet on the Western Front was directed by Lewis Milestone.

Instead, I click my phone off and curl into the smallest ball I can manage.

The Sound of Music was directed by Robert Wise.

It's not as small as I'd like.

CHAPTER SIX

A DESTITUTE VOLE IN A TACKY PAIR OF CARGO SHORTS

"Oh my god, hi, Peter!"

Lorne waves from the barstool next to the door of Marlowe's Diner as I emerge from my shift in the kitchen. Clad in my work attire of grease-stained jeans and T-shirt, I resist the urge to cover myself with my hands. My hair stands painfully on end after being released from a hairnet and baseball cap. Twangy country music floats softly though Marlowe's in the post-lunch lull, and I'm intensely aware of the fact that I smell of bacon grease and home fries.

"Oh, hey!" I wave.

Is there some way to tell who has been creeping your Poster page? Some app that everyone but me must know about? Some new reason for me to live the rest of my life in a cave with bad internet connection?

Lorne closes the book he's reading and motions for me to sit as he sips his coffee. The brown walls and wicker decor of Marlowe's scream *uncool,* and I flinch at the country bumpkin energies I must be giving off. I drop onto the stool next to his, and my eyes light up at the bright orange copy of *How Music Works* by David Byrne that Lorne has just bookmarked.

"Oh, wow," I marvel, instantly cringing at my overly earnest delivery. "I love David Byrne. And Talking Heads."

Lorne nods as if this is the only reasonable thing to say on the matter.

"Totally. Everybody only talks about "Psycho Killer," which isn't even very good if you ask me. Totally goofy art rock, which I guess is how they started off. But nobody talks about the fact that David Byrne is a certified genius when it comes to the actual *design* of the music. I've been trying to diversify my musical palette lately, but I always end up coming back to David Byrne, you know?" I don't really know, but I nod as if I do. I really only *like* Talking Heads, and I only know their hits. You know, like "Psycho Killer."

"I didn't know you work here," Lorne observes. "Looks like we're both slinging fries for the summer."

"Totally. Just saving up for college, you know?"

"Yeah, me too."

The twang of a new country-pop ballad strikes up over the speakers.

"Not much when it comes to music selection, though," I offer.

Lorne smiles, and I stare into the depths of his dimples, forgetting where I am for a second. I smile in a way that must scream *I'm going to cut your face off and wear it over my face.*

My phone buzzes in my pocket.

"I have to go," I manage. "But it was nice to see you."

"It's nice to see you, too! I'm really excited about this show you're all putting together. Let me know when it's happening and I'll be there," Lorne says, grinning.

"You should give me your number," I say before I can stop myself. When Lorne only nods amiably, I breathe again and soldier on. "I'll send you the poster and stuff, you know, when we have one."

Before Lorne can say a word, I've passed him my phone, which is ringing again, Alan's name popping up in bright green. I silence it and Lorne types in his name and number.

"See you around!" Lorne waves and I leave without a word, nearly smacking right into a pair of construction workers clomping through Marlowe's front door.

Tilly beams from the passenger seat while Alan revs the car to life.

"Excuse me," he crows as I drop into the back seat. "Did you see my one true love inside Marlowe's?"

A strange rush tingles up my fingers while I click my seatbelt shut. "I did," I say breezily, as if I've forgotten about it already. When the car pulls away from the sidewalk, I drop lower into my seat as Lorne's faint outline appears in the front windows of Marlowe's.

Tilly turns to glare at me dramatically, shock written large across her face. "And did you talk to him? Put in a good word for Ms. Culture? You know, about how massive her dick is and how—"

"Okay, Tilbert," Alan cuts in. "That's quite enough with the trading card stats, thank you."

"No," I say. "I just said hi on my way out."

I consider telling them what really happened but drop it when I remember that Alan has a proven track record of making something about *you* become something about *Alan*, like the time I turned green from nausea after too many spinning rides at the Spring Fair. I lay in the grass near the horse track, trying my best not to pass out. Alan sat nearby, performing an original monologue about how he was pretty sure he'd gotten a splinter from the Tilt-A-Whirl, and now that he thought of it, he was feeling pretty nauseous, too.

The chorus to "Never Gonna Give You Up" springs from Tilly's pocket and she makes a sour face at the screen before inhaling deeply.

"Hi, Grandma," she says as she presses the phone to her ear. "No, I'm just out helping Alan with something. Yeah. Uh huh. No, I probably won't be home in time. I know . . . yeah, I know. Okay. All right, well, I'll talk to you soon then. Yup."

Tilly isn't an overly *girly* kind of girl, if only because Alan takes up most of the estrogen in the room. But when Tilly's grandmother calls, Tilly becomes Little Miss Mason. Her voice pitches up and she's always more than happy to do whatever her grandmother needs, whether it's picking up a prescription, coming home early, or doing that old people thing where they sweep their walkways with a wooden broom. Tilly's grandmother doesn't even like doing that herself. She gives the sweeping-outside-despite-the-fact-that-it-is-outside duty to Tilly.

"Sure, Grandma. All right, I love you too."

Tilly hangs up and Alan turns the radio on while we sit in silence. The town turns into fields and farms around us. Tilly fiddles with an errant string on her cutoffs.

In the rearview mirror, Alan raises an eyebrow.

Can you believe that woman? he says through our invisible intercom.

What's going on? I ask with a look.

Girl, do not get me started.

"If we weren't on a mission of the utmost importance, I'd be abandoning the both of you and ordering me and Lorne a milkshake," Alan says dreamily, poking Tilly. "You know, the kind you drink with two straws."

Tilly's only response is a distant smile.

My phone burns a hole in my pocket, Lorne's number sitting in there like the final piece of evidence in an Agatha Christie story. I fiddle with the door handle, antsy and on edge as if Alan might somehow sense the addition to my recent contacts. But so what? It's my business alone which boys I exchange numbers with. Sure, the boy in question does complicate matters a little, given that Alan has already called shotgun on him. But if Alan and Lorne end up entwined in a summer romance, I'll eat my hat. And I don't even wear hats.

***

"I'll be honest, Peter," says Bailey Hayes. "When Aggie told me that you had signed on to be our producer, I was skeptical. You *are* the main character of

Poster right now, after all."

Bailey stretches out along her immaculately cushioned bay windows, pink throws and glittery pillows piled high about her. Her wavy blonde hair is piled even higher. Bailey might just be the opposite of Cora Copia. In her sapphire sundress, glinting jewels, and yellow hair, Bailey is bright and blaring. What she lacks in height, she makes up for in heels. We'd arrived to find Bailey in her full getup and waiting for us at her ornate front doors, the kind of doors that get thrown open dramatically at the beginning of a British period drama. It wasn't a shock to find her waiting on our arrival because her laneway is long enough to host a small marathon. Bailey's family lives on a property that you could go so far as to call an estate, complete with hedge maze, infinity pool, an assortment of all-terrain vehicles, and a faux-rustic guest house. Bailey appraises me with a calculating eye and I'm sure that all she sees is a destitute vole in a tacky pair of cargo shorts.

"But Cora and Nifoal swear by you. And if you've got their vote of confidence, then you have mine."

I exhale, trying not to breathe too hard around the expensive linens and draperies that make up Bailey's bedroom. Alan sits on the edge of her bed, perched delicately atop a black and white chevron comforter. It looks more expensive than the contents of my bedroom combined.

"That's great," I say at last.

And it is great. I half expected Bailey to greet me with a pair of tap shoes.

"I was so excited to chat," Bailey continues. "With you, and the whole team. Aggie, girl, how is your channel coming along?"

"It's going great," Alan smiles.

"Why haven't you come out with any new videos lately?" Bailey asks, batting her lashes.

"Oh," says Alan, "I have. Once, sometimes twice a week."

"That's so odd," Bailey muses. "Haven't seen it come across my feed. But that's smaller channels for you. It's honestly messed up how the algorithm treats you guys."

Tilly's hand closes over Alan's as his calm veneer threatens to crack.

"You're the producer," Bailey says, her eyes locking onto me again. "So I have some possibilities to run by you."

I nod as Alan flashes me a thumbs-up. Is this going incredibly well, or did I hit the floor of that gazebo hard enough to induce some kind of hallucinatory state?

"My mother knows literally everybody, including all these super boring and desperate people who work for the county. These absolute chicken fingers who are, like, forty five, but think they're cultural because they go to craft markets and community theater. Mama Striks will for sure be able to hook us up with, like, a venue. I'm thinking the town hall?"

Alan is close to hyperventilating, his hands fluttering in unfettered excitement.

"That sounds amazing."

"Ugh, I'm so glad you think so!" Bailey gasps. "This is fantastic. But we'll gab over the boring details after the interview."

Nobody says anything. I look from Bailey to Alan blankly while a woozy sense of impending doom begins to settle over me. My ego is already bruising at the tone of her voice.

"What interview?"

Bailey grins like a cat about to pounce. "Were my terms not clear?"

Alan plucks at a stray hair on his jeans. "So," he begins. "About that . . ."

"All I'm asking for is an interview, Peter."

Bailey brushes a lock of wig from her face, her pink nails combing deeply through the blonde mane. I consider ripping it off her head, but Bailey would love nothing more than the drama of a real-life wig-snatch.

While Cora Copia is a creepy spider-boy in a dress, Bailey Hayes is a *woman*. Her real name is Bailey Strickland, heir to the uber-loaded Strickland Energy Company. When he's not playing golf on a helicarrier or hunting the last known leprechaun on a secret rich-people island, Bailey is a high-fantasy drag queen. With her cinched waist and jutting jaw bones, it's impossible to see her as anything but a girl with money to burn.

She also happens to have a wildly successful YouTube channel.

"I never agreed to an interview," I inform Bailey, my sense of diplomacy beginning to strain.

Alan jumps up to intervene, but Bailey easily shushes him. And as angry as I am right now, I can't help but admire how quickly she was able to do that.

"Look, ladies. You know I'd love to perform. My followers have been screaming for a live performance all year. But if the other Rural Realness girls are getting their little dance solos, then Ms. Hayes will certainly be getting hers."

I grind my teeth, considering the corner I've been backed into. Appeasing Bailey Hayes, loath as I might be to even try, is the right move. Pity sales from her Poster followers alone could sell the show out in no time.

"Why do I get the feeling that you won't be interviewing me about my fashion choices?"

Bailey titters, glossy lips gleaming. "All I want is to hear your side of the story, Peter. Tell my viewers what really happened with Brison Dallas that day." Her drawn-on eyebrows arch casually, as if she's only asked me to pass the finishing powder. "At least do it for the publicity, darling."

Alan smiles, begging me to overlook the trap he's set for me. There it is. The shoe finally drops. The sequined, perfectly sized shoe. I walk back through Bailey's bedroom, and I'm through her front doors before Alan catches up to me, the gravel driveway crunching beneath our shoes.

"I forgot to mention—" Alan begins.

"You're forgetting to mention a lot lately," I lob over my shoulder. "And I'm starting to think it's intentional."

Alan wheels me around, which I don't mind, because I'm already a little out of breath.

"Not intentional. Strategic."

"Those are the same thing!"

"You don't play well with others, Peter! Excuse me if I have to wiggle the truth to accommodate."

"I *wanted* to be your producer, Alan. Stop acting like you're pulling me along, kicking and screaming."

"Then *stop* kicking and screaming! Try to play nice for a change!"

A gardener, snipping slowly with garden shears, slips quietly behind a hedge. I get the feeling he's used to the doors around here being thrown open dramatically.

"I *do* play nice."

"If you played nice, Bailey wouldn't have anything to interview you about."

A directionless, impotent surge of fury flashes through me, so I crumple my lips into my mouth to hold back the words that would turn this argument into a blowout.

"Fine," I concede. "But stop lying to me."

"*Fine*," Alan whispers. "Then you need to stop acting like you're above all this."

I scoff. "I do *not* think I'm above all this."

Alan's eyes narrow into a flat disbelief that isn't up for debate.

"I don't!" I insist. "I just don't think that taking advantage of your best friend is a good look."

"Oh, please. If I didn't pull stunts like this, you'd never leave the house in the first place."

"If I'm going to be the producer, you're going to have to actually *let* me produce."

"So produce."

"I'm trying!" I say. "But it's a little hard to get any traction when Aggie Culture decides to just make all the decisions in secret. It's *The Mason County Drag Extravaganza*, not the *Aggie Culture Solo Experience*."

"So stop leaving me solo!"

I exhale in a display of disbelief. Of course Alan thinks this whole thing has been nothing but him. This is Aggie Culture's world, and Peter should just be grateful to live in it.

"Yeah," I say as I walk past him. "Sorry I've done absolutely nothing for you this entire time."

I crunch my way back up to the house, the crystalline front doors bouncing the sun into my eyes as I go.

CHAPTER SEVEN

CREATURE FROM THE PROBLEMATIC LAGOON

"Hey, honeys, it's your fave drag diva, Ms. Bailey Hayes," Bailey announces down the barrel of the camera. She's changed into a purple blazer and matching skirt with a ruffled white blouse, the total picture of a news professional.

"Today's about a different kind of energy. As you all know, being involved with my community here in my *quaint* home of Mason County, well, it's super important to me. And today I have brought onto my show a local character who has found himself mixed up in quite the controversy. His name is, of course, Peter Thompkin. And he's been called, by some, a homophobe, a bigot, anti-mental health, and deeply triggering. I've brought him on today to address some of these issues. Peter, welcome to the show."

I'm already sweating beneath Bailey's lighting. Having the real estate to turn an entire room of your house into a film studio is one thing, but making me sweat like a hot-take-generating pig-boy is another. I play the part of the contrite talk show guest while Alan waves me on from off camera. Tilly just stares in wide-eyed amazement, holding back a barking laugh.

"Yeah," I say. "Thanks for having me."

"Let's get right to it," Bailey begins, putting on her best anchor voice. "You've found yourself in some hot water after a verbal altercation with a well-known classmate of yours, Brison Dallas. Brison recently lost his father to mental health–related causes. Which, according to a video making the rounds, you leveled against him. You went so far as to encourage Brison to commit suicide, is that correct?"

My palms begin to sweat in a way that I suspect has nothing to do with the heat.

"I wouldn't say I *encouraged*—"

"But you did bring it up," Bailey quickly points out.

"So what happened was—"

"Let me ask you something, Peter." Bailey leans in and smoothes her skirt, a hard-hitting journalist if ever there was one. "Do you have any experience with mental health?"

I blink.

"Everybody has experiences with mental health. That's like asking if I have experience with dental health."

Alan's face falls into his hands while Tilly rubs his back consolingly.

I can sense Bailey's restrained smile. She couldn't be happier that I refuse to play into the trap she's laying so brazenly. Still, I can't force myself into giving her an inch. It feels like she's holding out one of those old-timey dunce hats for me to wear. She can offer it all she wants, but white just isn't my color.

"Let's back things up a touch because we have an exclusive announcement for the queers and allies of Mason County, don't we, Peter?"

I relax slightly. Publicity. Think of the optics.

"We do, Bailey, yes."

"And you could have taken this exclusive to *other* channels, maybe ones with more of a, shall we say, local viewership. Why choose Bailey Hayes?"

Alan looks up through his fingers, the color draining from his face.

"That's a great question, Bailey," I say with a polite talk-show laugh.

"You're producing something that you're calling *The First Annual Mason County Drag Extravaganza*."

"Yes! A night of performances by the queens of Rural Realness, yourself included, right here in Mason."

"And are you at all worried that the controversy around your name might be a deal-breaker for your potential audience?"

"I think that the context around that video is important," I offer, grasping for a conversational life raft.

"Do you consider what you did an act of bigotry?" Bailey asks, eyes squinted in a display of journalistic integrity.

"*I'm* gay, Bailey."

"Sure," she allows. "But have you ever encountered the concept of *internalized* homophobia? Because gay people are perfectly capable of being problematic entirely on their own."

"That's actually the point I'm trying to make," I explain. "Brison had been bullying my friend Alan over his outfit choices for, like, a week before school let out. Alan was doing this, I don't know, performance art thing, where he wore outfits in the colors of the Pride flag—"

"And it made you uncomfortable to be around such bold displays of LGBTQ+ identity?" Bailey asks.

Knowing that it's the last thing I should do, I openly roll my eyes. "I was defending my friend, actually."

Bailey considers this, making a meal of her empathetic display.

"Of course you were," she simpers. "And you've come on my channel to apologize."

I halt, nearly laughing at how brazen this has all been. Bailey has finally played her hand. This has been her game this entire time. She wants an apology. Everyone loves an apology video, after all. They love it almost as much as they love to tear it apart, which means a swarm of views, reposts, and comments for Ms. Bailey Hayes. It doesn't matter if her viewers believe the apology. What matters is that they click on it.

"I've come to set the record straight," I announce.

Bailey's gleaming fingernails settle on her chin, that smile finally blooming across her face.

What are you doing? Alan's face screams across the room.

What does it look like? mine replies.

"Brison started this when he targeted my best friend," I explain. "You mentioned internalized homophobia, Bailey, and I think that was a great point. Brison can't seem to stand himself any more than the rest of us can stand him. So, Brison, if you're watching, I am sorry. I'm sorry that you felt the need to humiliate Alan Goode every day for a week straight just so you could feel better about yourself. And I'm extra sorry because even that probably didn't work."

***

Alan doesn't even look at me on the ride home. The sun is setting but still beating down ripples of heat that lace the asphalt. Tilly's eyes catch mine in the rearview mirror and then flit to Alan's. Her foot taps an anxious staccato while she finds something, anything, to fill the silence.

"I thought you looked really nice on camera, Peter," she says without conviction. "And it'll be great publicity, won't it? For the show, I mean." She fiddles with a twirl of fabric on her shorts. It tears with a faint ripping sound. Just as I'm considering if I can survive throwing myself from a moving car, Alan's phone rings. The words *Bailey Strickland* scroll across the display. Regarding me with a stern glance, Alan answers.

"Hey, hun!" he says airily over the speakerphone. "Peter and I were just chatting and I think he's actually really sorry for the way he—"

"Sure, sure," Bailey interjects. "Look, babies. I'm watching the stream back and I gotta say, we might have a hit on our hands."

I slink further into the pleather of the back seat, hoping to dissolve into a cloud of nothing.

"Really?" Alan asks, suddenly jubilant.

"Trust me, this is absolute clickbait. The comments section went wild, people on Brison's side, people on Peter's side. I've already gained a hundred followers since you hightailed it out of here."

The transport truck approaching from the other side of the road is beginning to look very appealing.

"And," Bailey continues, "I've decided that, since Peter *did* get me some quality clickable content wherein he makes a total ass of himself, I will join this drag show of yours."

"Drag *extravaganza*," Alan corrects her.

"Let my work my magic on my mother, and she'll work her magic on the dye jobs running town hall. 'Kay?"

"Totally 'kay!" Alan exclaims, grimacing at his own word choice.

"Okay!" Bailey trills. "Byeee!"

The phone beeps and Alan shifts in his seat, unwilling to let me in on his obvious elation.

"This is great news!" Tilly cheers, her words deflating in the otherwise cheerless atmosphere.

I stare into the distance, watching as the Mason town limits draw closer. "Great news."

"Fantastic news," Alan concurs.

I keep my eyes from catching his in the rearview mirror. From the driver's seat, I feel Alan doing the same.

***

A bat flits past my window, the summer heat swelling and resigning me to the wooden floorboards of my bedroom. My phone lies above me on the edge of my bed, but I decide not to touch it. And then I decide not to touch it again. I don't last a third time.

The livestream, cut down to nothing but my final remarks, fills the top of my Poster feed.

> **@brisondallaz** Hey, @ptkns1358. U mad bro?

> **@macnzeefkya** lol what is this gay ass shit?

> **@KlarisssaBTon** Not shocked.

> **@AggeeCltr** There are two sides to every story. @ptkns1358 is my hero.

Something about this last post sends me off the deep end. I toss my phone back onto my bed. Alan had trapped me in a moment of gotcha journalism only a few hours ago, but now I'm his knight in shining armor? I shouldn't be surprised. Alan gets to be the brave victim in this version. Not the psychopathic narcissist who needs the world to revolve around him at all times.

"Excuse me," Alan had asked that afternoon. "Did you see my one true love inside Marlowe's?" As if the only thing I'd be doing with Lorne would be putting in a good word for Alan. As if Peter could never be flirting with a boy. The trap that Alan and Bailey had set for me this afternoon circles my thoughts until it's the only thing I can focus on. You know, besides the image of me as some scaly Creature from the Problematic Lagoon.

I've been painted into a tight corner, and it's not escaping me that Alan just grabbed a paint brush. I'd felt something like guilt on our car ride to Bailey's, knowing that I'd lied to Alan about getting Lorne's number. I don't anymore.

My back peels off the wood as I pull myself up. I retrieve my phone, tap the new number sitting under *Lorne :)*, and type:

Hey, it's Peter.
You free tomorrow
night?

CHAPTER EIGHT
WATERLOGGED POOL GOBLIN

"Philosophy?" I ask.

Lorne nods and rummages around for the last of the Dairy Freeze fries.

"So you're going to, what? Sit around and wonder if the shade of green you're seeing is the same shade of green that I'm seeing?

"For four years, yes." He laughs through that crooked smile.

Lorne and I sit at a beat-up picnic table behind the fenced-off public pool, closed past sundown. The park beside us is empty and dark, the vibrant reds and blues of the slides and playground equipment shining dully against the distant streetlights. Lorne finds the last fry, and I try to act like I do this all the time.

"What does one do with a degree in philosophy?"

Lorne casts his hands to the sky. "I think that question is an act of philosophy itself. And what does one do with a degree in . . . what do you want to study?"

"I don't know," I say at last. "English, I think."

Lorne squints, making a show of his own perplexity. "English, the language you're currently speaking?"

"As in, you know, writing and like . . . reading and shit."

"You want a degree in writing and reading?"

"And shit."

"How *is* the glass house you live in, sir? Is it breezy?"

We both laugh, and for a second I forget just how nervous I've been since we sat down. "I never thought about college in terms of, like, picking a major."

Lorne sits back in amazement. "You thought you'd just go and hang out around campus being vaguely artsy?"

"I always knew I would go to college," I say firmly. "That's why I've been subjecting myself to cooking home fries for hillbillies."

"Let's say," Lorne says, "that you had to choose a major right now. What would it be?"

I resist the urge to lick the salty grease off my fingers while I ponder the question. The answer comes to me easier than I'd expected.

"Film," I say. "Maybe a film major."

Lorne nods, taking this as a win.

"You make movies?"

I shake my head.

"But you *want* to make movies?"

"I want to make . . ." I trail off, beginning to wish that I'd kept this to myself. "I want to make *things*, I guess. Movies are just the thing I know the most about."

"You're making a drag show," Lorne offers.

"I'm making a fool of myself is what I'm making," I say. "If there's a major for that, I'd get straight As."

"Okay, okay," Lorne relents. "So you're still figuring out the finer details."

"It could be worse." My nerves are fading under a growing sense of ease. "I could be Alan. He doesn't even want to go to college."

Lorne crumples the paper bag between his hands. "What does he want to do?"

"He wants to be a professional drag queen. Which is great, but it's always seemed to me that he's ignoring the amount of unpaid work you probably have to do before the money comes in."

Lorne nods. "Maybe he just wants to take a year off before he decides what to do next."

"That's the problem," I say. "He takes one year off, maybe he travels a bit. But, in all likelihood, he ends up stuck in Mason County with even less direction than he has now."

"And that's the worst thing that could happen? Being stuck in Mason County?" Lorne says through a sly grin.

"Yes. Now you're getting it."

Lorne places his hands on the table only a few inches from my own. A thrill passes up my arms and I shiver despite the heat.

"I think it's sweet how much you worry about him," Lorne says at last.

I almost laugh. Does Lorne think Alan and I are dating? He wouldn't be the first person to think we've coupled off.

"Yeah, well . . . he's my best friend," I reply uneasily. "People sometimes think that we're dating just cuz we're some of the only gays around. Which is funny."

A silence follows. I've ruined the night, haven't I? I shouldn't have said that. I shouldn't have said anything. This was a mistake. Not just going out tonight but thinking I'm anywhere close to being in the same league as Lorne. I should have stayed home and googled far-off nunneries willing to take in gay teenage boys. A life of quiet, sexless worshipping has to be a better option than this. At least nuns are used to the guy they're obsessed with not calling them back.

The shiver begins to inch from anticipation toward trepidation.

"What's funny about you dating Alan?" Lorne asks lightly, a crispness creeping into his voice. He surveys me over his now-steepled fingers, the very picture of a therapist studying a client.

"Oh, come on," I cajole, trying for a laugh and landing nowhere close. "He's my best friend, but Alan is a *ridiculous* person. Everything with him is a total pageant. And if he can't reach pageant status he'll settle for *parade*."

"So you would never have feelings for someone like Alan?" Lorne enquires from behind his fingers again.

Why am I being interrogated?

"I don't know about someone *like* Alan. But not Alan."

"Is it because of how he looks, or ... ?"

I fall speechless and kick myself for opening my mouth in the first place. Someone like Lorne doesn't want to hang out with a lumpy pizza-face like me in the first place. My back sweat becomes accusatory. I'm a bridge troll. The first bridge troll to join a nunnery.

"No," I say at last. "But he's my best friend. It'd be like dating my brother. Or, you know, if Aggie is around, like dating my own sister."

The joke doesn't land, but Lorne's eyes narrow in understanding. The moment grows stale between us. I'm Uma Thurman in *Kill Bill*'s ninja battle, slaying the good vibes with my katana of blandness and poor social grace.

"I just think we have to be careful about the way we talk about Alan, you know?" Lorne suggests. "It can come off kind of homophobic or even fat-phobic."

"Oh, not at all," I splutter. "That's not it at all, I just—"

"No, I know that's not what you *meant*," Lorne assures me easily. His hand slides onto mine. Maybe he won't even notice how cold and clammy it has become. "But intent and delivery can be *so* different," he continues with an air of cool generosity. "And we need to be building Alan up, not letting our preconceived notions punch him down, right?"

"Totally," I say, trying to reassure him. "I mean, I do nothing but build him up. One time he called me from a dressing room to ask me if his ass looked good in a new pair of jeans. And it wasn't even a video call."

"I just think we all have a lot of internalized hate that we need to start reckoning with, right? For instance, I've decided that I'll never sleep with someone of the same body type twice in a row."

A bird chirps in the tree beside us.

I have absolutely no idea how to respond to this.

"Let's go swimming," Lorne announces, effectively snapping the moment shut.

Bewildered, I survey the pool and the empty park beside it. My heart begins to cool its racing, nursing itself after Lorne's tonal whiplash.

"Totally," I say. "But it's closed."

"You're right. It is."

Lorne stands from the picnic table and ambles toward the fence. He glances back to the street to make sure nobody is watching and before I know it, he's launched himself onto the gray mesh. The fence sways with *clinks* and *tings* as he hauls himself up and over its vertical length, but he lands with a satisfied gasp on the other side.

"Are you coming?" he calls softly.

I'm about to find some excuse, but then Lorne strips his shirt off with a grin and I think that maybe swimming is a great idea after all.

***

The water is cold, but I drop into it quickly, not eager to show off my premature love handles and hairy nipples. I watch the dim backyards on the other side of the weather-worn changing rooms, more than a little apprehensive. Lorne, on the other hand, is enjoying the possibility of getting spotted, making laps and splashing just a little louder than he needs to while I cling to the gritty edge of the pool.

"Come on," he stage-whispers.

A bat flitters through the sky, and the illicit nature of it all finally sends a delightful shock to my fingertips. I push off and join Lorne in the center, my doggy-paddling arms already aching from the effort.

"You should know that I'm not a very good swimmer," I manage through sharp breaths.

Lorne yelps as I draw closer, floating easily on his back as I struggle like a drowning monkey to do the same. "You grew up next to a lake. Shouldn't you be Aquaman?"

"Those are the Port Anders kids, thank you very much," I explain wetly. "They grow up going to the beach whenever they want. For the rest of us, it's not so easy."

Lorne reaches out and buoys me up with a hand under my back. His breath smells like french fries, and I don't hate it. "I was almost a lifeguard. I'll make sure you don't drown."

"*Almost* a lifeguard?

"It got too corporate." He grins.

I'd be swooning if I wasn't too busy trying not to choke on pool water. Lorne effortlessly swims off again, and I try not to sink to the bottom of the pool.

"I have a question for you," proposes Lorne.

A jumble of nerves goes off in my stomach. This is it. This is the moment. There are a million questions that Lorne could ask, but *Can I kiss you?* is the clear front-runner. He glides close again and I tread water choppily, my stomach a nest of horny butterflies. He could need to check my body type off his list, and I don't even mind being a box for him to check.

"Totally."

Lorne swims closer. "It's about Brison."

With that, the butterflies burst into flames. A light moves across the wall of the changing rooms. On the street, we spy the unmistakable black and white of a cop car ambling its way down the street on the other side of the park. Part of me is terrified, and part of me is just glad that something, anything, got in the way of whatever Lorne had to say about Brison fucking Dallas.

Lorne holds his finger to his lips.

Our clothes sit like traitorous lumps on the deck, my red sneakers pointing an accusatory finger toward the water. The car stops and the engine purrs in the near distance. Music blasts from within, and a bland country twang floats over the water. The Mason County Police Department is the kind of workplace that eagerly welcomes the Luke Degraphs and Luke Andersons of the world. It's not hard to imagine what this officer would make of two scantily clad teenage boys huddled together in a pool, trespassing.

What would Alan do in this situation?

Then the cop car speeds off with a squeal of tires.

Lorne claps a hand over his mouth. "Oh my god!" he whispers. "That was wild!"

I laugh as quietly as I can, feeling his breath on my face again. Visions of us hauled off in a cop car are replaced by visions of us doing something much different. Lorne studies my face and I study his. I want to run my thumb along his stupid little sideways smirk. I want to put my fingers through his hair and hold the back of his head. A weightless feeling spreads over me. All I have to do is lean over and act like I know what I'm doing.

Water sloshes across my face and I wince as Lorne hauls himself out of the pool. He hops over to his shorts as if he does this sort of thing all the time. He waits expectantly for me to join him, shaking his hair dry like a dog. But I'm frozen in the water. Getting out of the pool right now would be a special kind of mortifying. The physical result of our breathy proximity is currently on full display, and my unrequested boner isn't exactly the image I want to leave him with.

I consider letting go of the ledge and sinking to the bottom. I'll live there. I'm sure it will be a simpler life. I'll be the scary water goblin living in the deep end of Mason's public pool. Legend will tell that if you approach me on a full moon, I will grant you one wish that will go horrifically and ironically awry.

"So are you going to soak all night, or should we get out of here before that cop comes back?"

I sigh. "Okay, but turn around."

Lorne turns to watch the street and we both hastily wrangle our shorts back on. In another reality, this moment could be something close to sexy. But in the current reality, where I'm wet, freezing, and visibly jiggling, I'm more of a waterlogged pool goblin than a merman.

"I should get back home," Lorne tells me when we are safely on the other side of the fence. He brushes the wet hair out of his face, and I can't help but imagine myself doing it instead. My phone rings in my pocket, but I let it go to voice mail.

"My clothes are getting pretty gross and stuff," he adds apologetically.

"Totally. So gross. I guess I'll head home, too."

We reach the street.

"All right," Lorne declares solemnly. "Have a good night."

He nods sagely and turns to walk off into the night. I just stand there, not sure how I'm supposed to feel about anything. Does he hate me? Had he considered kissing me before deciding not to? Had my terrible swimming been a huge turnoff? I'm boring. That's it. He'd thrown trespassing into the mix just to make *something* interesting happened tonight. No, it's that thing I said about Alan. Something about it had turned Lorne off the whole endeavor. Something about my homophobic, fat-phobic tone has shown Lorne that I'm just some ignorant hick who thinks he's cultured by merit of being one of the few gays around. A better looking, smarter guy with even an ounce of charm would have ended tonight with in-pool kissing. I begin walking home, turning the night over in my head and feeling increasingly like trash. Wet trash. Wet trash at the bottom of a public pool. I retrieve my phone to find a series of texts from Alan, several of them containing both rage and puke emojis. I scroll to the last text.

> Oh my god, get your flat little ass over here.

CHAPTER NINE
HOMO HUMPTY DUMPTY

Alan ushers me to the couch as I arrive in his basement, his phone already cued up with the latest Bailey Hayes video drop. My shorts itch damply as I sit to watch.

"The thing is, Bailey, I don't blame Peter," Brison says from the luxurious comfort of Bailey Hayes's studio. His hair is slicked back and he's wearing tight yellow shorts and one of those billowy, vaguely eastern-looking shirts. The kind you get from a boutique chain store that specializes in making you look well traveled even though you hate spicy food. "You can't blame someone for the ignorance they've inherited."

Tilly sits curled on the other side of the couch, writhing in discomfort.

"Intersectionality is *so* important when talking about this kind of thing," Bailey muses, sipping languidly from a metal straw. She clicks her claws against her glittery goblet. "Because, as you know, Peter self-identifies as gay."

Brison chuckles softly at this, as if listening to a child's ramblings. "I guess I just try to give grace to the other queer folks in our community,

Bailey. But what Peter did was not graceful."

"He was the one ragging on you for wearing Pride colors, and now he's suddenly Mr. Enlightened?" I seethe. "He's the one who was bullying the gay kid!"

"Well, the *other* gay kid," Alan corrects.

"The *other* other gay kid, thank you! Why does everyone forget I'm also a homo? Just because I'm not all, you know, done up like Brison or a freaking drag queen—"

"It wouldn't hurt your image, actually," Alan interjects. "Doing drag, I mean. It'd show that you're not such a stuck-up bitch toward the rest of the gays."

"I am *not* a stuck-up bitch."

"Well . . ." Alan and Tilly say in unison.

"I'm not this gay-hating gay they want everyone to think I am."

"No," Tilly allows. "But you do tend to be sort of . . ."

"You can, every now and then . . ." Alan tries.

"You just do this thing sometimes—"

"This thing where you're like . . ." Alan continues, "I'm gay, but I'm not *that* kind of gay."

My breathing shortens and I rein it in, refusing to show just how poked and prodded I feel. "Just because I don't want to do drag doesn't make me a homophobe."

Tilly shakes her head and takes my hands. "Nobody is saying that, Peter. But . . ." She weighs her options, glancing between me and Alan in a classic piece of Tilly choreography. She plays at being a no-nonsense badass, and for the most part she is. But a lot of the time she's also our peacekeeper. "You can sometimes, whether you mean to or not, act like you're better than other people."

"It's true," agrees Alan, a doctor about to deliver a life-altering diagnosis. "You think you're better than the heteros because, well, you are."

The three of us nod in tandem, facts being facts and all.

"But you also think you're better than the really *gay*-acting gays because you think we're all just being so goddamn basic all the time."

"I never said that," I stress.

"You don't have to," Alan points out. "It's just how you act. And it can be a little . . ."

"Intense?" Tilly offers.

"Off-putting," Alan confirms.

I laugh hollowly, refusing to engage. "I'm going to press play," I tell my friends, "because at least then I can *expect* to be completely attacked."

"Peter's involvement with the upcoming *Drag Extravaganza* may prove to be triggering for you," Bailey is saying through a mask of brave empathy. "Do you feel like it will be a safe space for you to attend?"

Brison is pensive for a moment while stewing in his own quiet bravery. "This is a huge moment for Mason County, Bailey. And I'm *so* excited." He smiles at the camera and my stomach lurches. "Even Peter Thompkin can't ruin that for me."

I scream into a musty yellow pillow.

"Who cares what Brison is saying about you?" Tilly shrugs. "He's super rich, super popular, and just gave the Extravaganza a ringing endorsement. This is a good thing!"

"For you!" I shout from within my cushion fortress. "For me it's just another *ringing* declaration that Peter Thompkin should be launched into the sun."

"Maybe," Alan muses. "But maybe that's going to make this entire thing blow up. I know I'm an idealist, but I'm not clueless. Throwing a drag show in the middle of Mason County and expecting it to fill up is a tall order. People probably see us as some act of charity or like some weird branch of community theater." His pacing shifts from *frantic* to *thoughtful*. "Anyone coming to see our show is probably seeing it as an act of community service. As in, *God bless those kids for putting on their little show.* And then they feel good about themselves for coming. Because they gave their five bucks to a social cause in their community and bore witness to the LGBTQ community creating a big, beautiful display."

The Extravaganza seems sillier than it ever has. It feels like the little song and dance your cousins make you watch while you're stuck at the kid's table. Yes, we all know that it's terrible. But it's cute that they're trying.

"But people don't want to feel like they're watching the Humane Society put on some fashion show for all the adoptable cats," Alan continues.

"Which I would buy tickets to *immediately*," says Tilly.

"They want to feel like they're witnessing an event. They want *drama*. They want *Tube Mommies*."

"Mmmm!" Tilly agrees, her interest piqued at the mention of her favorite reality show.

"Nobody watches *Tube Mommies* because they feel like they're doing something important for their community. They do it so they can watch the mothers of YouTube child stars throw drinks in each other's faces and say their catchphrases every ten minutes. They want petty behavior. They want gossip. And *that* is what's gonna sell tickets to our show."

"I'm sorry," I say, bafflement written clearly across my face. "Did everyone forget about the *drama* that happened during Nifoal's video shoot? We only narrowly escaped having our asses handed to us, and I have a feeling that this might constitute asking for it."

"Apples and oranges, Peter." Alan dismisses with a wave. "This is internet drama. Nothing bad has ever happened in the *real* world because of the internet."

"I don't even know where to begin with that," I mumble.

"But now that you mention it, that is a great idea."

I search Alan's face. Clearly I've missed something. He pulls up his phone and presses play on a video that I recognize immediately. My stout frame fills much of the screen, and Alan and Skinhead are visible on the left. There's some muffled audio and a scuffle before I fall out of frame like homo Humpty Dumpty.

Then the baseball bat appears.

"What's that got to do with anything?"

"It's evidence that Brison isn't the center of the gay universe!" Alan concludes. "The rest of us are dealing with some harsh realities, too."

"Sure," I say slowly. "But it's also a video of me falling on my damn ass. You don't think there's enough Peter Thompkin content online right now?"

Alan rolls his eyes while Tilly intervenes.

"We'll cut it down," she suggests. "So you can't see Peter falling."

"No," Alan insists. "They need to see what really happened."

"I've had enough of the world seeing me for a while, thanks."

"If we cut that we completely erase the context!" Alan pushes. "Then it's just me threatening some random guy. I'm *defending* you, Peter."

"Then we just don't post it."

"You're being too precious. Besides, this shows you in a sympathetic light. Isn't that a good thing?"

I feel like a mangled wad of something left on a bathroom floor. Alan isn't wrong. But I hate when he spins things like this. He wants to post the video because it'll fan the flames. Because he gets to play the weapon-wielding vigilante while I fall over like a toddler and cower behind Nifoal's boots.

But Alan isn't one to let go of an idea. He once fell asleep with the French channel playing overnight and spent a week convinced he'd absorbed conversational French. He went on believing it until Madame Racine let him know that he'd called her a dried-up hog peasant. So I relent.

"Fine."

Flopping down on the couch, Alan presses record on his own phone and stares daggers down the barrel of the camera. "This is a quick note to my good friend Brison Dallas," he begins. "I am *so* glad that you're going to be joining us at *The First Annual Mason County Drag Extravaganza*. And we agree that this really is *such* an important moment for queer people here in Mason County. But I also want to dispute your claims about my close and personal friend Peter Thompkin. Peter is, himself, a queer person who is nothing but supportive of his queer community, and he has been integral in the process so far. You'll also see from the video that I'm about to play, taken by Ms. Nifoal Dressage, that both Peter and I have been the victims of hate ourselves. Maybe giving this a quick watch will change your perspective because we wouldn't dream of perpetuating this kind of violence against our fellow gay," Alan finishes, blowing a kiss.

"Can't wait to see you at the show, August 28 at the Mason Town Hall at 8 p.m., tickets on sale now."

Alan presses stop. "Honestly," he exhales. "Do I have to do everything around here?"

***

My father squints at a blue tin of coffee before placing it back on the shelf and then adjusts his glasses to read a green one. Buying a new brand of anything requires a good ten minutes of deliberation for my dad, which has given my mom time to play Alan's video again. It's only been out for twenty-four hours but has already made its way into my mother's inbox.

"Can you please stop watching that?" I ask, already longing for death beneath the fluorescent supermarket lighting. An old lady in a calamine-pink blouse ambles between us, and she is the only thing stopping me from hurling my mother's phone toward the produce section.

Mom clicks it off, and the video of Alan with a baseball bat goes blank. My father eyes me wearily as he drops the green coffee tin into the cart.

"I still don't get it," he says.

I have no doubt that he's telling the truth.

"They're doing fashion shows, Andrew," explains my mother.

We turn into the dairy section. My parents are walking slower than usual, making me want to peel off my skin and flop onto the floor in a pile of organs and exasperation.

"They're not *fashion shows*, Mom."

"Well, that boy was wearing a dress and makeup," Mom replies, raising her hands in defeat. "What else am I supposed to call it?" She stops to pick up a tub of cottage cheese before frowning at my father. "You know, this went up by a *dollar*."

My father doesn't so much as glance at the cottage cheese.

"You're not wearing dresses, though," he says.

It straddles a place between a question and a statement, the way anything vaguely related to the word *gay* does.

"No," I reply thinly. But how would this conversation be going if I were? A headache is forming behind my eyes. Mom's friend Carol-Anne has e-mailed her a link to Alan's clapback video, and in doing so she ruined my entire day. Do people still leave bags of flaming dog shit on front porches?

"I don't think I like this, Peter," my mom worries aloud.

"I know, Mom, a whole dollar."

"No, the video."

"They weren't going to do anything." I shrug. "They were just trying to act tough."

Of course this is a lie, but my gut is telling me to play things as casual as possible. Is lying to your parents this easy for straight people?

"It's a joke, Mary," Dad assures her. "They're not really putting on a show like that." He hefts a jug of orange juice into the cart and I feel a familiar indignation rising.

"A joke?" she repeats, clearly not convinced.

"Like Gerald Corres," Dad says by way of explanation.

Mom examines the yogurt selection, looking for a sale.

"Who's Gerald Corres?" I ask half-heartedly.

"He's someone we went to school with," Mom explains. "Do we like Balkan style? Greek yogurt is getting so expensive."

"Gerald used to pull jokes all the time, Pete," Dad elaborates.

"They weren't *jokes*, Andrew."

"Well," he concedes, "he was always having a laugh, wasn't he?" Dad looks to me as if I was there, as if we're sharing a fond memory of our time in high school. "Gerald was always a bit weird, right?"

"Not *weird*. Different."

"Weird clothes," Dad explains. "Not afraid to be a bit girlier than most guys, you know?"

"And you never let him forget it," Mom says distantly, dropping the Balkan yogurt in the cart.

"We were having a good time, Mary."

"What did you do?" I ask.

"Oh, we razzed him a few times. But he loved it. This one time, Gerald comes to school dressed exactly like our old librarian, Ms. Klunchki. Other than his facial hair you could have sworn there were two of her."

Mom smiles at the memory, her face softening at the mental image.

The only problem is that Rural Realness isn't putting on dresses to get a laugh. They're putting on dresses *and* getting a laugh. They're performers. They're artists.

"Well, this isn't a joke," I inform them as we begin walking toward the cashiers. "We're putting on a show. We've got the town hall booked and everything."

Soft, tinkling top-forty music plays in the distance. The beeping of barcodes takes over as my parents fall into a standard Thompkin silence. Somehow the quiet fills me with a deeper annoyance than their questions got close to. For once I don't feel like dropping it.

"It was Alan's idea," I volunteer. "I'm just, you know, the producer."

We turn into a lineup and Dad squints at me, exasperated doubt written across his face.

"A *producer*? What does that even mean?"

"I'm helping them make it happen."

"Them?"

"Peter. Tilly. Friends. Why is this so hard for the two of you to grasp?"

"These men in the park," my mother asks. "You didn't know them?"

"No."

"And they still harassed you?"

"If someone does that to you again, Peter, you punch his lights out. You hear me?"

"Yes, Dad, I'll keep that in mind—"

"I just don't like this, Peter," says Mom.

"You don't like *what*, exactly?"

It slips out with more force than I intend. With more volume than I intend, as well. Mom's face tightens into the universal sign for *that's enough, Peter.* My father is suddenly very curious about the gum options lined up beside us. It's clear that I'm getting close to making a scene and that I've stepped too far from the polite docility that my parents keep while outside the home. Not that it's any different than the one they keep while *inside* the home.

Mom pointedly lowers her voice. "I don't like the way you and your friends are inviting this kind of response," she says, smiling and waving to another family. "Hi, Beth!" she calls airily. She turns back to me, her smile still in place. "People haven't taken well to, you know, what you're doing, and I just worry..."

Mom trails off, and I'm in no rush to keep talking. What my parents are saying lands with a wet thud between us as we approach the counter. I'm left with the fuzzy outline of this Gerald Corres in dusty librarian drag. Whatever the *razzing* had been, it's obvious that Gerald was less in on the joke than my father would like to believe.

It isn't hard to imagine a teenage version of my father in the video of me, Alan, and Nifoal in the gazebo. And my father isn't the one holding the baseball bat.

CHAPTER TEN
A VICIOUS FAT VELOCIRAPTOR

@daneebroh lol wut is this shit for real

@pinergorl07 yes!! yes yes yes! so important to platform queer voices in mason. other than the invoement of @ptkns1358 this is ahmazingg

@fiercemma33 This Is Not The Mason County I Know And Love. These Children Need Help, Not A Stage. Are We Going To Stand For This In Our Town Hall?

The botched video of the Cora Copia ft. Aggie Culture number has been repurposed by Alan in what, I must admit, is a clever act of marketing. Their number is quickly interrupted by the scattering of the alpacas in the background. Cora and Aggie rush to the camera as it hits a smoosh-faced freeze frame. Text fills the screen in candy floss pink.

THE FIRST ANNUAL MASON COUNTY DRAG EXTRAVAGANZA

AUGUST 28, MASON TOWN HALL, 8 P.M.! TICKETS ON SALE NOW!

While it makes its way across the internet, alongside the video of Alan nearly smashing that guy's skull like a pumpkin, so do the hot takes. Hours slip by as I scroll and refresh, scroll and refresh, watching as my Poster handle is attacked by curated showings of outrage from people I've never even met. At first I expect to develop a numbness to it, but it never arrives. My feed is full of text bars that read *what is the world coming to, these kids need to get a job,* or *this is sick.* Most of the Poster accounts behind them have bios that read something like *proud dad of four telling it like it is.*

A Clockwork Orange was directed by Stanley Kubrick. *Taxi Driver* was directed by Martin Scorsese.

My hand is developing a recurring cramp from its constant swiping up, up, up.

Jaws was directed by Steven Spielberg.

***

"At least wear some lip gloss," Alan requests from the driver's seat, worrying over me like I'm a toddler refusing to eat.

I bat his hand away, and he drops a stack of flyers in my lap with a dismissive flick of the wrist. Alan checks his makeup in the mirror while Tilly does the same from the passenger seat. We're parked on the grass out in the dark countryside, the only lights coming from the party already blazing around a barn at the foot of a dirt lane. I shift in my seat apprehensively.

"I'm not the main attraction," I remind him. "That's your job."

"Honey, when you look as good as I do, you're *always* the main attraction," Alan drawls, fixing the black robe draped over his shoulders.

"You're sure JJ and the band are cool with this?" Tilly asks as she touches up her drawn-on eyebrows. Her eyes have been made severe and angular with the addition of a long, arching eye wing and slashes of pink that stretch to her forehead. Her cheeks have been deepened with a chocolatey contouring and raspberry blush, and I start craving ice cream.

I think through tonight's scheme again, doing my best to sidestep the obvious pitfalls. The plan, though simple, has the very real chance of being met with the same kind of setbacks we found ourselves facing in the Port Anders gazebo. Probably even worse, given that last time we had evenly matched numbers. In the party raging up the drive, we're just three queers against an army of drunk heterosexual teenagers.

I decide not to think about it and shake away the nerves that are now dampening the flyers beneath my palms.

"JJ said the entire band was up for it," I say. "Anyway, he still owes me."

"Aw," Allen cooes. "Did you pop JJ's cherry?"

"Did you give JJ his OG BJ?" Tilly gasps, squealing and clasping Alan's shoulder in joy.

"Of course!" I wail in my best sex kitten affect. "I KO'd JJ's V-I-R-G-I-N-I—"

Alan screams while Tilly tosses a dried-up makeup wipe at my face.

"I helped him study for an English test last semester. And he said he'd pay me back sometime."

The truth is that I had an inkling that the next time JJ and I studied English, it would look more like tonight's Rural Realness Spelling Bee. But despite the vaguely artsy image that JJ cultivates, he doesn't have any interest in boys. I learned this when I invited him over to screen *Pink Flamingos* and was told that we could be friends, but he's "just not interested in dudes."

He got a B plus on the test.

"It's a shame," says Alan. "You'd make such *musical* test-tube babies. You could be a traveling band!"

"I don't play an instrument, Alan."

"I know," he says, touching up his lip liner. "But someone has to work the merch table."

"Who's throwing this thing anyway?" I ask, changing the subject.

"Mandy VanderVorn," Tilly replies.

"And we know this Mandy how?"

"Everybody knows her," Alan says. "She was in bio with us last year."

"It's not ringing a bell." I shrug, fanning myself with my stack of flyers.

Alan eyes me with skepticism through the rearview mirror. "Do you *actually* not remember any of our classmates, or is this some act you put on to show how cool and unbothered you are by us mere mortals?"

"I don't remember her!"

"There are only, like, a hundred people in our year. Not remembering them doesn't make you cool, it makes you pretentious."

I clutch my chest in mock pain. "I can't believe you would say this to me, Albert."

Alan turns, his face in full makeup, while the rest sits cozy in a T-shirt and jeans. "Stop vexing me. Mother can't handle the stress lines in her makeup. I need you in full charming mode once you enter this party."

"We're calling this a party now? I thought this was just an excuse for the heteros to get sloppy in their natural habitat while contracting Lyme disease."

"*No* Lyme disease jokes! Everyone in that party is going to have a peepaw or geegaw just swimming in it. And don't do that thing you always do. I love you, but you can't do it tonight."

I gasp and look about the car. Certainly Aggie is speaking to some invisible passenger and not me, the embodiment of grace and decorum.

"What *thing* do I do?"

Tilly and Alan exchange a look.

"You know," Tilly says carefully. "That thing where you're dead silent until you're not, and then you say something completely devastating and people run away screaming."

Alan nods. Clearly Tilly has summed it up perfectly.

"That was one time."

"It wasn't though," Alan says with a grimace. "Remember that time you told Brie Kelland that she only wanted to form a drama club so she wouldn't be the most annoying person in school?"

I glance out the window to avoid their combined eye contact. To be honest, I'd forgotten that one. But it's not like I'd been off the mark. One time Brie came to school dressed as a 1920s Parisian beggar to promote the *original song cycle* she would be workshopping at the upcoming coffee house cabaret. It was, and I say this objectively, annoying.

"I'll be good, Moms."

"Well," Alan says as I open the car door. "We'll see."

"After our little gazebo adventure, this kind of feels like testing fate."

"It's called guerrilla marketing, Peter. You just go out there with the in-your-face confidence of a gorilla. It's about getting butts in seats."

"The only butts involved will be ours when we get our asses kicked."

"Don't worry, baby girl," Tilly says. "Just call Rita Rustique and I'll come running. Just, you know, not before my call time."

They wave as I close the door, Alan blasting the speakers with searing techno music as the two continue their conversation without me. I make my way up the lane, the sounds of the party floating over the property. The air is filled with country pop, screams, and testosterone-fueled shouting from the kind of guy who thinks that being loud equals being funny. So, all of them.

I shrink back a little when I reach the gravel circle that makes up the yard. A hill leads up to the barn, with a farmhouse sitting opposite. The fields around us are dark and cavernous, but illuminated by the floodlights are a mass of people from the high schools of Mason County. I watch as a group of guys one year ahead of me, who by now have technically graduated, project videos on the barn's front wall. They include a long series of sports fails that involve skiers breaking legs, hockey skates cutting skin, and even a spandex-clad someone flying out of a bobsled. The boys howl in laughter, wolves surrounding their meal.

The music cuts out with a static-fueled jangle of noise. Across the yard is a van. The back of the van is open, and spewing out a web of black cords. A sparse silver drum set sits on the ground in front of it. This is JJ & The Refrigerators, the only reason I'm putting my life on the line in the first place.

A beanpole with dark hair down to his shoulder blades emerges from the van door before taking his place at the seat of the drums. A tentative crowd begins to form in the greasy yellow light, and the drummer is joined by a bass player with a shaved head and over-drawn black lipstick. She's the girl who deals mushrooms out of her backpack beside the track and field pit every day during lunch. She strums a warning thrum while their lead guitarist joins in, his mop of blonde hair the only discernible feature aside from the chin jutting out of it. This is Jamie Johannes.

"We're JJ & The Refrigerators," Jamie mumbles into his mic. "This is a post-structural, anti-capitalist tribute to the concept of . . . music."

Beanpole counts them in, and the three launch into what I would also describe as music. Punk music, maybe? In our study sessions he'd told me that the band's musical style was deconstructionist post-punk. He also told me that his favorite color was "energy drink color." I really should have taken the hint.

Our deal, made via text message last night, was that The Refrigerators will play four songs before it happens. Aggie and Rita, I was told, should be standing by on the third. The screeching of The Refrigerators gets louder and I move closer, figuring that I can offload a stack of flyers before I find a wooden barrel of some kind to hide in for the rest of the evening. But then someone steps into the smoky cluster of music lovers and my legs lock up beneath me.

Brison Dallas checks his phone, craning his neck in his search for someone. His tank top is nothing but a shelf for his muscles, his entire outfit an H&M rack repurposed to display his prime-time-teen body. My shirt, on the other hand, is once again displaying my visible underboob dampness.

"Oh my *god*, Peter Thompkin?"

I turn to find a girl in razor-straight bangs and a paisley dress stomping over to meet me. I happily turn my back to the van and move to join her. Anything to get away from Brison and the complete Novocaine sensation his presence is injecting into my brain.

Sylvie Burns waves and throws a hug on me before I can resist. With her, I don't even mind all that terribly. In a world where Alan Goode didn't scoop me up in the first week of ninth grade, Sylvie and I might have become best friends. Sylvie never takes the boys in our school seriously, and not in that *oh my gosh, Brad! You're so bad, stop it!* kind of way. Straight boys hate nothing more than girls who don't humor the way they suck the air out of the room. So, as a gay boy who hates the hetero ones for their grandstanding lifestyles, I consider Sylvie a partner in crime. She grabs my hand and pulls me back toward a group of people, which seems to be made entirely of ninth-grade girls who all give off matching noncommittally-alternative vibes. Nose rings and undercuts abound but not in a way that couldn't be worked around if needed. They're the Diet Doctor Pepper of girls with a generally artsy vibe, and they're crowding Sylvie as if they might absorb some of her coolness by proximity.

"Guys, do you know Peter? He's, like, the funniest person at school."

The group murmurs a few apathetic greetings.

"I don't know if I'm the funniest," I say, shrugging.

"Oh my god, no, he is though," Sylvie tells her flock. "One time he said to Colby Devine, *You sure say a lot of shit about how girls look for someone who looks like an off-brand Troll doll."*

The ninth-graders laugh with a calculated distance. I chuckle gamely to cover the way I'm racking my brain, trying to find any memory of this. Am I less quiet than I give myself credit for? Am I breaking my own rule on the regular? I know I have a reputation, but surely it's been blown out of proportion thanks to The Very Awful and Dreadful Thing That Peter Said to Brison Dallas on That Video. Am I really just this vicious, fat velociraptor? Hiding in the bushes to cut the mental Achilles tendons of unsuspecting teens?

"Aren't you the guy that told Brison Dallas he should kill himself?" asks a girl with an eyebrow ring. For a moment I consider ripping it off her face.

I quickly press a flyer into everyone's hands. "If you liked that show, you're going to love this one," I say grandly.

"I heard about this," says one of the girls. "Are you really doing a drag show in Mason? That's, like, literally insane."

"Yeah. Totally insane. You should come."

"I love drag," another chimes in. "I'm obsessed with *Dragathon.*"

"Of course," agrees Eyebrow Ring. "My cousin is gay and he says that I'm, like, such an ally that I'm allowed to say the word *faggot* if I want to."

"You're not," I tell her. "You're really not."

Without a second glance, I walk off. JJ's second song begins to wind down as I hide myself behind the dark side of the barn. When I grab my phone to text Alan, my chest lurches at the sight of a new text from Lorne.

> I can't believe you guys got murdered by an alpaca farmer, but this video does not lie.

The sweat pooling on my lower back turns cold. I find myself chattering under the same kind of nerves I'd felt the other day beside the pool. I think for a moment, typing and then deleting, typing and then deleting.

I like to think that he at least fed us to the alpacas. I served more use in my death than I ever did in life.

Yes, it's a tragedy. But those alpacas gotta eat.

Please tell me you're at this god-awful barn party.

I send Alan his cue and wait for Lorne's response. The text dots bounce up and down then settle again. A girl leading a guy by the hand stumbles past me and they apologize through their shared giggles. They walk off into the dark, and he glances back at me with a thumbs-up.

"Oh, good lord. Don't drag me into it." I shudder.

Song three picks up and I check my phone again, the dots still motionless.

Rounding the corner of the barn, I catch myself from running directly into another couple pinned against the barn wall, its dust and dirt already crusting along their shorts. The guy's bristly half-formed mustache pushes against her thin lips, and I may as well be a squirrel scampering by for how much they notice me. I may not register on whatever planet of horniness the two are on, but I apologize before walking away as fast as possible. The heteros are hooking up wherever I look. Sloppy make outs and socially acceptable public fondling are rampant. I feel Chrissy and Brison somewhere in the crowd, cackling in delight at the virginal energies emitting from my pudgy form. I must look like a crumbling garden gnome, standing dejectedly by a flower bed with dead eyes and creepy little hands. I have nearly as much sex appeal. My phone remains blank.

This is stupid. I'm stupid. Lorne would never in a million years go for someone who looks or talks like me. I know nothing about sex. Where am I even supposed to have sex? My house? The same house that my parents live in? Even if Lorne deigns to sleep with me, how am I going to pull that one off? Do I sneak him up the stairs after my parents fall asleep? Hope they don't need a glass of water while we're mid-coitus just down the hall? And if not at home, then where? Take him to a meadow somewhere and roll around in the grass? The mosquitoes and wasps have gotten worse around town this summer. The mechanics of regular under-the-sheets sex are baffling enough without bringing mosquito bites and wasp stings into the equation. Song four begins, and when a fight breaks out in the gravel not far from me, I retreat backward. I feel like a child, like my nether regions were built to be shame inducing by merit of their heterodeviation. I'm a classically trained bassoonist who has studied for years without even touching a bassoon. Sure, I can tell you all about the notes, but I bet I'll totally beef it when I go to toot that big ol' horn. Maybe a bassoon is a bad example here. I couldn't pick out a bassoon from a lineup of tough-looking woodwinds. I picture trying to kiss Lorne and emitting nothing but flat bassoon honks.

"I guess you think you're pretty clever, don't you?" someone calls from behind me, her voice the audio equivalent of pizza burn.

I turn, sighing loud enough to be heard over the clang of JJ and his band. "Hello, Chrissy."

CHAPTER ELEVEN

A TEMPER-DEFICIENT TODDLER WHO JUST INCITED A HATE CRIME

Chrissy is holding a can of Bud Light Lime and wearing an obnoxiously long crystal necklace that I'm sure she ascribes some watered-down spiritual significance to. Brison leans on the nearby fence, his tanned legs on full display.

Our eyes lock uneasily before Chrissy reels me back in.

"I loved your little interview with Bailey," she says through an ironic smile. And sure, I'm annoyed, but I'm also kind of impressed. Irony isn't a concept you'd expect Chrissy to understand. "You're probably *so* stoked that you've been able to use my best friend's suffering as a joke," she continues. "And to what? Sell tickets to your little show?"

I picture myself flinging the remaining flyers into her face and running, but my aim is isn't any better than my ability to run.

"Talk to Bailey. I'm sure her secretarial staff know your secretarial staff."

"I just think it's funny, you know," Chrissy says, not even needing me present for the rehearsed statement she's unloading. "It's just funny that you two love to act like you're the only gays in the school when the most *beloved* gay student is suffering, and you can't even be bothered to stop kicking him while he's down."

Brison rubs his eyes and tries to look busy. Shouldn't he be joining in the fun?

"You weren't so concerned about gay students when you made Alan your fashion punching bag, if I remember correctly."

Chrissy laughs flatly.

"We were making a joke, Peter. Sorry if you are both such drama queens that you had to spin it out of proportion. You know, there are people with *real* problems in this school, so get over yourselves for five minutes and take notice."

"Can you let Brison speak for himself? I'm sure he'd love to tell me about all the real problems he has. Counting all that money must be really hard on his dainty little fingertips."

"Don't talk about my *friend* that way, asshole," she hisses.

"Chrissy!" Brison calls from the fence. "This is so not worth my time. Besides, there's an entire pigpen on the other side of the farm. I'm sure Peter has a hookup to get to."

Brison's face is lit up by his phone, his haughty disinterest now shining in cold blue as he waits patiently to hear more about my evening plans.

"I'm not waiting for your sloppy seconds, Brison," I say. "But maybe cows are more your thing, seeing as you *are* besties with this one."

In the light of Brison's phone, I almost think I catch him smirking.

"You cannot talk to me like that!" Chrissy asserts with a jab of her finger. "It's anti-feminist."

"Oh my god, Chrissy!" Brison moans. "This is so boring, we're leaving."

"Yeah," I tell her. "Run along. Not that I'm not enjoying myself. I never feel smarter than when you open your mouth."

With a grunt, Chrissy pushes me. I stumble back and force myself not to rub at the pain she's ignited in my shoulder. Chrissy steps forward, eyes blazing.

"It's not fucking funny, Peter."

The vocal fry has cleared from Chrissy's voice. An alarming sincerity has replaced her usual snark, and I'm not sure I'm enjoying the tradeoff.

"I never said it was funny," I remind her. "You're the ones who thought Alan was a walking punchline."

"It's been really hard for Brison," she continues, her eyes searching mine. "You have no idea what he's going through right now."

I feel myself laughing defensively, at a loss for any other tactic. My face floods with something hot and embarrassing. I suddenly want to be anywhere but here.

Then Brison pops up behind her, dragging Chrissy away as she wipes away an angry tear.

"She's messy tonight," Brison explains with a shrug, as if neither of us has just accused the other of having intercourse with farm animals. Chrissy brushes him off, and for a moment it seems like Brison hates this as much as I do. For a second we're stuck together, bound by the woozy guilt seeping out between us. Chrissy's words continue to sting, pressing deeper like a cut after the initial shock.

"Everything okay over here?" asks a stony voice to our right.

An unsettlingly tall, chiseled body has lumbered into view, yellow back-light radiating around him like a hunky halo.

Andy Sanderson's freckled, rectangular face looks down at us, his orange hair blazing like an Irish caricature leapt off the page. Andy's arms flex in warning, like a peacock exhibiting its plumage before some kind of screechy bird fight. Behind him stand the equally colossal forms of Blake Roy and Kirk Monray, completing their signature triangle of buffness. The three are a trio rarely seen alone, like a creatine-soaked hydra. They're famous at Mason Central for being the three guys who are always in the tiny school

gym on the first floor, spotting one another and screaming violent encour-
agement. Huffing and puffing in a way that isn't exactly not porny. Part of
me wants to spray them with a power washer, but another part of me wants
to spray them with a regular hose while they all make out.

"Yeah. We were just having a little chat," Chrissy says coolly.

She flicks her can at my chest and stalks off into the party mob.

"What the hell is wrong with the people in this place?" I call after her.
"Do you all get some sort of sick thrill from littering cheap beer?"

The Three Broskateers regard me with sympathy while Brison takes after
Chrissy. My phone vibrates, and I hold it up apologetically, all too happy for
the excuse to leave The Triathlonic Trio scratching their heads in confusion.

"Sorry," I say. "Gotta take this."

> No, I'm not. Needed some
> me time . . . meditation
> time. Hope it's fun tho!

I tap the text box. I'm going to text the hell out of Chrissy's cousin. And
just to spite her, I'm going to have actual, person-on-person, perfectly real,
virginity-destroying sex with him. Mosquitoes be damned. It's going to piss
Chrissy off so much that her stupid head will unscrew and fly off into the sun.

JJ & The Refrigerators finish their fourth song to a half-hearted round
of applause from the attendees. This, as I have been informed, is showtime.

"So, yeah," begins JJ, apparently having forgotten the presence of his
audience. "Alan Goode is going to do a thing now, or something," he says
with a nearly audible shrug. I frown, flooded with regret for the part I took
in his B plus.

The drummer plugs an aux cord into his phone as the guitar player
lights a smoke. JJ checks his texts, shaking the hair out of his face with disinterest. A chatter of confusion ripples through the crowd as headlights cast
a yellow light over the yard. Alan's car rolls into the center with a crunch of

stones and gravel, coming to a stop as the beginning to Madonna's "Like a Prayer" booms across the farmyard.

"The fuck is this?" a guy by the barn hoots.

There's a smattering of laughter as Madonna's vocals come in, accompanied by her backing choir. The wigged form of Aggie Culture remains in the driver's seat next to the slicked hair of Rita Rustique, the calls and jeers intensifying as the music swells. Rather than drawing further attention to myself, I decide to stuff the remaining flyers into my back pocket, slinking away to the shadows at the edge of the yard as the drums kick in. As I do, the car doors fly open. Two pairs of high heels emerge from beneath two black cloaks. Aggie and Rita step forward, covered in the black robes and white bibs of a nun. Cheers come up from the group of girls still hovering around Sylvie Burns, Sylvie herself taking the lead. Laughter, shocked and outright derisive, continues to sound from the edges of the party. The two really are a sight to behold, turning and posturing in the watery light of the headlights, Aggie's signature green wig glowing radioactively as she bites down on Madonna's vocals.

I watch while they treat the car as set dressing, lip-synching their sister act in shoes that have no business being near a field of cows. Rita Rustique pulls in a girl from my year, Janice O'Brian, spinning her before dipping her low to the ground. Janice squeals, dark hair cascading over her face as she is righted and sent lightly back toward her friends. Aggie crosses herself dramatically, scandalized by the Sapphic sin taking place in front of her very eyes. Madonna is joined again by her choir, prompting both queens to tear off their thin, cheap habits to reveal searingly red dresses underneath. Applause breaks out, with loud whooping from Sylvie's congregants.

"Oh hello," Aggie's voice says over a recording. "It recently came to our attention that we need god, not a stage. So go ahead and tell everyone in Mason County that we have both."

Through the crowd I spy Chrissy and Brison clapping along with everyone else. Chrissy's face curdles at the sight of me, but I only smile magnanimously as I hand out the rest of the flyers. They may be damp from being pressed against my ass, but all the flyers are snatched up by the time Aggie and Rita bring their performance to a close. Our audience presses closer, and Aggie shows off the construction of her tearaway robe while Rita fields giggly questions from a certain Janice O'Brian. I wave, and Aggie winks through a thick lacquer of eyeliner.

JJ appears from behind the van, nodding vacantly at the sight of me.

"That was pretty cool, I guess," he says distantly.

"Yeah," I say, watching him trudge heavily back into the van. "Totally."

It's obvious now that *Pink Flamingos* would have been wasted on JJ.

"What the fuck, JJ?" a deep voice calls from within the mess of partygoers.

Some thickly bearded guy steps into view with his noticeably younger girlfriend in tow. He looks like a lumberjack with rage issues. A professionally established lumberjack, I should say, because he's probably in his late-twenties. This guy looks like he's paying union dues and trying to get more fiber in his diet. He tosses a crumpled flyer at JJ's feet while his girlfriend rolls her eyes. This isn't her first time being his voice of reason.

"Oh," I say quietly to myself. "*That's* Mandy VanderVorn."

"You didn't say anything about . . ." Lumberjack regards us from under his Cro-Magnon brows, like we're a heap of garbage JJ has dumped on his lawn. "Anything about whatever the fuck *that* was when we said you could play the party."

JJ shrugs, which I'm beginning to see is his response to most things. "I owed him a solid," he says with a nod in my direction.

Lumber Jack and Lumber Jill turn to me now.

"We don't want this kind of sick shit at her party, all right?" he blusters, a vein bulging in his neck.

"Babe, it's fine," Mandy protests, pulling at his arm without conviction.

"We were just leaving," Rita Rustique says, suddenly at my side and pulling me toward the car.

"Wait, what?" I ask as she ushers me away. "You think *this* is sick?" I ask

Lumber-bro. "Take a look at the two of you in a mirror sometime. You look like you're picking her up from daycare."

"What the hell did you just say to me?" he roars.

Aggie throws the back door open, and I stumble over his feet while Rita tries to deposit me inside. Aggie catches me, and I wonder if the two of us are getting into our first fistfight. It'll be a good story if we actually survive. Just as I think we're about to have our hearts ripped out, *Temple of Doom*–style, Rita is closing the door and holding her hands out to keep Mandy's goon from getting any closer. I lay crumpled in the backseat, hastily stuffed into the car like a temper-deficient toddler who just incited a hate crime.

"Just back the fuck up, my guy," Rita's muffled voice tells him in no uncertain terms.

Andy, Blake, and Kirk show up then, the three of them pulling Lumberjack away from her.

"Whoa, bro, simmer down," Kirk demands as Mandy's boyfriend brushes them off.

Are these three just bloodhounds for drama? Do they show up to parties hoping to find a fight they can inject themselves into? They all reek of machismo and old gym shorts, and apparently, they've taken a special interest in the fisticuffs potential that surrounds Peter Thompkin. Kirk's back slams against the window and the car jolts backward. A bunch of guys that look a lot like Lumberjack materialize around us, and their group is suddenly locking horns with Andy's. Blake is pushed back into the crowd by some guy in a flannel shirt with the sleeves cut off, and Kirk is launching himself off the vehicle to pin Mandy's boyfriend into the dirt. It's not just my palms that are covered in a nervous sweat; now it's the rest of me.

Rita slams the door behind her as she takes the wheel. Aggie doesn't waste any time and throws himself over my lap in a heap of red fabric. The horn blasts as Rita bears down on it, making a few people step backward and enraging Mandy's boyfriend. Mandy, still unfazed, watches from a distance while inspecting her nails.

"Can we not end tonight with charges of manslaughter?" I yelp.

But Lumberjack's boys aren't moving. In fact, some of them are drawing even closer.

The swarm of people outside begins to grow denser and Rita flashes the high beams.

"We're going to die in here!" Aggie screams. "If any of us survives this, make sure that my parents respect my will. They're going to fight you on shooting my body out of a confetti cannon, but that's only because they haven't read the cost-benefit analysis!"

"Are you happy, Peter?" Rita asks, her eyes boring into mine through the rearview mirror.

"Me?" I duck lower into my seat. "What's this got to do with me?"

"You just *had* to get that dig in about Mandy's creepy uncle-boyfriend."

"Well," I say, shaking my head. "Was I wrong?"

"You just *had* to do the thing you always do," Rita says over the sounds of a smashing beer bottle.

"Fine!" I scream, sinking lower into my seat as Lumber-bro locks eyes with me again. "Maybe I *do* have a certain thing that I tend to do, on occasion, sometimes."

A shadow falls over my face, and I flinch.

"Are you serious, Mandy?" Sylvie is leaning against the car, stony faced. "Tell your woolly mammoth to cool his shit."

"Butt out, Sylvie," I hear from somewhere in the tumult. "Brad is just looking out for me!"

"If he was looking out for you, he'd probably know that a couple of drag queens showing up is the most interesting thing to happen at one of your parties since Mike Nordell broke his leg jumping off your roof. Seriously, what the hell is wrong with him?"

More bodies appear around the car, their backs blocking our view. Sylvie's ninth-graders form a circle around the vehicle, following their leader into battle. They keep their backs to us, most of them folding their arms and jutting out their jaws, just daring the guys in the brawl to get physical with a ninth-grade girl. Sylvie sees me and motions to stay put. Apparently her girls have this all taken care of.

"Do we know these people?" Rita asks.

Eyebrow Ring pushes one of Lumberjack's friends to the ground when he refuses to move, and suddenly he's screaming in her face. Without blinking, she walks forward while fanning an exaggerated yawn. He finally takes a step back.

"Not really," I reply. "But Eyebrow Ring over there can definitely say *faggot*."

Andy and Blake clear a path in front of the car, and Rita reams the gear shift out of park. Lumberjack is in Andy's face, screaming something about *his fucking property*. Andy watches passively, the way a docile rottweiler would humor a scrappy shih tzu.

"Ding ding ding!" Aggie announces. "I think that's our cue."

Rita blows a lock of gel-doused hair out of her eye and then we're flying through the yard, faces whipping past the window as Rita gets us the hell out of the snake pit that is this high school barn party. Aggie crosses herself again, saying a silent prayer for the nun's habits now lost to the mob. As glad as I am to be alive, I'm still a little annoyed that Andy and his boys got to save the day. It feels as if they've made me a prop in their buff-boy roadshow.

I watch the lights of the party disappear behind us, waiting for a new set of headlights to emerge to try to run us off the road. When none come, I sit back in my seat and remind myself to send Sylvie a fruit basket. Maybe her ladies-in-waiting are more interesting than I'd given them credit for, if only just a little.

"So what *is* the vibe on JJ?" Rita asks through the rearview mirror, sighing as if she does this every weekend. "You think he's DTF?"

CHAPTER TWELVE
A RESENTFUL HOBGOBLIN

@brisondallaz the best thing about the Drag Extravaganza so far has got to be watching @ptkns1358 fall on his ass

@pinergorl07 can we figure out who the assholes in this video are? and no im not talking about @ptkns1358

@kuhrisskai lmao yall losing your mind over guys that wanna dress like girls this is jokes

"Can someone show me to my dressing room?" Bailey asks nobody in particular. He drops his black Balenciaga tote bag to the floor and trots into the town hall as if he built the place with his own hands. The rest of The House of Rural Realness follow as he bounces ahead. Even out of drag, Bailey's face is adorned with soft pink eyeshadow, like a model with fashionable hay fever.

Joining us is Mason County's cultural director, Gerald Corres. I'd held my breath when the man in the grandfatherly slacks and business-casual tie had introduced himself on the sidewalk outside the town hall, steeling myself against an onslaught of something close to guilt. A guilt by association that is currently making the eggshells I'm walking on particularly fragile. Maybe Gerald doesn't know who my parents are. Or, better yet, maybe he doesn't even remember whatever happened between him and my father. Maybe I'm blowing the whole thing out of proportion. But it is hard to keep my thoughts from slipping toward picturing just what my dad's "razzing" of Gerald might have looked like.

With the team finally assembled, our combined queerness makes us look like the members of a gay Voltron, like we're about to connect into a Mecha Drag Queen large enough to fight a giant space lizard. Bailey may be prancing about like he owns the place and I'm sure that Alan is already calculating my next public humiliation, but even they can't ruin the afternoon. A giddy energy of possibility has taken over our freshly convened queer conglomerate, and even I'm not immune to its power. It is the fifteenth of August, with two weeks until our grand debut. We now have a stage, lights, and a growing sense that this might all be real. The show finally has a container to be kept in, an oven to bake inside. It feels kind of good.

"What about 'I Feel Pretty'?" Tilly suggests.

"That's perfect," agrees Cora, "because I'll look absolutely vile."

"It's pretty, witty, *and* gay," Nifoal reminds him, tenderly rubbing Cora's shoulder. "You've only got that last one."

Cora barks out a laugh and the three break into bubbly chatter.

"It's good to see you, Peter," Cora says. "Your skin is looking . . . quite well today."

His searching gaze works its way across my exposed epidermis while I cross my arms and wonder which part of me Cora will eat first.

"Thank you, Cora," I reply coolly.

Gerald claps his hands together in excitement and addresses the team.

"So the dressing room isn't so much a dressing *room* as it is a long hallway backstage. But! There are mirrors and lights, and we can even get some more from storage, probably, if we need to!" He beams like he's informed us that Santa will be arriving early this year.

Bailey's Cheshire grin grows larger. It's scarier than his frown, given the scorned-starlet-rage lurking below the surface. Alan made me watch this movie called *Mommie Dearest* one time, about how bug-eyed psychotic Joan Crawford had been. While not in the same ballpark of Faye Dunaway as movie star Joan Crawford, Bailey gives the distinct impression of being at least on the bench *of* the ballpark.

"I'm sure that I'll make do just fine," Bailey says, his eye twitching.

Tilly and Alan begin to discuss their Shania Twain number while we wander about and take in the place. The building isn't much to write home about, but it isn't without charm. It's an old building with all kinds of carved flourishes and historical plaques. The hall itself is a wide room with prehistoric wooden flooring and tall, arched windows on both sides. I haven't set foot inside the hall in years, but I do have vague memories of being dragged along to watch the annual Christmas play by the Mason Community Players. They were always slapstick comedies about sexily mistaken identities on Christmas Eve, sexy Christmas party murders, or sexy slamming-door romances between coworkers who are snowed in together. Those actors really had some steam to blow off around the holidays, come to think of it.

In the summer there would be parties with community group bands that always featured someone's grandfather playing the accordion or the guy who runs the auto parts shop playing the tuba despite the hairy mole right next to his upper lip. Now, the inside of the hall is sun-faded and dusty, its unwashed windows covered in musty curtains. Arts and culture are on life support in Mason County, and I'm getting the feeling that the only person around here trying to stop it from flatlining entirely is Gerald Corres.

But why would Gerald still live in Mason County after all the bullshit he had to put up with in high school? Planning my escape is one of the few things that keeps me from going full nuclear meltdown on everyone. Gerald just lives without that? Yes, eternally eyeing the exits of Mason may have contributed to me becoming a resentful hobgoblin subsisting only on the fear of those foolish enough to pass by my cave. But one of these days I'm going to get out of here, and it will be *because* of how protective and durable my hobgoblin exterior was this entire time. Gerald must have something that is keeping him going. Maybe he's the guy responsible for the string of arsons that have been popping up around town for the last few years. The secondhand furniture store burned down, followed by two houses, and then Verdeen's Garden Center last year. I observe Gerald, framed in the gauzy backlight of the window, imagining him tossing the match and walking away as the kerosene does its thing.

The performers hover around the boxy stage like bugs attracted to a zap light while I check my phone. Lorne's text thread is working its way to the bottom of the page, falling below Alan, Tilly, and my mother. My phone has more texts from my mother than the cute boy I'd splashed around with the other night. This does not bode well for my romantic future.

Bailey returns from backstage, dusting his hands off as if emerging from a coal mine. "We'll need a few more mirrors back there," he calculates, brushing bottle-blonde hair from his face. "But that's nothing I can't take care of. After all, I did just sell out our entire show."

An airy silence fills the hall before Bailey's words lock in place.

"Wait," Nifoal says slowly. "Is this for real? Because if you can lie about those lip injections, you can lie about anything."

"It was a lip *correction*, Nifoal. And it was of medical necessity."

"Can we back up?" I cut in. "To the part about the show *selling out*?"

Bailey's fingers scratch absently at the bridge of his nose while he scrolls through his phone with the other hand. "Our sales just ran out," Bailey reports, flashing his screen for the group to marvel at. "You'd be amazed what a little Poster drama can achieve."

Alan screams and begins to applaud with the force of some ancient thunder god, urging everyone to join suit. He makes an exhibition of it, the grin slashed across his face just a tad too broad.

Tilly raises an eyebrow my way, and I return one in kind.

Alan is happy, of course, but only Tilly and I can tell that he's seething on the inside. The Extravaganza is coming together without a hitch but not with founder and megastar Aggie Culture at the center of the story. Alan's applause intensifies, the sonic booms almost loud enough to rattle the windowpanes. Bailey's interview with Brison has been racking up the clicks while Alan's clapback is trailing at nearly a quarter of the views. Now the show is sold out, and all it took was Bailey Hayes playing up the drama. I've chosen not to tell Alan that the only thing his video achieved was to prompt a conversation with my parents in the dairy aisle that I'm currently trying to un-remember. I've opted to store it away with a few other choice memories that are better swept under my brain rug. There's the time my father told me that there are a few subjects he avoids with his friend Isaac, who happens to do Christian missionary work every other summer. *My situation*, apparently, is one of them. There's also the time my father yelled at my sister for putting nail polish on me after swimming lessons and the time my mother said that my grandmother just doesn't have the constitution to take the news of *who I am*. When Grandma asks about when I'll be bringing a girlfriend around, it's probably best to just play along.

"That's amazing, Bailey!" says Nifoal.

"Well," Bailey tuts, turning to Alan. "I'm sure your Madonna stunt did some of the heavy lifting."

Alan smiles thinly, clutching Bailey by the shoulder.

"Now," Gerald begins, all chipper. "Do you have anyone slated to work the door?"

"I do," Alan chimes. "My parents will do it."

"I was actually thinking," adds Bailey, "of some local fans who want to help out. I was thinking of getting them in, like, *full* drag and just having them be our door bitches. Don't you think that would be super fun?"

Alan pretends to contemplate this, stroking his chin with wincing thoughtfulness. "My parents have years of experience with event management. We even had a family folk trio for a short time before Dad fell out of love with the autoharp."

"Wait," I pipe up, already regretting it. "Shouldn't I be making the decision on that one? Being the producer and all."

The faces of the room turn to face me, and I get the feeling that I've stepped between two cowboys at high noon. A tumbleweed could bounce past at any moment. Alan's eyes find mine before narrowing in consternation.

What are you doing? my glare asks.

We're just talking, Peter, his replies.

"Just talking" is not how I'd describe this.

Sorry, what? Alan says through an imperceptible shrug. *I can't hear you.*

We're talking through a nonverbal friendship mind link. I know you can hear me!

"Of course," Bailey allows. "I'll defer to our esteemed producer."

Tilly restrains a rueful laugh while Cora and Nifoal simply regard the sharks gathering around a floundering swimmer, blood beginning to color the water. Gerald looks on with bland civility, blessedly oblivious.

"Let's give it to Alan's parents," I advise, melting beneath the heat of his glower.

"Fantastic!" Gerald exclaims, clapping his hands once more. Alan and Bailey simper warmly at one another, violence simmering below the surface.

Before any wig pulling can break out out, the doors to the hallway open behind us. Lumbering their way through the doorway come three inverted triangles. Andy Sanderson, Blake Roy, and Kirk Monray enter with businesslike gaits, scoping the room out as if assessing any structural damage.

"We'll need someone working the door backstage, obviously," Andy tells his boxy brethren, waving a curt hello to Gerald. They spread out through the room while the rest of us hold our breath. Instead of engaging with the local wildlife, I decide to stare expectantly and wait for them to leave, which is what I usually do when straight men land in my general area.

"Do we know them?" Cora asks, his spidery hands clutching at imaginary pearls.

"*Can* we know them?" demands Nifoal.

Gerald brightens.

"I forgot to mention it! These young men have volunteered their time to work as security for the event."

"I'm not sure this is necessary," I point out.

"I say we let them pitch their, uh, case." Nifoal coughs, suddenly losing his trademark eloquence.

"That's where you're wrong, my dude," Kirk says, rubbing his buzzed head sheepishly. The trio joins our group and I nudge Nifoal in the ribs, hoping he'll pick his jaw off the floor. "Not to, like, tell you how to run your thing or whatever. But after what happened at Mandy's party the other night, the guys and I realized that you could really use someone watching your back."

Marvelous. So not only did that video land with a wet thud in the Thompkin household, it also sent a one-sided invite to Blake and the Biceps.

"There were some unseen complications," I admit. "But I think we handled ourselves just fine."

Tilly and Alan train a unified skeptical glare in my direction, as if to remind me of Alan getting tossed onto my lap while Tilly played getaway driver.

"And you won't believe some of the things people are saying about you online," Blake goes on.

"Well, I think I *would* believe them," I try. "That's kind of my point—"

"Peter," Alan cuts in, shouldering his way forward. "Show some decorum. We have guests."

Alan extends a hand to Blake's beefy forearm, reaching out like The Creation of Adam through the sunlit dust motes. Blake swallows nervously.

"I can show you, actually," says Blake. He holds his phone out and scrolls through a series of screen grabs taken from what I can only assume to be a particularly heterosexual, polo-shirt-wearing corner of Poster.

@taylaorrilla48 man I cant believe their actually using Town Hall for that tranny shit someone should show up and protest it aint rite

@levans_supermom24 Honestly disappointed to hear that @MasonCountyCultural will be allowing a public display this inappropriate to be carried out in the Town Hall how am I going to explain this to my 4 step children?

@balindavandeen these kids need to get a real job and not expect us to pay just to watch them jump around in a dress and makeup shame on @MasonCountyCultural

@christlZurlOrd08 The bible make it clear that any man who puts on womans clothing is an abomination onto the lord. the war on christians has been going on far to long and we will be putting a stop to these degenerates.

> **@aaar0nbezer66** this is beyond messed up if your at all even sane you will show up with us too protest these sex lies being told in our town, dont have kids but if i did i wouldnt let them anywhere near these groomers

"There does seem to be enough reason to be cautious," Gerald says through a worried smile. "But I'm sure it won't amount to anything. I like to think of them like my uncle Rudy. He always said he was going to toss me into the bullpen to make a real man out of me, but he never did. Besides, those bulls and I became good friends. I think a few of them even thought of me as one of their own."

"People aren't actually going to show up and protest," I say firmly.

"Not to contradict you," pipes up Andy, "but that guy in the video trying to attack you with the baseball bat wasn't just talk."

"*We* had the baseball bat," Nifoal amends through a hormonal fog.

"Exactly," I say. "And we handled it just fine."

Tilly looks at me keenly, the way she did when she suggested that I not Do That Thing That I Do. Which, it seems, I have just done.

"Well," Alan trills. "I think it's lovely that they want to get involved."

"Delightful," Bailey says sharply, a hand landing on Alan's arm. "Allyship is so important."

"*So* integral."

It takes all I have not to scoff. So I allow myself some light eye-rolling, because this is deranged. Andy and his buds are only cashing in on this opportunity for social clout. They're probably just using us as easy fodder for their college essays. "That One Time I Helped the Gays After Never Showing an Ounce of Interest", their title pages will read. Andy will get accepted on an athletics scholarship and won't encounter another gay until his son comes out as a figure skater.

From the stage, Bailey pulls a pair of black stilettos from his bag and begins to clasp them around his wispy ankles.

"The show isn't until the end of the month, darling," Nifoal calls out. "But I guess you need as much practice as you can get."

"I'm calibrating, Slenderman," Bailey bites back.

The two snap at each other while the doors to the Mason Town Hall creak open again. Gerald's face falls as the *clap* of a chunky heel announces a new arrival.

CHAPTER THIRTEEN

A FUMBLING CAPYBARA

A small army, clad entirely in white, files into the room. A diminutive, lemony-blonde woman leads the charge, her asymmetrical bob like a Lego piece stuck atop her skull. The rest of her monochromatic militia, it seems, is made up of her husband and their many children. Several boys are already shoving each other to the floor while one of the girls fights off a sister's attempt to fix her hair. The baby strapped to her beleaguered husband's chest, at least, is quiet. The husband's hand passes through his thinning hair, also blonde, while he attempts to separate the boys and smooth out their matching collars. I attempt to count how many there are, but between the flailing arms, open-mouthed coughing, and red-faced wailing, it feels better to avert my view and hope they'll be gone the next time I look.

"Hello, Gerald," says the mother through a syrupy sweetness.

Gerald's eternal smile falters for a moment before jumping back to its factory settings. "Hello, Jenna." As if having a tooth pulled, Gerald turns to the husband. "Hello, Terrance," he says with an icy formality.

Terrance adjusts his boxy glasses on his nose. "Gerald," he replies.

A look passes between the members of team THORR.

It doesn't take much to clue into some people's gayness. This does save the heteros a lot of time that could accidentally be spent trying to talk to us about fantasy football or movies where bald men drive cars. But I get the feeling that nobody is chatting with Terrance about those things. Because Terrance, like me, has The Gay Voice.

"Has there been a mix-up?" Bailey asks, clopping down off the stage in his skyscraping stilettos. Bailey's legs, framed between pink short-shorts and dark heels, look like they could pry the door off a burning car. "Do you have the room rented for some kind of"—he takes in their creepy white outfits—"ceremony?"

Jenna's gaze lands on Bailey's shoes. Her forced gentility falters and she swallows hard before regarding us with obvious contempt.

"Well," Gerald says, consulting his schedule. "The Wilbur family does have this space booked in half an hour, but if we're all finished up here—"

"What *is* going on here, exactly?" Jenna asks, outrage burgeoning across her tightly wound features. "We do have the hall booked out for our yearly family photo. We just came a skooch early to see if we could get set up. McCaighleigh and Flynnleigh have their synchronized dirt biking class this afternoon and we don't want to fall behind schedule. But I have to say, Gerald," she continues, eyeing us with barely tempered revulsion, "I didn't expect to have to explain something like this to my children."

"*The First Annual Mason County Drag Extravaganza* is what's happening," Bailey informs Jenna with a dismissive flick of his hands. "But we didn't sanction a preview. So I hope you got your tickets in advance because *these* girls just became a bunch of sellouts."

Jenna scans the room for whatever *girls* Bailey is talking about, landing only on Tilly in her denim vest and combat boots.

"I'd say you sold out years ago, Bailey," Nifoal says through his detached glaze, "but I'd hate to imply that you have anything worth selling."

"I looked up how to sell your soul to the devil last summer," Cora offers with a shrug. "But the ram's horns were cost prohibitive, you know?"

Terrance, father of the year, claps his hands over the baby's ears.

"You're selling that thing?" Nifoal says, tittering. "Honey, you couldn't *give* me your soul with a Subway gift card."

"I'm sorry," Jenna cuts in, gathering the children behind her. "Is this some sort of . . ." She drops her voice to a whisper. "Some sort of satanic cross-dressing show?"

"Well," Gerald starts.

"Good Lord," Terrance gasps.

"Yes!" gasps Bailey. "Now you're getting it."

"I can't believe what I'm seeing, Gerald."

"Does the town council know about this?" Terrance inquires, hands still protecting the baby from any contagious gender-bendery.

"Of course. And as our town's cultural director, I'm overseeing their first—"

"This is *not* the kind of culture that is appropriate for a public space," contends Jenna.

"Excuse me?" Alan asks. He takes a step closer to Blake Roy, as if overnight Alan has become a delicate southern belle fixin' to faint.

Andy and his boys form a loose barricade, as if the horde of children are going to launch themselves into the air and descend on us with their teeth bared, ready for blood.

"Please don't raise your voice in front of my children," Jenna admonishes.

Tilly laughs, and The Great Blonde Bobcut stares daggers at her.

"Is she for real?" says Tilly. "Look, lady, you're giving a real *Footloose* vibe and I don't care for it."

Gerald only gets one syllable out before Jenna takes the floor again. "I'll have you know," she pronounces, "that a lot of people in this community would object to what you're doing here. And I should say that I don't believe it *proper* for a municipal space to be used for such a . . ."

Jenna casts a glance of distaste around the room. "Such a controversial performance. I do *not* believe that this speaks to the values that *my* government should uphold." Her beady crow-eyes fix on Gerald. "And you, Gerald. First you stop coming to church and now this? Now you're exposing *my children* to such inappropriate lifestyles?" she concludes with a self-satisfied flair.

"I should say that your booking wasn't for another twenty minutes," Gerald mumbles through the shock currently coloring his face.

"He should also say that nobody asked you." I scowl at her. "Or your creepy child-cult, for your opinion in the first place."

Jenna blinks back her building fury. The rage teeming through my system has boiled over and I'm getting that feeling again. The same feeling I'd had when I told Brison where he could shove it. Because right now, Jenna isn't just some lady demanding to speak to the manager. She is the embodiment of everything wrong with Mason County. She is the guy at Marlowe's who took one look at me and Alan waiting for our food before declaring to everyone around that, *well, that don't seem right to me.* She is the coach of the last soccer team my parents made me join who had said *you know this is the boy's team, right, Peter?* She is whatever happened between Gerald Corres and my own father. Behind her chemically starched bangs and silvery manicure, she is the very reason people like me hate their hometown.

"I will not be spoken to that way," Jenna spits out, clutching at her chunky turquoise necklace.

"Look, lady. You can be as offended as you want, but you're preaching to the wrong choir. Go take it up with your knitting circle or your, like, placenta cooking class, because nobody here cares." The words feel good on their way out, like scratching a bug bite or stretching a sore muscle. Like I've been waiting to do this for ages. "Do you lose more brain cells every time you pop out one of those Children of the Corn, or are you just so vapid that you think *everyone* is hanging off your every word? I'm bored just telling you to fuck off."

My heart pounds in my chest as I run out of steam. Gerald leans forward to get a word in while Terrance retreats, his hands shielding the baby as if the gays are about to snatch it away for a midafternoon snack. Not that eating a baby is something I'd put past Cora Copia.

Jenna turns with rage to Gerald. "The town council will be hearing about this."

She storms off, parting the pasty white sea that is her sickly-looking offspring. They make me feel ill just looking at them. It's like Jenna ran out of ink by the last few. They follow listlessly in tow, just another afternoon spent following their crusader mother on a holy war.

The doors close and I feel the group watching me.

"What?"

"Nothing," Andy says, breaking the hush. "But, like, damn. Maybe you guys don't need us after all."

***

Alan is groaning into his basement rug. I can't remember the last time it was cleaned, but I have seen Alan use a makeup brush after his dog Eugene tried to play fetch with it. His voice is muffled through its crustiness.

"If she were wearing a wig today, I'd have ripped it off."

"I don't know," I say from the couch. "I'm not convinced her Supercuts Deluxe helmet head isn't a wig."

"No, Peter. I'm talking about Bailey."

"Oh, right," Tilly remembers, her legs propped up on the coffee table. "That was . . . a moment."

Alan bolts upright, a monologue prepared.

"Can you believe that absolute *priss*? She thinks just because she booked the venue and just because she has more views on her little videos she gets to, you know . . . like . . . right?"

"Totally," I agree.

Alan nods, glad that someone in the room is making some sense. Tilly grunts a half-hearted affirmative from her end of the couch as she absent-mindedly scrolls through her phone.

"She thinks she's god's gift to cross-dressery. If I were *that* loaded, I'd be gooped for the gag bus, too. She doesn't have *talent*; she has her daddy's credit card. Rich people are so used to walking over everyone. Like this Jenna lady. That's not a family, it's a basketball team. And then she just storms in with the light of Christ, ready to smite us all? I *don't* think."

A tide of queasiness settles over me at the thought of this afternoon. With the rush out of my system, I feel nothing but stupidity for opening my mouth in the first place.

"Yeah," I wonder, "but they're not going to tell the town council that we, like, verbally assaulted her and her children, right?"

This could be bad. Jenna could get the whole operation shut down before we even hit dress rehearsal. I'd not only be the guy who Said That Thing to Brison Dallas, I'd be the guy who ran his mouth and got the drag show shut down.

"Maybe," Tilly considers, reaching to stroke my cheek. "But I don't care. The memory of you ripping that bitch to tatters is officially my new happy place."

"No," I mutter, standing to pace the basement. "They're going to be back. They're going to show up with pitchforks and torches and an army of Catholic moms wearing floral blouses and shoes from a nursing supply store."

"Good thing we have Andy and his boys, then," Tilly sighs, fanning herself sharply.

"Yes!" agrees Alan. "I always thought those three were total cavemen, but I'm kind of in love with them now. I was talking to Blake, and he's actually, like, super funny and cute."

Tilly watches with triumphant amusement from behind her phone, watching my lip curl and just daring me to Do That Thing I Always Do.

"Aren't you excited for our new security team, Peter?"

I glare, wondering for the umpteenth time how Tilly is able to read my mind like that.

"Oh my god!" Alan screams, rolling around and cradling his phone to his chest. He holds it out for us to see like Charlie Bucket holding the golden ticket. "Lorne wants to hang out with me tomorrow night!"

My heart flops into my shoes. Lorne's text thread has yet to work its way any closer to the top of my phone. Maybe I really did say something wrong. Maybe it's a simple matter of Alan being more interesting than I am. Maybe the image that Lorne has of me is closer to some sort of large rodent that can't swim than the one of an unconventionally handsome man of mystery I'd been trying to project. Like a fumbling capybara or a malfunctioning beaver.

Tilly tackles him and holds Alan's face between her hands.

"You're so amazing, you sexy bitch!"

Alan and Tilly attack each other with praise while a layer of anger descends on me without warning. This really is Alan's Grand Gay Summer, and I'm just a secondary character. The best friend who gets humiliated while doing the bidding of the protagonist. The same protagonist who gets to end the movie by getting the guy just because he crushed first. Well, maybe I'm crushing, too, Alan. And maybe my storyline isn't just there for comedic effect, despite how many times it does seem to involve me falling on my ass. I dig out my phone, opening my chat with Lorne.

> Hey! Rural Realness had the wildest day. You won't believe what happened. Let's go swimming soon and I'll tell you all about it?

CHAPTER FOURTEEN

SWISS CHEESE ON LEGS

"Hey, friendlies!"

From behind my phone screen, Chrissy greets her camera with a breathy earnestness, walking off a run in her athleisure wear. The queens are dressed nearly the same as they work on their opening number in the sunshine streaming through the windows of the town hall.

"What if we all enter together?" Bailey suggests.

"I think that's a *maybe*," Alan considers.

It's August 22, and the Extravaganza is only six days away. But right now, the most important thing to me is hate-watching Chrissy McPhee's latest Poster video.

"I'm just here to say that even though there's all this stuff going around online right now, it's so important that we all show our support for the *Drag Extravaganza*."

Whatever this version of Chrissy is, it's not one I've ever met. Her social media face is all tender-hearted profundity and solemn allyship. I loathe this Chrissy even more than the real one who once asked, in the middle of tenth-grade science while I was riding out a particularly bad acne flare, if I was confused when that rover landed on Mars instead of my face.

"I'm here to say that I stand with my LGBTQ+ friends, who need me more than ever. My best friend in the whole world is Brison Dallas, and he is one of the most beloved LGBTQ+ members of our high school community."

"Maybe it just needs to be a solo," Alan observes tightly from onstage.

"This is an issue of acceptance and love," Chrissy continues, her face contracting into a display of devout sincerity. "And we need to show the LGBTQ+ members of our community that we love them."

I scream inwardly at the thought of how *pleased* she must be with herself. At the moral high horse she is peering down from. Chrissy blows a kiss at the screen and I flinch away from her virtual affection, as if some of it might get in my hair. Then I do the worst thing you can do on the internet. I read the comments.

Love you girlie

YES! Your so brave and beautiful babes

What is this about? Call me pls. Love Aunt Cherlynne

SO important, bbgirl. Love always wins

@brisondallaz Love you forever, queen

I consider leaving a comment of my own before my attention is snapped stageside.

"So the thing is that you're *actually* insane," Alan hurls at Bailey, his scarlet heels kicking up dust as they click across the stage.

"It's just a suggestion," Bailey calls back, his hands landing sullenly on the hips of his pink booty-shorts. "And who decided that *you* were the choreographer?"

"I can't stay till eight, you guys," Cora interjects, his baritone easily cutting through the room. "Can we finish this?"

"I'm *trying* to work." Alan rolls up the legs of his black sweatpants. They're his favorite pair because they have the words *Broadway Bound!* printed in fading white down both legs. "It's just kind of hard to get anything done when *some of us* keep second-guessing everything I say."

Bailey steps out of his shoes and jabs a heel at the air as he speaks. "They're artistic choices, Alan. Am I not allowed to weigh in on what's going on here? Am I not a member of Rural Realness?"

"Of course you are. And part of that is respecting the fact that I'm the *mother*."

Bailey opens his mouth, but Alan holds up a finger.

"Don't you dare say a word about the venue or the tickets. Because we know. We're all *very* aware of the fact that you're rich and can buy whatever you like. But, for the rest of us, it isn't so easy, so why don't you just listen to the people who had to actually work for what they've achieved?"

Even I'm blown away by that one, which is probably saying something. We all watch in awkward horror as Bailey trots silently through the hall, shoeless and defeated. He shakes his head in disbelief, hands floating to his face to block the tears now beginning to fall. The doors swing closed behind him.

"What the hell, Alan?" Tilly demands, sliding the spiky black wig from her head.

"What?" Alan wipes daintily at the tears forming in his eyes. "So I'm just supposed to let Bailey walk all over me?"

"No. But you *are* supposed to act like the leader."

Alan blinks back tears as he slinks backstage.

"I'm gonna go talk to him," Tilly says. "Will one of you please go deal with Bailey?"

The other queens only shake their heads.

"I'm not getting in the middle of that," says Nifoal, shaking his head firmly. "Whichever side I pick is going to be, like, treasonous to the other queen."

"She's right," agrees Cora. "Alan still hasn't let go of the time I won tickets to

Florence and the Machine and I took my terminally ill cousin instead of him."

"Oh, how is Samantha?" Nifoal asks, brightening.

"She's thriving, honestly. Her name is Samanthala now, and she's running a compound for fourth-dimensional crystal witches outside Portland."

"I can *totally* see that for her."

I tap at my phone, watching Tilly from the corner of my eye. Maybe if I look busy, she'll forget I exist. Scrolling my text thread with Lorne, I write *Hey*, before deleting it. *You won't believe the drama over here*, I try, deleting it as well.

Tilly grabs my arm. "Go deal with Bailey."

"What?" I ask, still holding very still. "Why?"

"Because," Tilly orders, pushing me toward the doors, "you're the producer."

I search for something to say, some reason to duck out of this one. They can't leave me in charge of someone's emotional well-being. That's like asking Freddy Krueger to watch your kid while you pop out to the shop for a few minutes. When you come back to find the place a bloody mess, you only have yourself to blame.

But a minute later I'm pushing open the front doors leading onto Mason's one-street downtown. A transport truck whizzes past as I get to the sidewalk and search for Bailey's twiggy frame. Maybe he called in the family helicopter for an airlift home. Maybe he's across the street at the Salvation Army, terrifying the church ladies behind the counter and asking to see the fall collection. Or maybe he walked over to the corner and is eating his feelings at Marlowe's. Does Bailey eat carbs? The closest thing that Marlowe's has to a salad is of the taco variety, and the only reason it got on the menu was management's attempt at getting an ethnic food option.

When I do find Bailey, he's is in the alleyway beside the hall, framed by the tacky metal archway covered with the words *Lover's Lane* and gaudy metal leaves and flowers.

"This shit is supposed to be smearproof," Bailey whines, catching sight of me while trying to clean his leaking eyeliner.

I sit at the other end of the stairs and pass Bailey the red bandanna folded in my back pocket.

"You keep a hankie?" he asks through a stifled sob, gingerly taking my donation.

"I get sweaty. In general, but especially in August."

"I know," Bailey sniffles. "You really should talk to a dermatologist or something because those pores are *clogged*. Or at least let me give you a cover-up tutorial because some of those bad boys on your face look angry."

"It's stress. And the heat. And the sweat. But mostly the stress."

I don't tell Bailey that the three pimples forming under my nose have me considering taking a cheese grater to my face. If I'm going to look like a wedge of Swiss cheese on legs, I might as well act like it.

Bailey passes me the makeup-smeared hankie and I stuff it back into my pocket.

"*That* I understand," says Bailey, his voice slowly returning to normal. "And I know what you're going to say. Poor little rich boy, what the hell does he have to be stressed about?"

"I wasn't going to say that."

Sure, I had been thinking it, but I wasn't going to *say* it.

"I didn't exactly turn out how my parents expected," Bailey explains. "You probably get that. But when things started taking off with the channel, I thought, okay, maybe they'll at least be happy that I'm making something of myself. When your son starts wearing makeup and develops an expensive taste for heels, it's probably not the easiest thing. Unless you're, like, super progressive or whatever. And my parents like to think they're progressive, but they still donate money to stop windmills and solar power going up around here. And they vote conservative just to spite everyone who thinks they should pay real taxes."

"My family vacationed in an RV last year," I say flatly. "We borrowed it from my uncle, and I had to pull a dead raccoon out of the motor because my hands were the smallest."

"My dad is all about pulling yourself up by your bootstraps, whatever that really means," Bailey continues, unabated. "Which is hilarious because he inherited the business from my grandpa. Who, by the way, is a total Nazi freak. I walked into this side room in his study once and it was just full of, like, antique swastikas. So fuck him, right?"

"Yeah," I nod. "I'd say so."

"So I thought that me striking out on my own would at least mean something to my father. But all he ever does is act like I'm wasting my time on some stupid hobby. Not *once* has he asked me about my channel, or my videos, or even this show. Which is going to be totally historic, and he couldn't even give two shits."

Tilly may have had to force me into this conversation, but now that I'm here I'm not as mortified as I'd expected to be. Bailey Hayes is *all show, all the time*. A part of me is fascinated with this peek behind the designer curtain.

"Alan doesn't know what he's talking about. I bust my ass even though my entire family thinks I should just quit and start getting really into propane. Which, like, ew."

"Maybe you should tell Alan that," I offer.

I feel myself falter, tripping over the words as they pass my lips. There's a text thread sitting in my pocket that I haven't shared a word of with Alan. One that is complicated by the dibs he called on Lorne.

Bailey scoffs. "Tell Alan? No. Showing weakness in front of him is humiliating."

"I can tell him to ease up on his All-Seeing Mother routine."

"What?" Bailey frowns. "No, I mean, do you have any idea what it's like to bend over backward to impress that bitch and still have him snap back at you? It's the actual worst."

"Alan?" I ask through a laugh.

"Of course Alan," Bailey says. "He's the reason the rest of this claptrap little routine had the balls to step out of the shoe closet in the first place. If he hadn't dragged some drag into this glorified cornfield, none of us would have even bothered."

I reel, imagining Alan as a shining beacon of light and hope to little drag queens watching him from the middle of nowhere with nothing but their phone, a Wi-Fi connection, and a wig-filled dream.

"If you idolize him so much, then what the hell was that?"

"I did not say *idolize*, Peter. And this show needs to be perfect. I'm just trying to make it as perfect as possible. I think I deserve a little credit, don't I?"

A daycare group trundles by on the street, a line of toddlers waving at the strangers sitting on the alleyway steps. Bailey's face lights up a little, and he waves back, the women smiling politely before ushering their ducklings away from the visibly gay weirdos in Mason's only alleyway.

"I get why you're doing this show, Peter."

I laugh again, but he is stone-faced.

"You do?"

"Of course," Bailey says. "You're trying to reset your public image after all this drama with Brison and the fact that people think you're, you know, a self-hating gay."

He's right, of course. But it still sends a shock to my toes to feel someone look me in the eye and appraise me so clearly. Bailey might not be as self-obsessed as I'd imagined. Without his camera running, I might even find myself trusting him. What the hell is happening today?

Bailey stands up and breathes in deeply. "We've all got our reasons for being here. But you really shouldn't care so much what other people think."

Bailey retrieves his phone and begins to record.

"We're here backstage at *The First Annual Mason County Drag Extravaganza*," he smiles into the camera. "And despite the hate we've already been getting, this really is going to be a show to remember. Hope you got your tickets in advance, babes." He blows a kiss and ends the video, the smile falling from his face as he does.

***

Bailey and I return to find Gerald addressing the rest of the team.

" . . .Which is why the town council has agreed to continue allowing the donation of this space. All we ask is that you play a little nicer with folks who might have a . . . a thing or two to say otherwise. Like Jenna Wilbur and her . . . husband."

The word *husband* emerges strangled, like Gerald can barely believe it himself.

"You want us to be nicer to the bigots, Gerald?" Tilly asks ironically from the stage.

Alan regards us icily as we rejoin the team, he and Bailey avoiding eye contact with a practiced haughtiness.

"I wouldn't put it that way," Gerald fumbles. "But we do want you to, maybe, represent the Mason Town Hall with a bit more of a, well—"

"A grin and bear it attitude?" Nifoal suggests wryly.

"Maybe *patience*," Gerald suggests, "and *understanding*."

"Ew," Bailey jeers.

"Um, guys?"

Cora Copia is staring at his phone, which he turns to display with trepidation. "Have you seen this?"

A long post by Jenna Wilbur fills the screen.

"This performance is a violation of the beliefs of many, many Mason residents," Cora reads. "And our town council's financial support of it is quite frankly offensive to my faith, my beliefs, and my convictions."

"Girl loves her beliefs," Tilly deadpans, chewing at a hangnail.

"Which is why I am calling for a protest on the night of this objectionable performance. Join me and my husband at the town hall, where we will make sure that the god-abiding voices of Mason County are heard and accounted for by our municipal government."

We stare at Cora, the drama between Alan and Bailey dissipating now that a larger one is looming. I retrieve my handkerchief and mop at the nervous sweat forming on my brow. This is Brison Dallas all over again. I've ruined everything.

"I hope she wears that all-white number again," Bailey says. "It makes her look like a haunted porcelain doll."

CHAPTER FIFTEEN
POCKMARKED SISSY

"And then we show up to Jenna's church with our faces beat for the gods. Literally!" Alan shrieks, pushing me nearly into the street in a fit of hysterics.

"Yes!" I howl, grabbing his arm. "And you can have one of those church donation baskets for tips while you work the runway."

Alan screams and buckles over, the sidewalk scraping beneath his shoes. "Bitch, it's called an aisle."

My stomach aches as I devolve into a bleating donkey wail of laughter, waving for Alan to stop before I burst a blood vessel. Slowly we continue for home, our breathing returning to normal as the residual giggles begin to fade. Mason's heatwave continues unabated, turning my back into a sweat-filled Slip 'N Slide. But I don't mind it much with the sun setting and the sky turning into cotton candy on the horizon.

"People can't take her seriously, can they?" I ask after a while.

"I don't know." Alan shrugs. "A lot of people were posting about it. And then Gerald wants us to just shut up and play nice?" His face clouds over in a way I don't often see. The ticker-tape parade that is Alan Goode is gone for a beat, and I'm not sure I recognize the Alan standing in his place.

"Maybe it'll blow over," I try, watching his face.

"Maybe. But maybe we need to say something about it."

Alan smiles, the way he does when he's mid-scheme.

"Like what?"

"I don't know," Alan muses. "Maybe something that only a group of baby drag queens can get away with?"

He grins the way he does when he's scheming, and I feel my chest tighten.

"Like *what*?"

"Say what you will about Ms. Hayes—"

"Which you really did today, by the way," I remind him.

"But she knows how to weaponize drama, and I get the feeling that Mason County is hungry for another video."

We approach the turn onto Poplar Avenue, Alan's usual route home, and a familiar anxiety fills my chest. Alan is going to run wild with this idea, I can already tell. By tonight he'll have an entire video choreographed, including multiple costume changes and several color swatch options.

"Maybe we should just listen to Gerald on this one."

Alan laughs again, tenting his fingers faux maniacally.

"*You* of all people don't feel like publicly telling Sister-Wife Sandy to jump off a cliff?"

"Of course I do. But not if it means we lose the space."

"So we lose the space!" Alan concedes flamboyantly. "We'll just perform it in a parking lot. Or a barn. The internet loves rural chic."

"Or, you know, in the town hall. Where we have lights and seats and a sliver of self-respect."

"Imagine the publicity we'd get from getting kicked out of the town hall!" Alan announces, disappearing into the fantasy before my very eyes. "Absolute stunt queens, they'll call us, not to mention the—"

"Can you just take this seriously for one second?" I cut in, exasperated. "It might not look like it, but I've worked really hard to make this show happen. I don't want it all going to shit because you had to make a scene."

Alan arches an eyebrow and retreats a step, affronted and snitty.

"And I haven't worked hard?" he asks, gathering himself.

"Of course you have, but making public statements about how much you hate someone hasn't worked out very well for me, if you haven't noticed. And I'm the one who wouldn't play nice in the first place, so there's no way Octo-Mommy sees this as anything but another attack from yours truly. Can we please just not?"

Alan takes me in wearily. "All right," he shrugs. "I suppose you are the producer."

"Let's work it into the show," I say. I can feel that I've pushed too far, that Alan is smarting under the sting of my tone. "It'll be too late to shut us down by then."

"No," he replies breezily. "You're right. Let's just leave it."

"I'm serious. Why don't I come over and we can plan something ridiculous for Aggie to do after intermission? You could do a lip sync to her post. Or even," I chuckle, "you could come out in a blonde wig—"

"I can't," Alan trills. He checks his nails absently. "I'm seeing Lorne tonight. Remember?"

"Yeah, right. Totally."

Alan smiles thinly and turns to walk home.

"It's fine, Peter. Really," Alan assures me, turning his back with a quick wave.

I watch him go and feel the mosquitoes swarming at my ankles as night falls over the street.

***

"You have to be careful, Peter," my mother informs me, her face illuminated by the white glow of her tablet. My father channel surfs in his armchair while Mom scans Jenna Wilbur's post one more time, her glasses perched at the end of her nose.

"Careful about what?"

"Careful that you're not, you know, upsetting the applecart on your way to the market."

"What does that even *mean*?"

"It means that people around here talk, and it's easy to get a certain reputation," Mom explains, as if reiterating that one plus one equals two.

I exhale petulantly, folding my arms in the exact way I know my mother detests. "Well, maybe Jenna Wilbur and her husband should be getting a certain reputation for being creepy homophobes who can't mind their own business."

"Your father and I think that you should maybe reconsider some of this, is all," Mom clarifies, her tone moving upward toward a note of familial diplomacy.

I'm speechless. Of course it took the threat of an upset applecart for my parents to take an interest in what I've been doing lately.

"It sounds like people are going to show up, Peter," she continues.

"Of course they're going to show up!" I retort, my voice cracking. "We sold out. Standing room only. This is going to be the most attended event in Mason County that has nothing to do with tractors fighting other tractors."

"People are going to *protest*, Peter."

Mom puts her tablet aside and fixes her glasses while Dad turns off the TV. The last time he turned the TV off for something was the time Ally had decreed that she was leaving her soccer team to focus on her goals with the volleyball team. It was a moment that could not be cheapened with the sounds of a *Law and Order* rerun.

"And so what if they do?" I ask the room.

"Maybe you could do it online!" Mom suggests, as if I hadn't said a word. "That way you won't have people showing up to cause a commotion."

"Is that really the lesson you're trying to teach your child right now? If people get in my way I should give up?"

"Of course not," she counters testily. "But this kind of thing can get people very riled up. I just don't want anyone to get hurt or for anyone to get the wrong idea about you."

That iron-clad focus is back, and I narrow my eyes the way I do when I'm about to say something stupid but honest.

"No," I note. "You don't want them to get the wrong idea about *you*."

"That's enough, Peter," Dad warns from his recliner. "Can we all calm down?"

"You don't want them to get the idea that you raised an angry little faggot who doesn't know his place. And honestly, I'm getting tired of being told to play nice with the people who hate me for no good reason, which you always—"

"Nobody is *telling* you to do anything!" my father interjects. "But it wouldn't kill you to take your parents seriously every now and then."

I don't respond. Honestly, I'm not sure how. Thankfully, my father unmutes the TV and the nothing-filled chatter of *The Big Bang Theory* takes over. I opt to turn and leave the room.

I'm careful not to slam the door to my bedroom. The worst thing right now would be to give the impression that I'm nothing more than a moody teenager. I flop onto my bed and hide my face in my pillow. The line has been crossed. The very carefully maintained line that I've put a lot of effort into. My parents aren't supposed to intersect with any of my gay goings-on. They know that I'm gay, in theory. My parents knowing I'm gay in *practice* is another thing altogether, something that I will try to avoid until I'm at least in my early thirties. Maybe with a nice backyard and a partner who has a soft-boy name like Stephen (with a *ph* instead of a *v*, of course). Stephen builds sheds in his spare time and can barbecue well enough to make my dad forget that his son is a pockmarked sissy and not one of those muscly gays who runs marathons but is also really good at math.

For a moment I contemplate texting Lorne, but the idea of it feels like tossing a banana peel onto an already overflowing trash pile. Maybe I'll text

Alan instead. Sometimes he forgets that he's mad at me when I text him videos of rescue dogs befriending llamas or giraffes. But when I do check my phone, I regret it immediately.

> **@jenawfewrr23** I'm all for supporting this community, but isn't this organized by the guy who made a sui**de joke about @brisondallaz? @ptkns1358, when r u going to take accountibility?

> **@kriskrisser11** if u got tix 4 the mason county drag extravaganza that's fine or whatever but ask urself if you wanna be seen supporting known homophobe @ptkns1358

> **@tan_er_jamma** @brisondallaz is going to the drag extravaganza show which is cool i guess, and big ups to @MsBaileyHayes for using her platform to platform him with her platform, but is @ptkns1358 even going to show his face? deplatform him

It's like I'm trapped. The Jenna Wilbur fan club hates me, my parents are embarrassed by me, and now the entire reason I've been busting my ass on this stupid show is blowing up in my face. Is producing Mason's first-ever drag show not enough for the Brison Pity Party to leave me alone? This entire thing is a calculated act of public relations but the public are still demanding that my head be mounted in the town square.

The joke's on them, really. Nobody should have to stare at my face when they're just trying to walk to the paint store. Will my face still break out after my head's been separated from my neck? Maybe I'll have clear skin before the flesh-rot kicks in. I open my texts with Alan and reconsider for a moment before typing.

> You're right. Let's drag her to hell.

Of course, you can't please everyone. But thus far I've pleased no one. As if to reward the middle finger that I'm holding up to the world at large, a trio of swimmer emojis arrive on my phone.

> Tomorrow?

My stomach leaps, and I roll over to scream lightly into my pillow. This is it. This is the night, I decide. This night won't end like the last one. It will end with me kissing Lorne. Or maybe even Lorne kissing me. I deserve at least one good instance of tongue-on-tongue before my head gets mounted somewhere within tomato-throwing distance.

> Tomorrow.

CHAPTER SIXTEEN

A BACNE-RIDDEN SEA LION WAITING FOR HIS SLOP

"And we're sure they're not home?" I ask again, readying myself to hop over the fence. Lorne has already landed easily on the other side of the pea-green slats, naked torso flashing against the dark.

"They're having my aunt check in on the plants for them until tomorrow," he reassures me.

I heft myself up, arms quaking weakly, air crushed out of me as my stomach balloons against the fence. Timidly, I roll over and try to land daintily. But then I stumble over a root while holding my arms over my wobbling belly. Lorne is too busy descending the steps of the pool to notice, so I take the opportunity to shake my feet free of dirt and my general jiggling goes unnoticed. Lorne's hips descend into the water and I try not to stare. How is his belly button so flat? Mine looks like one of those giant toothy worm monsters from *Dune*. In the near distance, the lights from Chrissy's house shine bright and accusatory, lighting the cavernous depths of my freakish navel.

"It really is wild, you know," Lorne says over the gentle splash of the water. "People shouldn't be allowed to be this rich. There should be a wealth cap, right?

I wince as I wade into the chill of the shallow end, deciding not to point out that the house in which Lorne has been staying all summer isn't exactly a shack. We're only able to pool hop in a house that has its own outdoor kitchen because Cousin Chrissy lives on Blackberry Avenue, the street with the largest houses in town. At least two of the houses are attached to horse pens, and more than a few have boats in their driveways.

Lorne does a lap, and I tread water while wondering if I should ask about Alan. But how do you ask that kind of thing? *Hey, did you have fun hanging out with Alan? Did you guys talk about me? He didn't tell you about the time I busted the seam in my pants just by sneezing, did he?*

No. I won't. These are not questions that will lead to me rounding any of the bases. Are the bases the same for gay people? Baseball feels like a straights-only affair. Then again, there might be nothing gayer than a bunch of guys wearing matching outfits with tight pants and jaunty little caps.

"So what's going on with this Brison Dallas drama?"

Water jumps up my nose as I try to contain my surprise. I bob like a potato and try to play cool. "Honestly, it's all kind of blown out of proportion," I explain, forcing nonchalance hard enough to burst a blood vessel in my forehead. "Brison and Chrissy were giving Alan a hard time about this . . . this Pride flag outfit thing he was wearing . . ."

"Yeah," says Lorne. "They can be kind of harsh, right?"

"Exactly!"

I exhale in relief, relaxing a bit and poking a toe into the drop to the deep end.

"And it sounds like Alan was just, like, trying to be visible as a queer person," Lorne considers.

"Sure," I agree. "Not that he's ever had a problem with that." I laugh.

A distant flicker of disapproval flashes across Lorne's face.

"Not that there's anything wrong with it," I continue. "Being visibly queer or whatever."

Does Lorne think I'm making a fat joke? He *for sure* thinks that I'm making a fat joke. But how? My stomach looks more like a washing machine than a washboard. Lorne can't think I'd go that far. Maybe he can. Maybe Alan *did* tell him about my long habit of saying terrible things about people that go on to ruin my life, like this one, right now. I'm not going to be rounding any bases tonight. I'm going to be stuck in the parking lot without any special baseball pants or fancy caps.

Is it just me, or is baseball kind of hot?

"You have a lot of anger inside you, Peter," Lorne says sagely from the deep end.

"I what?"

Lorne swims toward me, now close enough to touch. Is that what he's planning on doing? Water is dripping from his shoulders and collecting in his clavicle and I'm staring at his neck like a horny vampire, aren't I?

"Can I propose something?" Lorne asks quietly.

Oh my god. It's happening. Yes, my weird quip about Alan might have cast a bit of a pall over tonight's proceedings, but Lorne seems graciously willing to overlook my offense. It's generous of him. Magnanimous, even. My throat constricts beneath my nerves, but I manage to croak out a reply. "Yeah, totally."

"Philosophy is what I plan on studying," Lorne explains with hushed gravitas. "But what I really am, at heart, is an energy reader."

I nod, patiently waiting for the joke.

Lorne nods, too. Because apparently there is none.

"Wow," I muster.

"And with your consent," Lorne continues solemnly, "I'd like to read your energies."

Lorne holds his palms up to my chest. The somber intensity of this moment is nearly too much for me to handle. There's been a distinct lack of ironic detachment throughout this entire exchange. This alone should be enough to make me break out into hives or projectile vomit while my head spins around. When it comes to sincerity, I'm like one of those trained rats that can find bombs. I sniff it out from miles away, diffuse it as quickly as possible, and then go home to eat some cheese. But Lorne *has* just offered to touch me. And what is touching if not a gateway drug to first base? Or is it second base? A government body of some kind needs to publish an official report on the bases system and then write an addendum for the homos. I don't think that's asking too much of our elected officials.

"Sure," I say at last. "You totally have my consent."

Lorne lays his hands on my chest and I shiver.

"Too cold?" he asks.

"Nope," I reply as casually as possible.

Lorne closes his eyes, so I close mine. Water drips from his arms, landing with a soft *plunk*. We breathe and exhale, repeating it a few times as his hands relax across my chest and then my shoulders. It feels good at first, but my reluctance turns to annoyance when I consider his words again. It doesn't take a vibe wizard to see that I have *anger inside me*. Of course I do. I'm not some gay buddha, even if our stomachs do look alike.

"You're threatened by Alan," Lorne reads ceremoniously, his wet hands now placed soundly above my floppy man tits. "Why is that?"

"Oh," I say through closed eyes. "I don't think I am."

"That's not what your energies are telling me."

"I drank like an entire pot of coffee at work today, so it might be that."

"And you love to deflect with humor. It's a coping mechanism," Lorne deduces with a Sherlockian flair. "Which I respect. But one of these days you're going to have to let those walls down. Because it makes sense. Alan lives his true self for everyone to see. He knows what his life's purpose is. That can be hard for people to deal with. Maybe even hard for *you* to deal with."

The icy chill is gone. My neck is beginning to sweat. Lorne is clearly just making this up as he goes. I'm not jealous of Alan. Alan and I are apples and oranges. We're two fruits who just shouldn't be compared.

"You have a lot of tension at home," Lorne says after my pointed silence. "With your parents."

I'm a small-town gay teen. Yes, I have tension with my parents. It'd be weird if I *didn't* have tension with my parents. Just because Alan's parents *Live, Laugh, Love* their gay son doesn't mean the rest of us are living every day like a very gay episode of *Sesame Street*.

"And you want to apologize," Lorne concludes.

His hands splash back into the water. I open my eyes.

"Apologize?"

Lorne nods empathetically. "For what happened with Brison."

I laugh, but it's clear that Lorne is stuck in a state of serene openheartedness. It's beginning to wear on me, and it's getting in the way of the mission at hand. "I'm still waiting for Brison to apologize."

"Taking accountability is so powerful, Peter."

I splash water his way with a flick of my wrist, trying for playful. I can salvage this, even if Lorne is determined to ruin the mood.

"Sure. And Brison can account for how much of an asshole he was to Alan."

"I don't think this is about Alan."

"What?" I laugh. "Of course it's about Alan."

"I think this is about you." Lorne wades closer to me. My back is against the side of the pool now. "There's something I say sometimes. *Hurt people hurt people.* Does that make any sense?"

I stretch my arms to either side, leaning back and hoping that Lorne will take the hint. Any hint, really.

"Wait, you think you made that up?"

Lorne wrinkles his brow, clearly not used to being questioned while in process.

"Yeah, I made it up."

"Hurt people hurt people," I repeat. "That was you?"

"Yes."

"I don't think it was."

"I'm only a novice energy healer, but it's clear to me that there is a lot to be healed here, Peter," he says dulcetly.

"I thought you said you were an energy *reader*," I say, successfully holding back a laugh for maybe the first time in my life. This has to be a joke, right?

"Exactly," Lorne says with a nod. "And reading is the first step to healing this kind of hurt."

Oh my god. Lorne is an idiot. He's been an idiot this entire time. I only thought he was smart because he talked about liking philosophy. He didn't even talk about any particular philosophers—he just talked about generally enjoying the concept. That's like saying you like hiking when, really, you just enjoy the idea of some no-nonsense boots and a chunky bag of trail mix.

"I'm not hurt," I say through my dawning realization.

"That's not what I'm getting."

Lorne's hand is back on my chest, which I'm not mad about. Yes, he's a dummy who has probably licked a salt lamp or two. But he's hot, goddamn it, and I've put in the legwork.

"I've been thinking about apologizing," I lie. "Really considering it, actually. But I've been kind of distracted lately."

Lorne just stands there, dripping.

"Distracted by you," I try again, distantly aware of how cheesy this must sound. Something warm and sharp kicks up in my stomach and crackles to the edge of my fingers. Crickets chirp in the yard. The poolside fridge below the awning hums to life and Lorne's hand grows warm against my skin. The flirtation hovers open-ended in the chlorine-tinged air.

"I'd really like to kiss you," I say.

My lips go numb.

The moment trails by, bloated and dull. Maybe I blew it. Maybe I look like one of those gray sea lions turning aimlessly in the water, waiting for the zookeeper to toss in some fish chunks. I bob there, a bacne-ridden sea lion waiting for his slop. Lorne says nothing, considering if he feels like tossing me some fish heads.

"All right."

My heart threatens to rip out of my chest *Alien*-style. Batter up.

I lean in and press my lips quickly to his, smelling whatever spiced and musky products his hair must be full of. The kiss lasts a second, his closed lips pressing back noncommittally like a handshake of the mouths. Lorne nods as I pull away, my washing machine body now tumbling full of weird chemical feelings.

Then a car pulls into the driveway.

Lorne's hand flies to my mouth. The engine turns off and voices drift through open windows. The warm and fuzzy teenage tingles shatter, reforming into a swirling mass of apprehension as I watch Lorne glide over to the ladder and pull himself out. He looks back to see me turning to stone in the water and mouths *let's go*, as he makes his tiptoed escape through the garden. I follow, trying desperately not to splash. The car door closes outside the gate and I take the steps carefully, pool water dripping in audible accusation. I crash through the garden as quietly as I can, my heel igniting in pain as something prickly and green squashes beneath it.

"It was a perfectly fine resort," a man's voice laments from the driveway. "But it's just *not* fresh seafood if I can't see the fear in its eyes, you know?"

The homeowners rummage through the back seats, and I waste no time in heaving up and over the fence, jutting out a leg to catch myself but still landing with a thud on my side. Twigs dig into my arm and I turn to see Lorne already hustling toward Chrissy's house at a crouched run, his pale skin shining alabaster in the moonlight. The couple make their way up the lawn, and I exhale gratefully at the sound of their keys jingling in the front door. Soaked and slipping, I right myself and scuttle toward the tree we left our shirts under. Lorne pulls a black T-shirt on, and I dress hastily, more than happy to cover myself after his tepid, almost medical mouth to mouth.

Lorne smiles weakly and looks back to Chrissy's house, as if I've kept him from something more important. He's close enough to kiss again. Maybe the moment isn't over until I say it is. I lean in for round two to find nothing but open air as Lorne steps back. A truck appears, turning into the driveway and catching the two of us in its super-powered high beams. Brison Dallas steps out of the passenger seat, his beach-casual outfit looking perfectly crisp, his dark hair swept back without a hair misplaced.

My shoes squelch fartily beneath me.

"Oh," calls a voice. "Hello, Peter." Chrissy rounds the corner of her truck, the keys dangling from a fresh set of nails.

"Be nice, sweet cousin," Lorne chastises her.

"I was just going, actually," I tell them.

Chrissy raises an eyebrow, almost disappointed. Brison says nothing.

I turn and walk away. Lorne calls his goodbye from the lawn, but the three of them are already walking up to the house, Chrissy's clunky laugh filling the empty air. My face burns with something I'd rather not feel right now. Would Lorne have returned that second attempt if Chrissy hadn't crashed her truck into the moment?

The crickets sound off as I make my way home, chiming in on the fact that I'm just some gross, horny negative space where a person should be. The worst part is how *needy* I feel, as if Lorne had been doing me a favor by returning my romantic advances by rote. As if the stink of effort emanating from my pores had made him feel sorry enough to politely let my lips touch his. I'm pretty sure most people's first kiss doesn't feel like a charitable act. I hadn't been naive enough to expect an orchestra-swelling movie moment filled with fireworks and confetti. But how has moving from being theoretically gay to being a practicing gay made me feel like even more of a floating blob of sexlessness? How have I waited *this* long to cross the most basic of milestones only to fail so utterly?

My heels begin to blister in my damp shoes. I don't have an answer for myself.

CHAPTER SEVENTEEN

VILE HATE-SPEWING RAGE MACHINE

It is August 27, and The House of Rural Realness is standing under the full stage lights of the Mason Town Hall. The hall is filled with folding chairs, which we sweatily pulled up two flights of stairs to represent a full audience. In the dark, Gerald Corres and I are flies on the wall of the soap opera still simmering between Aggie Culture and Bailey Hayes. Aggie and Bailey take opposite sides of the stage as the queens warm up, stretching while pointedly avoiding the sight of one another. Tonight, the girls look more like a very gay dance crew than a team of drag queens, but their wigs and shoes are still being worn for rehearsal purposes.

After announcing her intent to have a unified look for the Extravaganza's final number, Bailey had arrived with silver hand-sewn sashes and a notable hint of pride.

"I don't do silver," says Nifoal. She discards the shimmery sash to the side of the stage with a flick of her wrist.

"It's unfortunate, but true," Cora agrees, tossing her sash to form a pile. "They're not really in keeping with my general vibe."

Aggie takes notice but remains silent during her calf stretch, an eyebrow raised in wordless glee.

"I think they're really nice, Bailey!" Rita tries.

"I'm going for a Miss Mason look," Bailey explains. "Like we're pageant girls. It's a gag."

"Totally," nods Nifoal. "I'm just not gag*ging*, you know?"

"Yes," Cora agrees. "It's giving *Drop Dead Gorgeous* vibes but Cora Copia's is more *Dead and Gorgeous*. Can I at least cover mine in brain splatter?"

"Leave it to Cora to need fake brains," Nifoal deadpans. "God knows she doesn't have any of her own."

Cora smacks Nifoal's arm while mid-stretch. "I don't need brains. I'm a look queen," she says haughtily.

"Yeah, a *look fucking dumb* queen," Nifoal brays.

The two scream in laughter and continue to pelt each other with camped-up insults. It's the one part of drag I think I'd be good at.

"I think the sashes are fun," says Rita. "They're ridiculous, right?"

"Exactly!" says Bailey. "And anyway, you bitches think I'm just a credit card in heels. But here I am sewing garments for your busted asses, and this is the thanks I get?"

"I vote we wear them," Rita says with a smile.

Through the windows comes the distant sound of a car alarm. Nifoal adjusts the strap on her heels. Bailey casts her eyes across the stage, conviction slowly falling from her face. "Okay," she relents, her eyes scanning the floor. "Never mind, I guess." Bailey clops across the stage to collect the discarded sashes, patting them off with exaggerated effect. She folds them carefully and pushes a blonde lock from her face. The car alarm wails on.

"I also vote that we wear them."

The group turns to Aggie, now finished her warm-up. She shrugs and picks at a nail.

"You're drag queens. Stop taking yourself so seriously."

Aggie busies herself with her shoes, playing at being nonplussed while avoiding Bailey's thankful gaze.

"Great," Rita concludes. "Three to two. Done. Can we record now?"

"Yes!" I call out. "Let's record, ladies."

The queens break into chatter as they ready themselves for tonight's promo shoot. Aggie fusses over Cora's hair and I wonder if she's in the forgiving mood tonight. The non-kiss with Lorne is festering at the back of my mind. Maybe I won't even tell Alan. Maybe I shouldn't. But hadn't he been the one so insistent that I put myself out there? Wasn't he the one acting like I'm some boy-deprived anti-gay?

"And we're sure there's nothing too bothersome in this routine?" Gerald inquires from the aisle. *Bothersome* meaning anything that might get us in trouble with the town council. *Bothersome* meaning anything that might cause Jenna Wilbur's Prayer Party to clutch their pearls even tighter.

"Not that I've been told," I reply. "But they might still be making a few last-minute adjustments."

Gerald sweats visibly and trots back up the aisle to fret in private, his smile thinning but still present. It's not like I can blame him. Responding to Jenna's protest was one thing, but doing it in a literal song and dance is another. Technically this is a test run, with Gerald having the final decision over it getting posted online. I wonder if my mom will get this video in her inbox, too. Maybe I even hope that she does.

Aggie gives me the cue and I press play on the laptop, which we've hooked into the hall's ancient sound system. I start recording on my phone, and the music kicks in as the queens take the stage again. One by one, each of them strikes a battle-ready pose from the cover of a movie poster. A movie that, for the record, I would watch.

So, calls a simpering voice from over the speakers. It's Nifoal Dressage, booming in a sultry sibilance. *I heard The House of Rural Realness has been getting some naysayers.*

It's true, whispers Cora Copia. *Isn't that so hecked up?*

You bet your sweet bippy, replies Nifoal. *Cuz saying neigh is my thing.*

A whip cracks, followed by the whinny of a horse. *Let's tell these girls what's what!* declares Cora.

Or even better! says Nifoal. *Let's tell them who's who.*

Cora's face lights up, her typical placidity erupting into a smolder. The hair on my arms and neck stands on end as team THORR comes to life. Cora's vocals stream from the speakers while she mouths along in delight.

My name is Cora Copia, I'm gonna make a mess of ya,
Cuz your hair is making me gag.
I'd never trust a Jenna wearing white and wearing pleather,
Not to mention that knockoff bag.

Rita steps forward, her hair slicked back and her heels the highest in the bunch.

They call me Rita Rustique and I'm anything but rusty,
Unlike your backward views.
My girls are fab and flawless, but please don't think they're clawless,
Cuz bitch, we are coming for you.

My hand claps over my mouth as I laugh behind the camera. Nifoal takes center stage with a delightful sneer.

My name's Nifoal
And I'm gonna take a stroll
All over your busted bangs.
This horse has hooves
You think they're cute?
Well don't cuz this mare has fangs.

Nifoal hisses, and the drum machine takes over while the three reveal Bailey, positively gleaming in her rightful place as the center of attention.

Hi, I'm Bailey!
And you can blow me
Cuz your bigotry is getting me down.
You made me sad,
And feel real mad,
So delete it, you dried-up clown.
Yes your hair is bad,
But you should be glad
That I don't have more to say.
Cuz I could say more,
But that would just bore.
Okay fine, her husband's gay.

The video shakes as I hold back my laughter, and the queens gather for the final verse of Mother Aggie Culture. But the dancing stops as the girls catch sight of something in the audience. I pause the music and Aggie steps forward, shading her eyes from the light.

"Something wrong, Gerald?"

Gerald's face is in shadow, but it's easy to tell that his trademark smile has disappeared entirely.

"I thought we'd agreed that we would conduct ourselves with behavior that represents the town hall with some grace and poise?"

It's like someone has pulled the switch on Gerald. Nobody says a word. The mounting anxiety in the room is enough to make my stomach knot.

"It's just a stupid clapback video, Gerald," I say limply. "It'll drum up some last-minute buzz for the show."

Gerald shakes his head wearily. "Look, poke fun at Jenna all you want, but you have to know when to leave things be. And talking about Terrance that way is *not* acceptable."

"They showed up in *our* venue and gave us a full *god hates fags* routine," I say, pushing back.

"Yeah," Nifoal says from under the stage lights. "Besides, her husband, like, *has* to be gay, doesn't he?"

"For sure," agrees Cora.

"He's at least bi-curious," says Nifoal.

"There wasn't a hint of curiosity in that kitty cat, darling," Cora says, laughing.

"That's enough!" Gerald booms.

Silence fills the room. Gerald being anything but aggressively pleasant is one thing, but this is something else entirely.

"There are a lot of things . . ." Gerald trails off. He sits heavily in the nearest chair. "There are a lot of things that you don't understand yet. About being a . . . being gay around here. I'm not going to lecture you, because it's not your fault, but you need to understand that you're . . ."

Gerald searches for his words, and out of respect, or reticence, everyone lets him. "You're probably all going to leave Mason County and go live wonderful lives where you get to be yourself, with a group of friends who let you do that, because it's easy for them to see who you are and what is so great about you. But some people stay here, for a lot of different reasons. And it's not so easy for them. Some of them can't even see that part of themselves. And sometimes if they do, they try to get rid of it." Gerald stands and walks toward us, his indignation deflating as his face comes into view. "We can get up onstage and pat ourselves on the back for how funny and daring we're being. And you should. You're all very talented and brave for doing this in the first place," Gerald tells us, his face softening. "But speak for yourselves. And be the bigger person when you can be."

Then he runs out of steam. His grand speech doesn't land on *triumphant lesson to be learned* so much as it lands on an ellipsis. Embarrassment stings my face as I avoid eye contact with the rest of the team. I guess we may have gone too far with this one. But I still feel like throwing a folding chair through the window.

People keep telling me to be quiet. Even I do. But the thought of Jenna Wilbur walking in here and telling us how to behave doesn't leave me feeling quiet. Gerald has said a lot, but it's clear that there's more he isn't saying. It's clear that the defeated Gerald sitting in front of us is a lot closer to the real Gerald than the peppy smile machine we met on our first day here. I feel kind of sick, watching Gerald shift so entirely. It feels shameful, like we're just children playing too roughly to notice that we've broken a favorite toy. It's ugly, whatever this moment is. Gerald and Terrance, and even Nifoal's weird Man Meet guy, are another possible version of ourselves. Versions where we don't take the path covered in rhinestones and sequins. Cora removes her shoes, and the rest of the queens do the same, if only to fill a few minutes with practicality.

When Bailey speaks up, her tone is devoid of her usual venom. "We'll just forget about it," she offers.

The rest of the group nod in silent agreement. Rita grabs Aggie's hand when she opens her mouth to protest, shaking her head lightly. Gerald considers his options as the white noise of the room dials up a notch. He takes us in, the queens in their high heels and me with a brow furrowed into infinity.

"Maybe we just cut that last line," Gerald says thoughtfully. "I did like the part about the hooves."

Cora chuckles darkly, and Nifoal laughs with shock.

"Are you sure?" Rita asks.

"Yeah, I think so. Besides," Gerald says, taking us all in. "Jenna should have known better than to piss off a bunch of drag queens."

***

"You know what? I'm just going to invite my grandma to the show and leave it at that," Tilly announces, stuffing her phone into her backpack.

The night's rehearsal has concluded, and the three of us are sitting below the concrete swan in the courtyard outside the town hall. Water trickles weakly from the swan's beak and dribbles down to the fountain below, the edge of which Tilly is perched on. Other than a few guys toting a case of Bud Light outside the greasy glass storefront of Pizzaville (the worst and only pizza place in Mason), the main strip is quiet and dark.

With the final rehearsal for the extravaganza in the can, my nervous anticipation for tomorrow has begun to eke toward a stoic nervousness. Tilly's grandmother is the least of our problems. We've got protesters slated to show up outside the hall in under twenty-four hours.

"At least she's not telling you to quit," I offer.

"Yeah. But she's not telling me anything," says Tilly. "She won't talk to me."

The silent treatment has been pervading the Thompkin household on all sides since last week. I nod, knowing exactly what she means. Alan says nothing, his all-but-perfect parents excluding him from commiseration.

"The protest is really freaking her out," Tilly explains. "She's convinced that people will think she doesn't know how to raise her own grandchild. On top of, you know, vague religious bullshit."

"Have you tried talking to her?" Alan suggests, and I nearly laugh at the idea. Talking first is how you lose the game. What kind of familial utopia is Alan living in?

"You don't know how long she can hold her silence. Once, she didn't talk to me for a week when I took the Lord's name in vain for stubbing my toe on the couch."

"Well, you're always welcome to my parents," says Alan, opening his arms.

"Yes, please." Tilly laughs, tossing her arms around him. "I'd say I'm the daughter they never had, but Aggie is more than enough daughter for them."

"They truly are blessed, aren't they?"

Tilly kisses us both on the cheek and waves as she walks across the street, passing Marlowe's Diner and making her way home. Alan and I turn to walk home ourselves, his eyes locked on his phone screen.

"Isn't it all kind of, like, insane?" he asks distantly.

"Yeah. Wild."

"I'm glad you signed off on the tonight's video," Alan carries on, scrolling rapidly. "Even though I totally knew you would."

Aggie Culture's larger-than-life eyebrows flash across the screen. Alan must be losing his mind at the sheer perfection of it all. For once, the rest of Mason is as obsessed with Aggie Culture as Alan is.

"Knew I would *what*?" I ask, masking my irritation. I hate Alan's I Know Peter Better Than Peter Knows Himself routine.

"Oh, you know," Alan replies breezily. Smugly, even.

"No," I say dully. "I don't."

Alan stores his phone and shakes his head, as if I'm a child asking why the sky is blue. "Know thyself, Peter. You can't ignore the chance to be absolutely sadistic to someone who was asking for it."

I blink. I *do* know myself. In fact, I might even be surprising myself lately. I may be jumping fences, hopping into pools, and kissing cute boys.

"I'd argue that I'm ignoring a chance right now."

"It's catnip for you," Alan insists with a laugh. "Like how I can't ignore a massive heel or the shortest member of a boy band."

"I'm not, like, this vile hate-spewing rage machine, you know," I contend, finding myself standing firmly on this hill and ready to die on it.

"Girl, you're *my* vile hate-spewing rage machine." Alan lovingly pats my hair and I brush him off. "And you're allowed to be, okay? Nobody is stopping you. We love you just the way you are." He begins to list things on his fingers. "Small-town boy who hates his town, drag-show producer who hates drag, gay guy who hates other gays."

My patience begins to evaporate.

"Let's talk game plan for tomorrow night, vis-à-vis my future boyfriend," Alan continues. "Obviously I need to find a moment alone with him before I make my move. Once I de-drag, of course. Our first kiss needs to be simple, authentic, you know?"

"Let's just focus on the show," I say.

Maybe it shouldn't shock me that my attempt at romance had felt like a facial charley horse. Alan had decreed my romantic future on the day we met Lorne at the Dairy Freeze.

"Which flavor of lip balm will Lorne like the best? Is cherry too on the nose?"

It really is that easy for Alan, isn't it? The show will go off without a hitch, spiteful Peter will be his obedient guard dog, and Lorne will fall deeply in love with both Alan Goode and Aggie Culture. Alan will prance through it all, bright eyed and optimistic, while Peter remains a short, fat raincloud who ruins everything he touches.

"And try to play nice," Alan says abruptly. "Lorne is coming with Brison, and everyone is going to be *gagging* for a rematch."

The words, when they arrive, bubble up from some deep pit at the bottom of my stomach. They burn cleanly on the way out. They feel good.

"I kissed Lorne."

I say it plainly, factually. Alan's face drops along with his shoulders. The air has been let out of the party balloon that is Alan Goode.

"What?"

"It just sort of happened," I lie. "The other night. I wasn't going to say anything because he clearly wasn't into it. Or me. But if you're planning on, you know, getting him alone, or whatever, I thought you should know."

"You kissed Lorne," Alan repeats, not sure he's understanding correctly.

"Yeah."

Alan nods and processes the information, his face impassive.

"Okay," he says slowly, calculating. "Okay."

We near his turn onto Poplar Avenue, and Alan folds his arms.

"I'll see you tomorrow, then," he says tersely.

"Yeah," I say, just as brusque. "I'll see you tomorrow."

Alan turns and begins to walk home. For a second I think to call out to him. I should catch up and apologize for going behind his back. For using my first kiss as a weapon against my best friend.

But I'm just a vile hate-spewing rage machine. On the lawn next to me, a sprinkler clicks to life as Alan's footsteps fade.

CHAPTER EIGHTEEN
SAUSAGE-FINGERED NANCY BOY

I study myself in the mirror, scraping my hair back despite its refusal to stay in place. It pops up irregularly, making my head look fat. Then again, at least my head will match my gut.

The spiral of self-hate that I'm riding like a bucking bronco has carried me through the day in an irritable stupor. Hovering over all of it is the mental image of Alan's face last night. The way he'd gone blank behind the eyes, shutting off entirely. I was sure that I'd wake up on the day of the show to a cascading list of last-minute requirements. Maybe Bailey would require me to do cartwheels on the back of a moving flatbed truck while wearing heels and fending off a horde of feral raccoons. Or perhaps Cora Copia would need me to feed his pet bear while smothered in honey and riding a unicycle. Neither text arrived. What did arrive was a deepening sense of dread that has stayed with me all day.

My parents fall silent as I enter the kitchen. My presence has been enough to bring everything in the house to a muted standstill since blowing up at them.

My father tinkers with a cabinet hinge at the table while my mother scrolls absently through her tablet. Commercials blare from the television.

"What time do you think you'll be home?" my mom asks lightly.

"I'm not sure. Late, probably."

"All right," she says. "Phone if you need a ride."

"It's just down at the town hall."

"I know. But you let us know."

Shoes for the whole family at half the price, at The Shoe Barn! a voice announces on the TV. My dad curses under his breath at the hinge and flings the screwdriver onto the table. I slide my shoes on. Someone across the street revs their lawnmower. I don't ask my parents if they will be in attendance tonight. Not because they'll say no but because they won't say anything at all.

"Gerald Corres will be there tonight."

My father looks up, surprised.

"He's Mason County's cultural director, you know," I say.

This isn't news to my mother. A house doesn't sell in Mason without Mary Thompkin knowing who sold and who bought. A death doesn't occur without her knowing the cause and location and without her quietly leaving a sympathy card in the mailbox of the bereft. But my father, head eternally buried in some tinkering project or the television, isn't a cog in the Mason rumor mill.

"Really?" he asks.

"Yeah," I confirm, trying to measure their reactions. Mom scrolls her tablet some more while Dad returns to his hinge. I wait for either of them to say something. It's not that I want them to come to the show tonight. I don't. I don't need to give my mother ammunition for a backhanded compliment wrapped in a character judgment.

The costumes were nice, but did they have to curse so much?

I don't need to give my father live examples of mincing faggotry for him to be visibly uncomfortable with into perpetuity.

So where did those boys get all their . . . hair? he will ask, pained.

"You could come, if you wanted."

My mother looks up, apparently as surprised as I am. Maybe I just want them to tell me honestly that they're not comfortable attending. And that an undisturbed applecart is more important to them than supporting me.

"Well," Mom says, considering her screen. "I didn't think you wanted us to."

Dad's hands have stopped fiddling, but his eyes haven't left the table. Both of them wait for me to make the next move.

"It's fine," I say with a shrug. "You don't have to."

I don't wait around to hear anything else. The screen door closes behind me with a dull slam.

***

"This looks like it took a while."

Alan regards me coldly while I take in the decorations now blanketing the hall.

The place is done up like a very gay birthday present. Paper rainbows and glittering streamers hang around lights, windows, and the stage itself. A flurry of construction paper cutouts of lips, fans, dresses, shoes, and wigs are arranged on the doors to the hall beneath the banner that reads *The First Annual Mason County Drag Extravaganza!* Plastic beads, paper lanterns, flowing fabrics, and paper doilies have exploded across the walls, tables, and doors of the hall. Long rolls of colored crepe paper have been draped across the backs of the chairs, turning even our audience seating into a rainbow. The lip of the stage is festooned with leftover costumes taken from Alan's drag wardrobe, forming a rainbow for the queens to literally dance on. Strung atop them as a final touch is Alan's extensive feather boa collection.

"I've been here since noon," Alan says from his perch on the stage.

"It's really good, Alan."

"Thanks."

I take another circle of the room and wait for Alan to divulge his process in great detail. He doesn't. Maybe I should apologize. Then again, maybe he should.

"Listen, Alan," I begin.

"Oh. My. God," someone squeals from the doorway. Bailey drops two duffel bags at his feet, taking in the hall over the rim of his bespoke sunglasses. "This is actually perfect."

"Thank you," Alan says with reserve. "I'm really happy with it."

"I'm wondering, though," Bailey ponders, reaching into a plastic bag, "if we can add just one final piece?"

Bailey unrolls a bright poster with a flourish, revealing an image of team THORR done up in their rehearsal drag, smiling or otherwise smoldering for the camera. When this was taken I had been standing in the doorway, writing and rewriting a text to Lorne that I'd never sent. For some reason, I can't even focus on the picture. All I can see in it is my own absence.

"I want to apologize, Bailey," Alan says, eyes still on the poster.

Bailey allows the poster to curl on itself again while his hand flies to his heart.

"For what I said about you. It was uncalled for, and it was unprofessional. And I think you're wonderful, and you've done so much for the whole team, and I—"

Bailey's arms wrap around Alan before he disappears into Alan's return bear hug. Then they're both crying.

"I'm sorry," Bailey sobs from the depths of Alan's chest. "I'm sorry that I made things more difficult for you than you needed. I just really care about this show."

"I know you do," Alan says deeply, clutching Bailey closer and wiping the tears with the heel of his palm. "And that means *so* much to me."

"*You* mean so much to me!" Bailey cries. "I totally look up to you and I've been so, like, scared to even show that, you know?"

Alan breaks their embrace to present a look of disbelief.

"Oh my god, no! I look up to you, though—"

"Shut up."

"No, I really do."

"Oh my god, I freaking love you."

"I freaking love you, girl."

"You've done so much for this community."

"Are you kidding me?" Alan sniffles. "*You've* done so much for this community. We wouldn't be here if it wasn't for your channel. You're, like, way better at this all than I am, and I think I'm just jealous of you, which is so messed up because we need to be lifting each other up, not, like, competing—"

"I could never ever compete with you!"

"That's what I'm saying—we don't need to!"

They rip through their affirmations urgently, finally surfacing for air from the depths of their resentment. Alan and Bailey melt into pools of emotion before me, exhaling deeply before cry-laughing as they attempt to clean their reddened faces.

"Okay," Bailey says, taking a deep breath. "Let's do a freaking show."

"Yes!" Alan cheers.

Alan turns to me, and I watch as the love drains from his face again, replaced with the same blank look as before.

"I think you should be backstage tonight," he says stonily.

I search his face for an explanation, or even a modicum of what he's just had with Bailey. Alan is my best friend. Shouldn't I get to cry it out with him, too? Or whatever my equivalent of crying is. Crying has never been my thing. It's like my tear ducts never showed up for job training.

"It's still too dark backstage," Alan explains plainly. "Someone needs to pass us the right props and costume pieces."

That deepening sense of dread sinks even lower.

"We haven't rehearsed that, Alan."

I try to hide the alarm in my voice as Alan plucks at the purple pashmina he's hung off the end of the stage.

"It'll be fine," Alan says, not worried at all. "You're the producer. You know the show better than anyone, right?" He beams plastically before leaving to help Bailey with his bags, the two of them now the very best of friends.

I could say no. But that's not a door that Alan has left open. It's a test, isn't it? A test of whether Peter is a team player or not. A test of whether Peter actually cares about this show, about whether he was actually paying attention this entire time instead of just standing at the back and drafting texts to Alan's crush. He wants me to look like a bumbling, sausage-fingered nancy boy who is all talk and no talent. Instead of just *feeling* like the bumbling, sausage-fingered nancy boy who is all talk and no talent that I normally do.

If this is a test, it's one that Alan wants me to fail.

***

"Does the riding crop come in off the *top* of *Rocky Horror* or at the end?" I call after Nifoal.

She turns to slide between me and the backstage entrance. "Toss it to me at the end!" she trills, breaking from her vocal warmup, and then takes the stage with the rest of the girls, dropping her neck into a spinal stretch.

"Totally," I mumble. "Me and my famously good aim will just toss it to you at the end."

Our basket of props is overflowing, but with the costumes and makeup cluttering the makeup stations, I don't have anywhere else to lay them out. Tilly appears behind me, the base of her makeup drying on her cheeks and a baseball bat held at her side.

"We already have security," I say. "You might remember them, the glazed hams on stilts?"

Tilly hands me the bat and motions for me to slot it into the basket.

"You really are off in the clouds most of the time, aren't you?" she asks lovingly.

I slide the bat next to the riding crop and squint in confusion. "What are you talking about?"

Tilly pats my face and returns to the stage, laughing softly to herself. Not that it bothers me, but it seems I've missed an inside joke or two. But Alan won't get the pleasure of seeing me sweat over this final hoop to jump. He'll only see my normal amount of sweat, currently working double time in the cramped side stage. Half-glowing light bulbs line a set of four dressing-room mirrors set above a drooping ledge and some plastic folding chairs. The air is stale and humid back here, and Alan's intently avoided eye contact is becoming the single thing I can focus on. Of course, I'm spending tonight focused on nothing but Alan Goode. Of course, being the literal star of the show wasn't enough for him. Alan also has to be the star of my brain at the same time. He's mad at *me*? If anything, I should be mad at him for acting like everyone else and just expecting me to be the bland and supportive gay best friend in the movie who has no sexuality of his own. My high school tenure is running out by the minute, but sure, Alan, let me languish in my own nothingness a little more, just for you.

Not that it matters. Lorne might as well have given me a high five for all the sexual chemistry between us.

Something is very wrong. This is not how tonight is supposed to feel.

I stomp down the backstage steps and emerge into the audience again, waving feebly to Gerald as he makes polite small talk with Alan's parents at the hall's double doors. Even under the faint air conditioning, my shirt is still sticking to my back. I need air, I decide, and move to slip past the Goodes on my way to the staircase. I really should have known better.

"Peter! Aren't you just so excited?"

Alan's mom wraps me in a hug and squeezes the air out of my lungs, and I find myself tangled in her long, graying curls. She releases me and is replaced by Alan's father, who matches his son in size and body hair. I find myself locked in Jack Goode's arms, once again crushed by the Goode family vise grip. Gerald watches on, nursing his own recently compressed ribs.

"Of course," I wheeze.

"We're just so proud of you kids," says Jack, letting me go. "The entire family is. We've got relatives coming in from all over tonight. Nina and I haven't shut up about this show for weeks."

Nina rattles the battered old cashbox that she's brought along, a relic from her days of selling homemade, hemp baby carriers at flea markets.

"We're *so* excited to be a part of it, Peter," she informs me. "Jack even tried to do some makeup for tonight, but his eye just got too smoky."

"Nina's mother, she's been all in a tizzy about tonight, you know," Jack tells Gerald.

"Says she just doesn't like seeing her grandson stirring the pot," Nina elaborates.

"But she says, Nina, tell the boys what you said."

"I said, *Mother, some pots need to be stirred. Otherwise, you burn the soup.*"

"We used to attend sit-ins when we were in our twenties. Peter, do you know what a sit-in is?"

"But then you slow down," Nina continues. "And you have a kid and you're just glad that he's the one stirring the pot."

"We're so proud, Peter," says Jack emphatically. "Of all of you. When I think about what you've already accomplished, I just . . ."

Tears well in his puppy dog eyes, and for a moment he looks like Alan with forehead wrinkles.

"See, now you've got a show going on in the lobby, Peter!" Nina exclaims as she passes Jack a handkerchief from her back pocket. Jack dabs at his eyes and sniffles while Nina pats his back with a practiced nonchalance.

Team THORR laughs onstage, arms and legs extending in preshow warmup. I smile from the other side of the room, feeling like a random audience member at this point. Why does it seem like this entire night was put together by someone else? Shouldn't I be excited? It's happening. The people of Mason County will see that I'm more than just The Guy Who Said the Very Bad Thing to Brison Dallas. They'll see I'm not just some ruthless, self-hating gay. Look at this selfless act of giving! Look at this valuable space I've created for queer performers! Look how many rainbows this place is covered in! Surely you can't still think I'm a bad person.

Even if Alan's cold shoulder has me thinking the same thing.

"Should we leave your parents' tickets with you?" Nina asks. "Or just hold onto them to be picked up at the door?"

Jack scans his list and blanches at my parents' absence.

"I don't think they're coming," I admit, feeling Gerald's gaze burning into my face and doing everything I can not to return it. We've avoided the topic of my parents this entire time. If we can get through one more night, I can just pretend we never had to in the first place.

Jack and Nina exchange a look of grave parental concern. They mask it as well as any parents do, which is to say not well at all.

"Well," Nina says firmly. "We're going to have some fun tonight, aren't we?"

"We're going to have a great time," Jack echoes.

The Swole Squad emerges on the staircase with Andy in the lead. They're wearing matching black tracksuits and carrying walkie-talkies.

"We're gonna need a quick sweep of the perimeter before we open this place up for business," Andy intones. Like the others, he's wearing a pair of polarized sunglasses. The team splits apart to take stock of the otherwise empty hall. Blake Roy approaches me cautiously, slipping his sunglasses down like he's the damn Terminator.

"We've got a bit of a situation outside, Peter. Do you have a minute?

CHAPTER NINETEEN
TUBBY LITTLE JACK-IN-THE-BOX

Jenna's protesters are blocking the doors to the town hall.

Blake, Gerald, and I stand on the sidewalk and survey the watertight sea of bodies currently blocking the entrance. The sense of impending dread in my stomach has decided to put up its feet and stay a while.

Day is beginning to fade into night over Mason, casting long shadows over the already sinister faces of our newly acquired Homophobia Platoon. They're lined up around the front doors, holding hand-lettered cardboard signs. The clouds are hinting at rain, the air pressure is tightening, and a headache is forming behind my eyes.

"Now, Jenna," Gerald says waveringly. "I'll have to ask you all to please move aside and leave this entrance clear."

Cars roll past us on Mason's main strip, a few slowing to take in the display. Jenna's protest stands firm against our audience, which is growing by the minute and congregating under the swan fountain in the town square or milling about the steps of the library. Members of the extended Goode family, their features all very Alan-like, wave at me with concern written large across their faces.

"We're perfectly allowed to peacefully dissent, Gerald," Jenna replies, grinning like a wolf baring its teeth.

A good portion of Jenna's Human Wall of Hate is made up of her own family. Her many children stand by flimsily, wilting in the humidity while slapping and pushing at one another. *Boys Will Be Boys*, their signs read, and *Save the Glitter for the Craftbox!* The backward Rs are a bit on the nose, if you ask me. Next to the children are a few stern-looking teenage girls with crooked teeth, starched blouses, and skirts that fall militantly to their ankles. They hold signs proclaiming *Keep Your Sex Off Our Stage*, *No Perversion On Public Property*, and *GAY SEX WILL BURN GAYS IN HELL FOR THERE GAY SEX.*

I know that subtlety isn't the name of the game for a protest sign, but I still have a few notes on that last one.

The protest is rounded out by church-mom types standing, shoulder to shoulder, with unkempt men sporting oversized mustaches and T-shirts saying things like *Don't Mess with the Bull* and *Where's My Participation Trophy?*. They are joined by their fundamentalist female equivalent, a trio of severe-looking women wearing matching shirts, cracking with age, that all read *Abortion = The Silent Holocaust*. Capping off the Bigotry Brigade is a pair of leathery women in weathered bootcut jeans and greasy T-shirts, their thinning hair frizzing outward like a cartoon character holding a live wire. I'd have assumed they're a lesbian couple in need of a good moisturizer if they weren't holding signs that say *GENDER ISN'T A CONSTRUCT, IT'S A FACT* and *GO HOME DEVIANTS.*

"Blocking our entrance isn't peaceful," I tell Jenna. "Are you six years old? This is the protesting equivalent of saying *I'm Not Touching You.*

Jenna gathers herself up while her husband shushes the baby strapped to his chest. Jenna scowls, appalled that I'd raise my voice in front of their child.

"My children should not have to see this kind of thing in a public space!" she contends at top volume, loud enough to be heard by the Sinful Sallies and Sams in line to see *The Sin Show for Sinners*.

Tonight's audience has begun to fill the square, their attention firmly fixed on Jenna's unsanctioned opening act.

"Really?" I ask. "*You're* the one who dragged them along to this. You could have just left them home, but then who would you use to make a point that *nobody* cares about?"

"We're worried about you, Gerald," Jenna appeals, her face pinching with fake concern. "Ever since your mother passed, you've stopped coming to church. You've been on a path that Terry and I just can't support."

"He doesn't need your support," I tell her.

Gerald's palm lands on my shoulder and I fall silent. This is Gerald's big moment. This is when his genteel coating will wash away, revealing the proudly gay motherfucker beneath. Sure, Gerald may seem like Pooh Bear with pants on. But I have a feeling that he's about to take his paw out of that honey jar and claw Jenna's face off.

"You *are* allowed to protest, Jenna," Gerald says steadily. "But you're not allowed to break fire codes."

I frown. It's not the face-shredding I was hoping for.

"We're talking about moral codes, Gerald!" shrieks Jenna, eyeing our assembling ticket holders. They're almost as queerly adorned as the hall upstairs. Fluttering Pride flags, sparkly makeup, and neon tops pepper our waiting audience. I may be face-to-face with yet another bunch of barely literate homo-haters, but the exhibit of queer solidarity now filling the town square does stop my heart for half a second. Monica Whitehead waves timidly from the library steps amid a clutch of Mason Secondary students. Sylvie Burns catches sight of me and smiles nervously. They all watch with unease as our standoff develops.

"And we're talking," Jenna goes on, "about the town council giving a public space to an event that is *not* fit for public consumption."

"You all look like mole people who can't handle direct sunlight," I say, stepping in front of Gerald as he wrings his hands and stammers some kind of response. "But sure, you tell *me* what's fit for public consumption."

Gerald pulls me back harder than I'd expect. Blake puts himself between me and the guy with the biggest mustache, who has stepped menacingly out of line.

"That's quite enough, Jenna," Gerald asserts, some heat arriving in his voice. "I really don't want to get the police involved tonight."

Jenna's lofty smile only mutates, broadening into something from a slasher flick. "You can go right ahead, Gerald," she says. "You know Bill Leeman, don't you?" She motions to the man with the second biggest mustache, his sunken features and bloodhound eyes apparently also on loan from a B-movie horror.

"Howdy," Bill waves, his greeting holding the note of foreboding doom that every straight, middle-aged man is able to communicate with only a word. It's the same violence bottled inside every guy like him, the kind that threatens you before blaming you for feeling threatened in the first place.

"Bill is a member of the Mason County police force, after all," Jenna informs us, her eyes glazing over in triumph.

I watch Gerald's face fall as he shrinks under Officer Bill's imperious, acidic presence. The cop smirks behind his forest of facial hair and my headache disappears with a jolt of adrenaline. My shoes crunch on the sidewalk as I join Gerald's front line again.

"You've got a dirty cop in your fucking prayer circle, Jenna," I seethe. "And you want to talk to us about moral codes?"

"Well," Jenna gasps, her eyes flashing. "If you can't engage with us without *cursing* in front of a group of children, then I'm not sure that we have anything else to discuss."

I feel Blake pulling me toward the street, and watch as Gerald's arms fly up in the universal display of *why don't we all just calm down?*

"You're unexceptional, Jenna!" I holler. "You're boring!" I continue from behind Blake's grip. Jenna watches in astonished disproval, shaking her head as if to say *this is exactly what I'm talking about* and *these gays just don't know how to play nice with the rest of us.* "An interesting person doesn't have to pull a stunt like this to get people to notice them!"

"All right," says Blake, his voice rumbling through his chest as he pulls me back.

"What are you doing?"

I swat at Blake's tree-trunk arms while he ushers me up the street.

"Let's just cool off for a second." Blake deposits me at the window display of McCleary Realty.

"I'm fucking *cool*, Blake."

"Let's just breathe for a second," he suggests airily. "Kirk has this breathing exercise he leads us through sometimes, and I have to say that it tends to work wonders on my intrusive thoughts."

"I don't need to breathe."

"Sort of seems to me like you need to," Blake says lightly, his hands falling on my shoulders. It does feel kind of nice, actually. He's like a weighted blanket wearing Axe body spray. Blake inhales and shakes me a little until I do the same. We hold our breath and exhale while the sounds of Gerald's continued negotiation float down the street. The intersection lines up with cars. A couple and their baby carriage stroll by, footsteps smacking with their flip-flops. A seagull squawks on a rooftop somewhere, and Blake holds his hands on my shoulders. It doesn't feel the same as Lorne's hands on my chest. For one, I'm not harboring any urges to make out with Blake. But it is intimate, in a sense. Blake grips me a little tighter and the wrath that usually leads to me saying the first malicious thing that comes to mind begins to slink back into my darker corners. It's as if I've been curled up in the back of my own brain but now I can stretch out into the rest of my body. Blake slides his hands off me and holds out a questioning thumbs-up, which I return.

We stand there for a while, comfortably silent. My calm begins to recede as guilt sets in. I've been pretty harsh on Blake and his friends. Yes, they had showed up tonight dressed in questionable CIA Halloween costumes, but all they wanted to do was help some homos dance around in heels. There are people doing the literal opposite right now, and I find myself getting chilly in the harsh shadow that contrast is throwing.

"Cool," I say. "Thanks. Those guys are fucking assholes, so I needed that."

At once I feel distinctly embarrassed, intensely aware of how unhinged I'd been back there. Snapping like a savage, tubby little jack-in-the-box.

Blake absently turns the knobs on his walkie-talkie.

"Yeah. Well, you were right. They're doing a full "I'm Not Touching You." It's kind of embarrassing, to be honest. For them, I mean," he shrugs. "They think you're just a bunch of stupid kids, but they're the ones acting like it."

A couple of preteens trudge by wearing gaudy eye glitter and neon fishnet sleeves, chittering excitedly as they make their way toward the hall. I watch them go and hate Jenna all the more for what she's ruining. For what she's so gleefully treading on. As Blake and I stew in the unwelcome possibility of tonight being ruined, I'm beginning to see just how much stock I've placed in this evening. I'm starting to feel just how much I was looking forward to it. Not just as some way to overwrite the things being said about me online, and not just as some physical embodiment of the middle finger I feel like holding up to Mason County. But as a way to pop the cork on the gayer parts of this place, to speak up for ourselves in a way that sounds a lot more like laughter than chanting. Jenna and her people can protest all they want. But we were supposed to be too busy having a good time to notice.

Blake is right—it is embarrassing. Jenna and her busted disciples are playing like children. So maybe we should, too. If my sister hurling her Fairy Magic Barbie at my head and leaving a scar along my scalp taught me anything, it's that "I'm Not Touching" you is an incredibly effective way to provoke someone.

"You're kind of creeped out by Cora Copia, right?" I ask shrewdly.

"I mean, yeah," says Blake, his hand running over his stubble. "That's her thing."

"And would you ever describe Nifoal Dressage as *user friendly*?"

"No," Blake frowns. "No, I would not."

I pull my phone from the pocket of my shorts. "Good. Neither will Jenna."

***

For the first time in my life, the sight of a pickup truck doesn't make me duck for cover. Blake's rusty gray Chevy slides up and idles across from the front doors, where Gerald is still locked in a tense whisper-off with Jenna. From the driver's seat, Blake presses play on his phone and cranks the volume on the dash display. The synthetic staccato of Lady Gaga's "Applause" booms from the cab and cuts off the jabber of the protesters, who are now glowering while the audience in the square turns to take us in with newly captured attention.

"Did you have this on your phone already?" I holler over the roar of the music.

"Of course!" Blake calls back. "*Artpop* is criminally underrated!"

The doors to the Mason Town Hall crash open, revealing a duo of half-formed drag queens backed by the imposing forms of Andy and Kirk. Cora Copia, her shaved head shining in the setting sunlight, rakes a set of red rubber monster claws over a skimpy burgundy dress, her makeup still setting under a gossamer mask of finishing powder. Nifoal's long black dress billows at her ankles, and her sharp, equine features have been perfectly drawn. Wigless, lashless, and unpadded, Nifoal is still a gorgeous being beyond the binary that I can't keep my eyes off. But to the walking cups of vanilla pudding blocking the entrance, she might as well be *The Thing*'s titular character.

Jenna's children flock to their father as Cora takes the first verse, lip-synching while warmly beckoning the children to come back with her beastly digits. The youngest scream while the older children scatter toward the town square. Her mouth still running Gaga's vocals, Cora begins to welcome the few members of our hesitant audience toward the front doors.

Jenna Wilbur stands firm, fury building behind her chunky bangs.

Terrance Wilbur chases after his brood while the church ladies hold their place, signs held higher to ward against the oncoming wave of gender fuckery. Cora slinks closer, never making contact, while Nifoal rocks stone-faced to the beat. The men of the line square their shoulders, affronted but unwilling to allow their rock-solid masculinity to crumble beneath the effeminate freakishness clopping around them. Nifoal takes over for the chorus, clapping half-heartedly while Cora turns around to reveal an old-timey hooch jug with the words *PIG'S BLOOD* written in large red letters. She upends the jug into her mouth, gulping thirstily before displaying a lizard-like tongue now dripping with a thick red ooze.

Our audience is building a line now. They laugh as the church ladies split off at the sight of Cora's gaping maw with cries of huffing indignation. They've left the doorway open enough for Gerald to begin conducting our ticket holders inside. The Goode family politely greets the remaining lemon-faced protesters. Cora and Nifoal sandwich the remaining men of the protest between themselves, directing their lip syncs to one another as if Bill Leeman was never born, as if Push Broom mustache man and the leathery ashtray next to him are little more than nearby shrubs. Our lineup cheers as the song fades, and the queens take a languishing bow around the three remaining men.

"Thank you so much," Nifoal says, addressing her audience. "But a special thank-you to our costars!" She motions to Bill and his buddies, who do their best to act as if Nifoal isn't there. "It was hard for us to book the cast of *The Hills Have Eyes*, but weren't they great?"

Blake and I laugh alongside our audience, but Bill and his boys look as if they don't quite get the joke.

"But really," continues Nifoal, "it's so exciting to see these community members coming out to our show. Because I know coming out has been hard for them in the past."

This gets a laugh from the fishnet kids.

"Right? Let's show these boys that this is a safe space!" Nifoal rants sardonically. "Look, we all know that calling a homophobe *gay* is hack comedy. But I'll be damned if it doesn't get results, and I for one—"

"Are we going to have a problem, kid?" Bill cuts in, a dirty look fixed on his hound dog features.

"What?" Nifoal snickers. "No! No problems here, darling. You and your boyfriends are welcome to join us at any time, but please don't make out the second the lights go down. I know you'll be *dying* to—"

Push Broom jerks forward while Nifoal plants her heels, staring haughtily downward from her towering height. Nifoal doesn't move. Andy and Kirk arrive, driving a wedge between the two.

"That's enough, man," Andy tells Push Broom.

"They have a right to be here, I'll have you know," Jenna says frigidly.

"Oh, girl," Nifoal tuts sympathetically. "I bet you spend a lot of money for your hair to look that bad, don't you?"

Our lineup continues to file in while Jenna does all but stamp her foot and pout. Monica Whitehead and her friends step through the doors, followed by the frozen yogurt girl, who turns to whisper something to a friend at the sight of me. I grimace but keep my mouth shut. Even she can't ruin the wavering sensation of victory that I'm enjoying. Behind them are Bailey's parents, short in stature but high in cheekbone, and dressed in a manner that makes it clear they usually attend events with a higher ticket price. They step forward, and the next arrivals to round the corner of the hall make me flinch. Lorne and Brison move along with Chrissy in their wake, her phone held up to document her gaggle of gays for Poster posterity.

Brison notices me first and nods a curt hello. Lorne's eyes fall on mine and I smile wanly, that sinking feeling from our last pool hop blooming anew in my stomach. I think I'm going to be sick.

"You okay, Peter?"

I turn to find Blake still behind the wheel, his hand rubbing nervously at the stubble of his buzzcut.

"I'm good, yeah," I say lightly. "That was awesome. Thanks so much."

Blake nods sheepishly, suddenly very focused on his steering wheel. For some reason Blake has shifted into a nervousness I've never seen on him, skittish like a cat about to scale a tree.

"I just wanted to say," Blake tells his car horn, "I think that it's really great what you guys are doing here."

To my credit, I do refrain from rolling my eyes so hard that you can hear them scrape my skull. I ready myself for the standard *I'm not gay, but I think gay dudes are totally fine, but, like, no homo* routine.

"Yeah, thanks—"

"Cuz, like, I'm bi, myself, and it's all really inspiring," he finishes quickly.

I nod while my throat constricts, surprise flooding my face with red.

"Right," I find myself saying. "Well, yeah, for sure, I'm glad you're here."

Even though I'm stumbling over my words like a set of marathon hurdles, I do mean it. Blake nods some more and I glide off to watch the last of our line up make their way up the staircase and into the hall. The clouds darken as ozone tinges the air, the oncoming rain announcing itself with a far-off clap of thunder.

CHAPTER TWENTY

A PERPETUAL MOTION MACHINE OF NARCISSISTIC CYNICISM

A strange mix is still populating the town square. Students, married couples, people done up in dresses and colorful shirts, and a few people who look like they've just stepped off the farm. Two men in flannel, boots, and silver belt buckles stand nearby, laughing with Stella from Divine, the salon just down the street. For a moment I wonder what two Mason County farm boys are doing here, and if their matching flannel and jeans were a coordinated attempt. Then I recognize the bundle of green the guy on the right is holding.

"Hey!" one of them calls over. "I think this belongs to you."

Maybe I should have kept Blake by my side. Hot Alpaca Farmer is here, and he's approaching holding the same lime green feather boa I'd lost while fleeing his dogs.

"Looks like you might need it tonight," his friend says, laughing. "The girls didn't at least do your makeup?"

The friend is as hot as Hot Alpaca Farmer. He's got wavy brown hair, and with his cowboy boots, he looks like something straight out of a cowboy porn fantasy. You know. If you're into that kind of thing. Which I am not.

"You guys really should come knock on the door next time," Hot Alpaca Farmer offers as my stunned silence continues. "I'm sure the ladies would love their own solo."

Hot Alpaca Farmer hands over the boa and smiles kindly. It feels like a relic from a bygone era, like we snuck out to that alpaca field many years ago.

"I'm Michael," he says, searching my face as I continue to gawk. "And this is Frank."

"The ladies are the alpacas," Frank explains.

I shake their hands and introduce myself, watching as Frank places his hand lightly on Michael's lower back.

"To be fair," I tell them, shock rouging my face, "Alan didn't give me any information until we got there. And then we thought you were going to, like, kill us or something."

"Mike's a pussycat," Frank informs me. "He'd have invited you in for coffee and given you a tour of the farm."

"Well, thanks so much for coming."

"We wouldn't miss it," says Michael. "We're total *Dragathon* freaks."

My mind reels as Frank lays his hand on Michael's shoulder, at which point I notice his wedding band. Married gay farmers in the middle of Mason County are the last people I'd expect to find in a town square filled with a militia of homophobic children and women who hate having reproductive rights. It's also a pretty good tongue twister.

"Hey, look." Frank points past my shoulder, back toward the intersection. "You guys are famous."

A man with a familiar face is standing behind a camera and tripod, holding out a microphone. Framed with the town hall in the background, Trey MacLachlan from KCNM's *News at Six* is interviewing one of the incensed church ladies who just escaped the claws of Cora Copia.

The boa crumples beneath my fingers.

Trey finishes the interview as I approach. Sunday School Trunchbull shakes his hand before turning to join her God Squad once more, eyes held to the heavens in a proud attempt of pretending I don't exist.

"Hey there!" Trey calls with a TV-ready grin. "I'm—"

"Yeah," I cut in. "I know who you are. What the hell are you doing?"

Trey is clearly not used to being addressed with anything less than awe and reverence. His professionally placid features falter for a moment as he adjusts the collar.

"It's quite the story happening here," Trey informs me, eyebrows raised to indicate that there is no compliment higher than being noticed by him. "So I'm here getting all the sides. Are you watching the show tonight?"

"I'm *producing* the show tonight," I say. "And I never arranged any news coverage."

"Well," he stalls. "We at KCNM are huge supporters of the LGBTQ+ community, and—"

"How?" I ask.

Trey falters. "Excuse me?"

"How are you *huge* supporters?"

Trey fiddles with a button on his camera.

"Well—"

"Because it seems to me," I continue, "that actually supporting us would have involved being interested *before* a bunch of fundamentalist twats happened to show up and cause a ruckus. And then, here *you* are, interviewing them before you've even said a word to anyone inside. Does that sound supportive to you?"

I fold my arms over my chest and wait, thunder unfurling overhead again.

"Well now," Trey says through his plastic grin. "It's important to get an even, balanced account of the event itself. That's good journalism."

"Giving grown-ass bigots their own airtime to spout off hate isn't journalism, it's just secondhand homophobia."

Michael and Frank are keeping tabs on me from the doors, and maybe I am showing off for them just a little.

"What you have to understand is that—"

"If you really support us, you'll delete that video and come talk to some people who are *actually* here to support us." I shrug, entirely unbothered, thrilling at the way Trey is withering beneath me. For a second I wonder if KCNM's very own anchorman is going to punch me in the throat. When he speaks again, it's through near-gritted teeth.

"I'd love to interview some of your friends—"

"And I'd be happy to facilitate that as the producer of this event!" I croon, all smiles again. "As soon as you delete that interview."

Trey's eyes narrow in barely tempered rage.

"Of course. The KCNM team is a huge supporter of the LGBTQ+ community," he repeats robotically.

I watch as he opens the screen on the side of the camera and taps the most recent video. Jenna's Righteous Warrior of Christ disappears as Trey presses delete.

"Come meet some friends of mine," I invite Trey. "I'm sure they'd love to tell you all about how the KCNM team can be huge supporters of the LGBTQ+ community."

I'm showing a nearly boiled-over Trey up the stairwell when Gerald appears, his hands held in their worried praying mantis pose.

"Everything good out here?" he asks.

"We're golden, Gerald," I assure him. "Just peachy."

"Things got a little out of hand back there," Gerald begins, hands rubbing hard enough to spark a fire. "And I want to apologize for not intervening further."

"You didn't have to," I remind him. "That's what your security team is for."

Gerald considers this but continues to worry at his own knuckles.

"Still. As cultural director, I should have—"

"It all worked out fine. And the girls loved having their own moment to shine."

Gerald exhales and undoes his top button, sweating nearly as much as I am.

"Good," he allows. "I'm glad."

On the street, rain begins to splatter across the sidewalk, and the white roar of the storm closes over Mason. The humidity slackens, and both Gerald and I breathe a little easier while the last of our audience files inside with the kind of screams and laughter that are only possible when you've been caught in the rain. They make their way up the stairs toward the hall, the sounds of which are now filling the entranceway and mixing with Mason's watery ambience. Fat, splashy drops pummel the street as Jenna and her children appear in the doorway, flanked by the members of the Hate Horde.

Many choice words come to my mind, but it's Gerald who acts first.

"So sorry, Jenna," he says lightly, barring the door. "The hall is for ticket holders only this evening. Unless you felt like purchasing some standing-room tickets and joining us?" They stand on the sidewalk as the rain intensifies, the children's creepy blonde hair matting against their even creepier, milky foreheads.

"We won't be supporting this kind of thing with our own money, thank you very much."

"All right, Jenna," Gerald coos. "You folks have a good night."

He closes the left door while I take the right, cutting off Jenna's last protest with a wonderfully satisfying click. Gerald smiles serenely, and I cackle as the music from upstairs fills the building.

"I hope they don't get too wet out there," says Gerald.

"I know," I agree. "Can you believe this weather?"

***

"I know she won't be out there," says Rita, setting her wig, "but did you see my grandmother in the audience?"

The girls of Rural Realness study their handiwork in the powder-dusted mirrors, the backstage-turned-dressing-room stewing in the combined body heat of five drag queens. Tilly catches my eye in the mirror and I watch her face drop behind a sheet of indifference.

"Not that I saw, no," I reply, my gaze lingering on hers as I search for a buffer. "But it was pretty hectic out there, so maybe I missed her."

"Sure." Rita shrugs. "Maybe. Doesn't matter." She blinks back a faraway despondence and smiles broadly, snatching my hand and giving it a shake. "Anyway," she brightens, a long blue nail combing a strand of black wig away from her lashes. "I've got you bunch of homos, so what do I need her for?"

Aggie, now fully transformed and standing even taller in her green beehive, flicks a flat look in my direction before lighting up for Rita.

"Damn right, you beautiful bitch!" Aggie crows, clasping Rita's left hand.

The three of us are linked for a moment, and Rita laughs the way people do when tears are the other option. Then Aggie disengages to adjust her fake boobs, one of which is sagging out of its cup. Aggie Culture has said nothing to me since my arrival. She's punishing me and making it apparent with every withheld word.

"You guys won't believe what happened outside," I begin.

"We'll believe it after the show, Peter." Aggie dismisses me. "The queens need to focus."

"I know," I try again, brushing past her attempt to ice me out. "But Jenna is out there soaking wet, and we completely terrified her children—"

"Peter!"

Aggie glares at me through the mirror while the rest of the queens halt in a shared record scratch. I dissolve under Aggie's reprimand, like a child with my hand caught in the cookie jar. Our eyes lock and I chuckle in disbelief, my only instinct being to diffuse the situation.

What are you doing? I ask with the twitch of an eyebrow. When I wait for Alan's wordless response, it never comes.

"Save it for later, please," Aggie says in a low voice, shaking her head in disbelief. "We need to focus."

Cora adjusts her stacked silver-white wig. Bailey is suddenly very interested in checking her contour. Nifoal is deeply concerned with combing her long horse mane.

"Right," I say. "Fine."

"We'll celebrate after the show, sweetie," Rita assures me before smacking Aggie's shoulder with the back of her hand. Aggie makes it clear that she hasn't even noticed.

I descend the steps into the audience, my face flushed and my hands shaking. Maybe it's just nerves. Or maybe it's the fact that Alan can be a scornful bitch when he feels like it. I scan the hall, suddenly much larger with the addition of a sold-out audience. Tonight's preshow insanity might have been a lot to contend with, but at least it distracted me from the feeling of apprehension now revving to full once again. The feeling that I don't belong here, that this entire operation has been as transparent as I am.

"So, Peter," comes Trey MacLachlan's voice from beside me. I turn to find him with his mic out, his camera over his shoulder and rolling, and a grim journalistic determination set across his face. "You're the producer for tonight's festivities. Tell me, what does this event mean to you?"

My eyes land on Monica Whitehead and Sylvie Burns, on Chrissy and Blake. Each of them, I know in my gut, is only here to scoff and to see this stupid endeavor fail, which is exactly what I deserve in the first place. Thinking I could just sweep over the video of me and Brison was childish. I'm an idiot. I'm a perpetual motion machine of narcissistic cynicism. Trey MacLachlan holds the mic closer, his eyes all but rolling under the strain of his own disinterest. I scramble for something profound, something to adequately represent the intended weight of the evening. Something to hide the fact that all of this has been done in a cold and calculated attempt, by a cold and calculated person, to relaunch his tarnished public image.

"It's just really important, you know . . . for the community? And representation, like . . . of the community, you know? The queer community, I mean. In Mason County."

I feel my face turning white. I sink into the free-falling sensation of knowing that I'm doing something mortifying while being unable to stop it. Even Trey MacLachlan, professional purveyor of sound-bite bullshit, senses my half-baked conviction. He nods tepidly as I walk away and try to look busy, nodding to Andy as he confirms that the doors are secure, that the show is ready to start.

The audience is full, the queens are ready. So why do I still feel like I haven't been invited to the party?

CHAPTER TWENTY-ONE

THE INCREDIBLY OFF-PUTTING YOUNG MAN

"Oh, hello," a disembodied voice calls over the speakers. "I didn't see you there." The lights dim and the audience descends into silence when Aggie Culture speaks from the ancient announcer's microphone backstage. The queens gather around her, and I flatten myself against the wall, wiping my brow dry for the thousandth time tonight. Aggie grins through her exaggerated lips and passes the mic to Bailey Hayes, their shining press-on nails forming a kaleidoscopic burst of color as they merge.

A glittery figure emerges onto the stage while we watch from beyond the curtain. The stage warms as Rita drags the knob on the dusty lighting board to full, displaying Aggie Culture in all her green glory. Aggie's emerald dress and matching wig sparkle blindingly as the audience cheers. She shrugs with the mic clutched in her long nails. Aggie Culture has crowds screaming for her all the time, her shrug broadcasts. What's one more?

"You sure you're good with this?" Rita whispers as she passes me Alan's phone, glowing with tonight's playlist.

"Lights go up, song goes on," I say. "Easy."

The lighting and music for tonight *are* easy. It's the costumes and props that have my head buzzing with nerves. But Aggie has decided to throw Peter a curveball, and I'd rather get out onstage in full drag than let her see me fumble it. Oh my god, am I *obsessed* with baseball?

"It seems to me," Aggie continues, "that not everyone out there is gagging for this rural realness."

A riotous *boo* rolls across the hall and Aggie holds her palms to the sky as if to say *what is to be done with these silly little homophobes?*

"But you're gagging, aren't you?"

The audience erupts again, and I can hear Jack and Nina leading the call with unadulterated pride. Rita grips my hand and giggles with joyous disbelief while the rest of the girls link arms. Alan's cold shoulder may sting, but I still feel chills prickling my neck. Aggie has the audience eating out of her bejeweled hands, and the unified backstage swell of delight is difficult for even me to shy away from.

"There is a lot of hate in this world," Aggie concedes. "But if I had Jenna Wilbur's bangs, I'd also be full of hate. It's easy to pooh-pooh young people dressing up and putting on a little show. Because it takes a lot of bravery. And hate is a very un-brave thing, isn't it? So tonight we're going to be brave. We're going to be true to ourselves. You're going to be kind to your neighbor, and we girls up here are going to give you absolutely *everything*. Which is very kind of us, if you ask me.

The audience's applause drowns Aggie out as she looks backstage and winks to her drag babies. I press play on track one.

Shania Twain's "Man! I Feel Like a Woman" blasts from the sound system as the girls of Rural Realness pass through the stage door in their clacking heels. Rita Rustique gives me one last squeeze as she goes. Aggie places her mic back on the stand and attacks the lip sync, glittery dress twirling around her calves as she goes. One by one she is joined by Rita Rustique, Nifoal Dressage, Cora Copia, and finally Bailey Hayes, whose long blonde hair and tight blue corset have our audience screaming.

The girls dig into their choreography, which alternates between showing just how much leg there is going on with the majority of team THORR, and Bailey using her petite little body to perform something close to drag break dancing. Our audience loses their minds as Cora Copia and Bailey Hayes pop their legs out, going full-on timber into a unified death-drop. Rita Rustique pulls off her long black wig to reveal her natural hair. She retrieves a plastic mustache from her cleavage and fixes it to her upper lip in time with the song's final beat.

The applause is thunderous.

The curtain flutters as our queens flee the stage, and in the break of the fabric I catch sight of Lorne, who is clapping heartily with Brison and Chrissy. She places an arm around Brison, as if supporting him in the bravery it is taking him to be here in the first place. But maybe I don't care. Maybe I don't care that Lorne is here, watching the show that only sprang into being to impress him. Other than deep vexation toward Chrissy and her self-congratulatory performance of allyship, I don't feel much of anything. Whatever gross, carnal *thing* I've harbored for Lorne has been torpedoed by the perfunctory half-kiss we'd shared. Screw Lorne. Just because I *haven't* screwed Lorne doesn't mean I'm still the warbling mist of a person I'd been when he rolled into town. People are screaming for the second number, and I made that happen. I don't sit idly by while my teenage years pass me by. I make things happen.

"Now," Aggie says into the mic. "You might have heard about the drama that we gals had with some rough and tough types over in Port Anders."

The hall boos again and I feel a poke in the arm.

"Peter," Rita prods, nodding to the bucket of props next to me.

"Oh, yeah," I mutter, passing her the baseball bat poking out the top.

Rita walks onto the stage with it in her glittery hands, and I curse myself for already dropping the ball, praying that Aggie Culture hadn't noticed the fractional delay. Rita passes the bat to Aggie and waves goodbye to her audience with sultry intent, joining the rest of us backstage and delivering me a placating smile.

Aggie swings the bat and pops her tongue, watching the invisible ball fly off into the imaginary distance.

"The folks outside like to call us sinners, or heathens, or other things that sound like a lot of fun. But what they don't realize is that the queens of Rural Realness are full of spiritual belief! It's true. This is a sacred object to us girls. Her name is Helen Bunt."

The crowd laughs, but all I can do is stare at the baseball bat and wonder when it acquired its name. Which text to Lorne had I been busy writing and deleting, writing and deleting.

"Peter!" Cora whispers. She's standing to my right, closer than necessary even in our cramped backstage quarters. When I reach into the basket again, drawing out two wobbling horse-head masks, I feel Cora's eyes on the back of my neck. I offload the masks, and Cora takes them graciously.

"Thank you, Peter," she says. "Your service hasn't gone unnoticed this past month."

"Thank you, Cora."

"The girls and I all agree that you've been just . . . delicious."

She turns to take the stage alongside Rita Rustique, the two of them clomping with their masks held high as they form the lead of Nifoal's invisible horse carriage.

I realize two things in this moment:

1. Cora Copia really is going to mount my taxidermied body on her mantle.
2. My timing is off again, if only slightly.

A wave of embarrassment hits me at high tide. Aggie Culture continues her baseball pantomime while glancing quickly backstage, her eyes flitting across mine with reserved displeasure. Her glare perks up again as I tap play. The four begin Nifoal's cowboy-chic John Wayne number, bigger and better than our short-lived performance in the Port Anders gazebo. Part of me feels something close to nostalgia at the sight of the rubbery horse heads. Maybe even something close to a sense of ownership.

"Girl, you there?"

Bailey Hayes, blonde wig held out of the way, waits with the back of her neck exposed. She hands me a long, jewel-beaded necklace with the word *CHAOS* affixed in steely silver letters, and I drape it across her collarbone before clasping it at the back.

"And the cape," Bailey prompts me.

"I know," I reply, before promptly running into Bailey's makeup chair. It scrapes across the wooden slats of the floor while Bailey winces and I catch myself from tumbling in the claustrophobic space. Aggie Culture, currently turning on the spot, catches sight of my near spill. My fingers turn to stone as I grab the purple cape from the back of the chair and toss it over Bailey's head. The song fades and Bailey steps into her matching purple heels as applause takes over again.

"You kids having fun back here?" Nifoal asks as she saunters to her makeup station.

"I'm fine," I say under my breath.

Aggie introduces Bailey Hayes while I clutch the phone again, a spatter of sweat dripping from my eyebrow onto the screen. I thumb Bailey's mix and the soft opening piano of Kate Bush's "This Woman's Work" fills the house. As Bailey enters, I sense Aggie Culture standing behind me.

"You're doing great," I whisper.

"What's going on back here?" Aggie cuts in, carefully pulling the green dress over her wig and delicately dropping it into my arms.

"What?"

"Our entrances are late."

"Well, it's like I said," I explain. "We never rehearsed this."

Aggie hands me a pink dress with papery ruffles on the arm, and I bend to help her step into its bubblegum depths. Kate Bush's ghostly voice cuts out suddenly, replaced by the fuzzy bass of Britney Spears's "Work Bitch." Bailey tears away the purple smock to show the necklace, a yellow bra, and long black pants as she attacks the new song with the sharp focus of a military official

Aggie pulls the straps over her hairy shoulders. "It's fine if you can't do it, Peter."

Bailey works the audience into a frenzy, her long wig whipping and arcing as she gives the full Britney. My eyes lock with Aggie's again. In the cold of her disregard, it becomes clear just how warm her gaze used to be, how comfortable I used to be within it. The invisible best friend's mind link has been disconnected.

"I can do it," I say, attempting to laugh it off.

We wait in pointed silence as Bailey whirls through her finale. She exits and Cora Copia readies herself as the replacement, a black veil ballooned over her head to match the lacy black dress obscuring her bony frame. Bailey's applause begins to fade, and Aggie presses play on the next song without so much as a glance my way. Cora strides onstage to the thrum and wail of Led Zeppelin's "Immigrant Song" and I swallow the annoyance in my voice as best I can.

"I can *do* the music, Alan."

Cora unveils her face to show the pointy monster horns jutting out of her hair and a black pair of contacts now darkening her eyes into full dilation. Aggie stares fixedly ahead, and it's not hard for me to take the hint. I fold my arms and laugh under my breath, scolding myself for being surprised in the first place.

Rita Rustique places one hand between my shoulder blades and the other on Aggie Culture's unruffled shoulder. "Okay," she breathes. "I love you silly bitches, but you need to just hug out whatever this thing is, okay?"

Black streamers spout from Cora's nipples as she drops into the splits, and whatever Aggie would have said is buried under the roar of the crowd.

Rita's face falls as Aggie joins the fanfare, cheering while Cora bows in a twisted coil of lacy black fabric. I reach for the aux cord again, flicking through the playlist to cue up the next track, but I stop when Aggie's hand lands on mine. Cora has begun to strip off her funeral garb, eliciting a string of ironic catcalls from the teenaged members of our crowd.

"Not yet!" Aggie huffs, wresting the phone away.

My patience finally cracks, and I feel myself curling in at the edges. The urge to grab the phone out of Aggie's hands and hurl it to the floor rises and falls, and I nearly laugh at the absurdity of this entire night. The air is crowded with powder, glitter, and hair spray, but I'm huddled in a corner with the jittery focus of a pilot trying to land a crashing plane. Cora just shot crepe paper from her tits, but I'm standing by with the grim determination of the surgeon about to cut your brain open. Alan's lunacy is contagious, and I need to get as far away from it as possible.

"Fine!" I rasp, pulling myself free from our cramped huddle.

"What the hell, Aggie?" Rita asks.

I'm already leaving, traipsing down the stage stairs while Nifoal joins Cora for the last number before intermission. I can feel the audience watching me as I make my way down the far aisle, but I don't particularly care. I walk as fast as I can to the back of the hall, stewing hotly in everything I *should* have said while Cora and Nifoal jump into an athletic performance of "I Can Make You a Man" from *The Rocky Horror Picture Show*.

I could have said *Fine, Alan! I hope you and your control issues are very happy together.*

Cora leaps into Nifoal's arms, waving serenely.

I could have said *You're right, Alan. Next time I'll just wait for your permission to have a life of my own.*

Cora bends backward, holding herself in a grotesque, spine-tightening bridge before kicking her legs up into the waiting hands of Nifoal Dressage.

But no, I'd add, *you never will. God forbid somebody turn you down and inject some reality into Aggie Culture's Perfect Fantasy Land.*

Cora drops out of the handstand, and I gasp.

Her landing was off. She's landed harder than she did in rehearsal, and I'm certain that I've just seen Cora roll her ankle.

The two leave the stage with Cora awkwardly hopping, and I force myself to breathe again. I rush along the side of the audience, slip into the stageside door, and find the group huddling in the narrow hallway around Cora. She clutches her ankle on the floor.

"I definitely rolled it," she grimaces, her spiked brows now furrowed in pain.

"Okay," I stammer. "Just breathe."

Aggie snaps to action and strolls back onstage, fanning herself before throwing her arms wide for the audience's adoration.

"Now is the part of the show where we gals powder our noses," she proclaims. Cora gingerly slips off her black heels with a grimace.

"So take a moment to love thy neighbor, and we'll be back in twenty," Aggie concludes, blowing everyone a kiss.

Cora inspects her ankle cautiously. "I'll be fine after a bit of ice."

"No," asserts Rita. "No, you will not."

Gerald appears in the doorway, face dropping with concern as he takes us in.

"We need ice," I tell him.

Gerald nods with grim-faced authority and exits again.

"I'm so sorry, Peter," Cora says thickly. Even through her deathly clown-white foundation, it's easy to see that she's gone pale. "But you're going to have to go on for the grande finale."

She says it without a question mark. Shouldn't there be a question mark?

"It was choreographed for five people. It'll look like absolutely *nothing* if we don't have five, and you and Gerald are the only people who have seen the choreo enough to cobble it together."

I look around the room, waiting for somebody to disagree. Eyebrows rise around me in actual contemplation of this objectively terrible idea. This is bad. Very bad. Just the thought of this audience catching sight of me in drag is enough to make my stomach enter pre-puke mode. I'm not the kind of person you put onstage. I don't have stage presence. The best I could do is a freak show of some kind. The Incredibly Off-Putting Young Man or The Amazingly Sweaty Boy. Marvel as his boob sweat merges with his back sweat to form images of your future! Be warned: the first three rows will get wet.

"Then maybe Gerald should start getting ready for his debut," I offer weakly.

Bailey clicks her tongue. "The final number is the showstopper, Peter! We're trying to go out on a high note, not a fart noise."

"We can just cut the final song," I say thinly, my baseline sweat already tripling.

"You can do this, Peter!" Rita says, smiling, taking my hand in hers. "Besides, nobody is expecting perfection. Seeing a first-time queen will be a total gag, you know?"

"Exactly!" Cora manages, face twisting sorely. "People will be talking about it for ages."

I don't point out that this is exactly what I'd like to avoid.

Aggie watches dispassionately from the wings. She checks her lipstick in the mirror, as if waiting for me to bail, waiting for me to fuck up like I did with the props.

I'm looking directly at her when, knees beginning to tremble, I nod.

"Yeah. Okay."

"Get her into makeup," snaps Rita, all business.

"I'm on it," Bailey confirms, taking my arm and leading me to her chair. "I've been wanting to do this for weeks, if we're being honest," she whispers, smiling just a little too broadly given the gravitas of the situation. My heart begins to hammer. Bailey worries away at me, and I only remember to breathe when I need to speak again.

"I don't remember the choreo beat for beat, you guys."

"You don't need to," Bailey tuts as she brushes my eyebrows. "Oh, lord," she fusses. "We don't have time to block and redraw your brows but thank god you've got these big caterpillars that we can play with. And you've seen the choreo, like, a million times, Peter. All you have to do is watch Rita and mirror what she's doing."

As she begins to dab cool primer on my face, Gerald appears, now holding a tea towel full of ice.

"Okay," he says breathlessly. "I need to stress, as the adult in the room, that the show *does not* need to go on." Gerald surveys us gravely as my face is gooped and rubbed under Bailey's fingers. "Do you need to go to the hospital?" he asks Cora.

"So they can tell me to put some ice on it?" Cora scoffs. "No. This show is going on."

The sound of the hall fills our backstage as Gerald considers the second act. His eyes land on mine and then Cora's. Rita wraps her arms around Aggie's shoulders. Tonight might be all over. It might even save me from getting out on that stage and making an absolute clown of myself.

"Okay," Gerald says, taking a deep breath and slowly letting it out. "The show will go on."

The girls cheer, Nifoal planting a lipstick kiss on Cora's cheek while Rita shakes Aggie's shoulders hard enough to displace her wig. The temperature backstage is suddenly even hotter than before. Is it hard to breathe in here, or is it just me?

"You know," Bailey Hayes clucks in my ear. "I'm technically your drag mother now. And you are the *shadiest* bitch I've ever met. So I'm naming you Anna Mossity."

CHAPTER TWENTY-TWO

UNSPEAKABLY HORRIFIC LABORATORY MULLIGAN

Intermission is disappearing, our twenty minutes passing in what I'm pretty sure is closer to five. Cora sits in her chair with her leg elevated atop Nifoal's, who has vanished with Rita to locate a pillow of some kind for Cora's aching leg. Aggie waits wordlessly in the corner, locked into the flurry of Poster content swirling around *The First Annual Mason County Drag Extravaganza*. Since Bailey began to drag-ify me, Aggie has done her best to pretend I'm not there.

"This is a closed set, people!" Bailey calls over her shoulder, powdering my cheeks and making me cough. "Girl, don't breathe. You'll get clown lung."

Bailey moves to double-check my hack and slash contouring when I see exactly who she'd been talking to. Lorne has appeared in the doorway, grinning his sideways smirk.

"Sorry," he says. "I just wanted to come say hi. You folks are really killing it out there."

Aggie Culture pulls herself upright and flicks Lorne's chin with a giggle. "Oh, hello," she says, dripping sweetness. "If you were looking for me, all you had to do was ask."

Lorne laughs and claps Aggie on the shoulder. "I didn't know you were going onstage tonight, Peter."

Aggie makes mirror-enabled eye contact with me and snatches the moment back as fast as she can.

"Technical difficulties of the ankle variety, unfortunately."

"Oh my god!" exclaims Lorne, taking in the ice and towel wrapped around Cora's elevated ankle. "Is everyone okay?"

"Ms. Copia will have to sit out act two," says Aggie, all mother hen. "But Peter has elected to fill in for the final number."

"Wow," Lorne marvels. "That's really brave of you. Especially after all the hate you folks have been getting. If it were up to me, I'd say that your local representatives should host a round table about the open queer-phobia on display here. But, then again, you do have to wonder if that would be platforming oppressive voices."

Bailey clutches my shoulder, fanning herself, as Lorne continues to pontificate.

"It's about bodies in space, right? Both queer bodies and non-queer bodies. Allies need to be using their bodies to protect queer bodies in queer spaces. So, if those people outside decide to mess with you, just know that I've got your back. I guess I just wanted to come back here and show my allyship, you know?"

Maybe it's the powder clouding my face, or the terror of what I'm about to do, but the air has been entirely sucked from the room.

"Allyship?" I ask.

"Totally," he answers with a flicker of self-satisfaction.

"So you're not queer?" I continue, my voice wavering as my chest begins to pound with a heady mix of outrage and trepidation.

"I've always considered the A in LGBTQIA+ to be Ally, so in many ways I am a part of the community," he says easily. "But that *might* be asexual erasure, and I need to be using my privilege to uplift rather than erase—"

"So why did you kiss Peter?" Aggie asks quietly.

Bailey's hands fly to her mouth. Cora seems to be considering crawling to safety, ankle be damned. Personally, I'm hoping to discover a teleportation superpower that has lain dormant within me until this very moment.

"Well," Lorne replies, considering it with a nervous laugh. "I guess I just wouldn't want to invalidate anyone, you know?"

"I'm sorry," I say, brushing Bailey's hands away. "I'm so sorry . . ."

I'm laughing. Why am I laughing?

"You just thought you could lead me *and* Alan on for nearly a month because if you didn't you'd be, what, homophobic?"

Lorne shrugs, that glaze of gentle superiority washing across his face and just begging me to smack it off. But I do not. Because from some blessedly distant vantage point, I watch myself retaining my composure. I will not *do that thing I always do.*

"Look, I know just as well as you folks that straight folks can be totally problematic and make things really hard for queer folks who are just trying to live their totally normal lives—"

"Stop saying folks!" I blurt out.

Well, I tried. But at my core, I really am just a trigger-happy verbal wrecking ball.

"And we know our lives are *normal*; we don't need you to tell us that."

"Exactly. And if I'd turned you down, wouldn't I have just been another oppressive force invalidating you?" He shrugs for a third time, and I picture myself ripping his arms off at the shoulder.

"Oh my god. You're actually the worst. You're fucking insane."

"Peter, please. That word is pretty violent toward folks with mental health issues, and you really shouldn't—"

"So, what was your plan, exactly? Hang out with the local gays and then what? Give us the gift of your lukewarm make-out abilities? What did you think this was? Charity work?"

Lorne's eyebrows are nearly scraping the ceiling. "Sexuality is a spectrum, Peter. And I don't have to explain myself to you—"

"No! You didn't have to! But you just did! You're not an ally, Lorne! You're a tourist. You're a fucking tourist in our fucking spectrum with every intention to hop back out when you feel like it. You weren't *experimenting* or, like, *discovering* your sexuality. You were checking off a box. You're the worst. You're the actual worst."

"Yeah," Bailey says icily from behind me. "People say I'm the worst, but even I can tell that *you're* actually the worst."

"I never said I was straight," Lorne says breathlessly, his gaze falling to the floor.

"Then are you queer? Are you being anything but your own twisted version of *polite*?"

"Fine!" he erupts, throwing his hands skyward. "I'm not gay, I'm not queer, but I'm also not a problematic person, all right? And what you're doing right now is called *gatekeeping*."

"Oh, you are a *total* tourist," Bailey gasps.

"Maybe we are gatekeeping," I say, laughing hotly. "But it's only because when we open the gates to fuckheads like you, we end up feeling like complete shit about ourselves!"

Aggie says nothing. Lorne squints in disbelief, like we've missed the point entirely. Then he turns and stomps out of the dressing room. Rita and Nifoal trot up the stairs with a threadbare seat cushion, finding us in a queasy silence.

"They're getting restless out there," says Rita, eyeing us uneasily. "Should we get going?"

"Yeah," Aggie says, faraway. "Okay."

"I'm still going to need a few minutes," says Bailey, jumping back into action. "Think you can buy me some time?"

Aggie stares at me, quietly furious.

"I've got an idea."

Aggie Culture turns to take the stage again, the audience whooping and then settling as she does. Under the stage lights, she begins to work the audience.

"Who are these delightful young ladies in the front row?"

"Look," Bailey whispers under Aggie's magnified voice. "You know I love drama, but unless you two intend on filming this for my channel, you need to rein it in."

"I've been trying to!" I whisper scream. "Alan won't even look me in the eye."

"That girl loves deeply, bitch," Bailey says with a click of her tongue. "Which means she hurts deeply. So whatever is going on between you two must hurt a lot. Just get through the show and cry about it backstage like real drag queens do."

"I'm not a real drag queen," I remind her.

Bailey inspects her handiwork, an eyebrow raised in appreciation. "No. But you're close."

"I think it's time we address the elephant in the room," Aggie tells her adoring crowd. "Now, I know some of you have been following our very active online presence. That means I'm sure you've also been following our drama with a certain young man who is here in the audience. Brison Dallas, how are you doing?"

My jaw drops open and Bailey's hands falter. Shock dulls the dressing room around me.

"I'm great!" Brison calls back from his seat.

"Brison," Aggie says, giggling, "would you please join me up here for a come-to-Jesus moment? And no, not the kind that Jenna Wilbur wants us to be having."

I watch as Brison climbs onstage, craning my neck as Bailey guides me back into my seat. She pulls a long, pink wig from a plastic sleeve and slides the tabs over my meshed-down hair.

"Now, Brison. We're just meeting tonight for the first time, but you know my non-drag persona, is that right?"

"Yes, that's right!" Brison chuckles. He's enjoying it up there. Of course he is. Whatever laboratory he was grown in made sure to genetically encode him with stage-ready charm. I pull at a hangnail on my thumb, feeling once again like the unspeakably horrific laboratory mulligan someone tossed in the bio-trash.

"And everyone knows that you've had some beef with Peter Thompkin."

Bailey turns my chin to face her, bobby pins in her mouth as she fixes the wig to my scalp.

"I don't have beef with Peter, Aggie."

"You don't?"

"No."

"Even after going on Bailey Hayes's YouTube page and claiming otherwise?"

"Yeah," Brison begins. He considers his words for a moment. "But I think I was kind of just trying to screw with him a bit."

This gets laughs. Bailey tightens her grip on my chin and I rip a hunk of cuticle from my thumb.

"I had a lot of people telling me a lot of different things about how I should be, you know, responding, I guess," Brison says. "Online and stuff."

My thumb begins to bleed and I press my fingers against the sting.

"Brison, some people have accused Peter of only working on this production as a way to clean up his public image."

"I mean, I don't know," Brison says slowly. "I think that's kind of unfair, don't you?"

Wait. What? What is happening?

"He's yet to apologize," Aggie proffers, affecting her best Oprah voice. "Or take any real accountability for the damage he's done to the community. Instead, he's putting all his effort into trying to make everyone forget how triggering his attack was for you. And so close to your family's tragedy."

"I don't think I care if Peter *is* doing this to make up for it," Brison says with a laugh. "I think this show is great." The audience claps in agreement, jumping at the first chance to break the inexplicable tension that Aggie has been building while I consider slipping out the back and running forever. I'll steal a car, and I'll just drive north. I'll keep driving until I hit the ocean, and even then I'll just keep my foot on the pedal.

"*You* certainly are strong and resilient, Brison Dallas," Aggie says softly. "And I forgive you. Do you forgive me?"

Brison chuckles again. "I do, Aggie Culture."

"Well, let's all leave tonight knowing that we can *still* make amends for how we may have let our community . . . and our friends down."

The crowd cheers while Brison takes his seat again. Bailey pulls me to my feet despite how much I want to curl up into a ball and blip out of existence. She drops a pair of black flats into my hands.

"There's no way in hell I'm putting you out there in heels."

Bailey prances back onstage as the opening twang of her "Just Like Jesse James" routine with Rita Rustique begins. Aggie lowers herself gracefully into her seat and removes her green wig in favor of an electric blue updo.

"What the hell was that?" I ask tersely.

"I did what you couldn't," Aggie explains. "I apologized."

"You don't care about Brison Dallas. You just wanted to drag me in front of the entire audience."

"You knew I liked him," she spits, holding her new wig in place. "You knew I liked him and you kissed him anyway."

I breathe, my arms folding protectively over my still-naked chest. "You don't have exclusive rights on having a crush on a straight boy, Alan."

"No, but you went behind my back. And you know why? Because you *knew* what you were doing was shitty, Peter. And you thought I didn't stand a chance."

My face flushes hot. She's right, and I can't find a way to maneuver my way around it. I haven't said a word about Lorne all month. It was a lie by omission. I grit my teeth under Aggie's beam of shame.

"You think the fat boy can't get with someone like Lorne, so you might as well go for him yourself," she concludes venomously.

"I'm not exactly skinny."

"Admit it! You thought your silly fat sidekick had no business getting with the cultured boy from the big city."

"*You're* the sidekick?" I whisper, dumbfounded by Alan's ability to spin everything on its head. "You've been dragging me around on a leash all summer. You tell me to jump and I do. *Sure, Alan! Hopefully I can jump higher than the literal guard dogs trying to maul me.* You say, *Let's post this video of you falling on your literal ass online* and I say, *Sure, Alan, what's one more humiliating video of me going around the internet?*"

The Cher song is coming to an end. Aggie whisks herself back onstage, the fluttering of her dress serving as her final word. This glorified closet of a room is vibrating around me. Cora pretends that she hadn't heard every word while I throw myself back into Bailey's chair and turn my head from the mirror. I can't go out there looking like this. I can't go out there at all.

CHAPTER TWENTY-THREE
ANNA MOSSITY

"Bitch. What are you doing?"

Bailey exits stage right to find me removing the wig.

"I'm not doing this. Alan doesn't want me here and this *entire* thing is just one big Alan wet dream, so what's the point?"

Bailey's pointy fingers close around my shoulders, forcing me back into my seat as Nifoal joins Aggie onstage for their performance of "Just a Girl."

"Listen," Bailey says with a sigh. "I didn't do this show as an Alan Goode vanity project. I did it because there are people in this county who need to see that the faggots around here aren't going to just sit around quietly while the heteros have all the fun. I did it because my grandparents haven't talked to me since I started posting my videos and because my parents seem just fine to let them hate me while my grandfather still controls the business. I'm doing it because I do makeup better than any of the women in this place and because I look fucking good with long hair."

She sets to placing my wig again. Even in the heat of the pep talk Bailey moves with graceful skill.

"I don't know if this show will mean anything in the long run. Or my videos. Maybe we're just pretty dummies in corsets. But it makes being born in the wrong place, with the wrong people, feel bearable for a little while when you can show them how fucking *good* you are at being you. Or, you know, this painted-for-the-gods version of you."

Bailey places a finger under my chin and raises my face to the dim light. She stares into me through her neon-blue contacts.

"Besides. I'm your drag mother now. So be a good girl and listen to Mommy."

She rummages through her bag and unveils a paisley blue sundress that she tosses at me.

"There's no way in hell you're fitting into Cora's getup for the final number. But this might work."

She carefully places it over my head and finds a braided belt to cinch above my waist. If you ignore my hairy spider legs and the hair popping out from my armpits, I don't look half bad.

"You're my beautiful Frankenstein daughter," Bailey declares with a twinge of pride. "Now stuff these pads into your tights like you mean it."

Then she's gone again for her "Dancing Queen" solo.

Once I cram the almond-shaped padding under a pair of bike shorts, I consider myself carefully in the mirror. The foundation and concealer have smoothed over my splotchy skin. Bailey's lip liner has given shape to my nearly nonexistent lips, enlarging them in a coat of pomegranate red. My eyes are something new entirely. Even with my natural boy-brows capping them off prematurely, my eyes have been deepened and elongated, topped with a razor-thin wing on either side that seems more likely to have been applied by some tightly calibrated makeup machine than a teenage drag queen in the middle of her own show. Bailey really *is* good at what she does, because I could never have imagined this version of me. Despite my nerves, I take another good look at myself. I might even like what I see. Most of the time I hate how round and puffy my face looks, but Bailey has harnessed my round features by making them pop beneath the soft blush now shaping my cheekbones. The joint effort of the padding on my hips and belting above my waist are giving my normally bulging midsection some shape. Suddenly I don't have a gut, I have *curves*. It's not as if I shrunk at all. In fact, quite the opposite. But for the first time ever, someone has shown me how to add some definition to that part of my body. It feels kind of like my body has always been a set of barely legible sentences written with the nubby end of a pencil. But right now I am Anna Mossity, the *italicized* version of me. The letters didn't change, but they have become a lot more fun.

Rita is behind me now, grinning as she catches me in the act of unadulterated vanity.

"I think I'm going to puke," I tell her. "Or pass out. Hopefully in that order."

Rita grabs the sides of my wig. "Just come out and have some fun with your friends. That's all it is." And for a second I might actually believe her.

Bailey takes the stage and retrieves the microphone, waving regally.

"We have one final number for you tonight," she tells the hall. "But before we get on with it, I want to do two things. I want to say thank you to the best, and also the first, audience The House of Rural Realness has ever had."

She claps daintily as the audience whoops and hollers.

"And second, I'd like to introduce a queen who was born tonight during this very show. She's my first drag daughter but hopefully not my last. Her name is Anna Mossity, and she's a star in the making. But before you meet her, I want to introduce, once again, the buxom beauty who brought us gals together: Ms. Aggie Culture."

The soft opening piano notes of Dolly Parton's "Light of a Clear Blue Morning" drift from the speakers as Aggie emerges and swaps places with Bailey, who joins us in the wings and winks at me. Nifoal squeezes my shoulders. This is a bad idea. Maybe I can preemptively roll my ankle before our cue. Everyone knows I have zero coordination. As far as I can tell, this is the one time in my life it will ever work in my favor.

But then Dolly's voice fills the room and Aggie is mouthing along soulfully while raising her hands to the ceiling. For a moment I forget how much I want to push Alan/Aggie off the stage. For a moment I'm just another audience member watching a shiny, gorgeous drag queen doing the thing she's very good at.

The tempo kicks up a notch as Dolly sings to the heavens. Rita, Nifoal, and Bailey glide back onstage and then I'm with them, resisting the urge to shield my eyes. The audience is hard to see, but that's probably a good thing. I breathe in hard and try to focus on the choreography. We stand in line with Aggie in the middle and I do my best to mirror Rita, who is dancing beside me and making it look like the easiest thing she's ever done. It's a simple two-step at first then some raised jazz hands above your head. So far, so good. Everyone turns in, but I'm turning out and bumping against the star of the moment, Ms. Aggie Culture. The audience chuckles obligingly and Aggie smiles, brushing the wig out of my face and turning me back around to clasp palms with Rita.

"You're doing great," Rita whispers as we slow dance through the bridge.

Aggie is going gospel at center stage. The white glow of phone cameras lights up the audience, and my heart threatens to hammer out of my chest like a viscera-covered Woody the Woodpecker. The piano cascades as Dolly launches into the final leg of the song and we turn our backs to the audience. The knots in my stomach tighten as I step directly on Aggie's heel, pulling the shoe off her foot as I do.

Aggie rights herself, patting me on the head like a concerned mother. The audience eats it up, and I wonder distantly if death by pure embarrassment is possible under these exact circumstances. This is a nightmare. Worse than a nightmare. At least in those I'm not wearing a sundress. They're laughing *with* Aggie, but they're laughing *at* me. Chrissy, Brison, and especially Lorne must be cackling. The yogurt girl must be readying a fresh barrage of berry gloop to aim directly at my wig. I'd wanted to change my public image, hadn't I? Well, here you go, Peter. Now everyone will talk about the time you ruined Mason's very first drag show with your dancing inability. I'm beginning to understand why Carrie chose a telepathic murder spree over living her own public humiliation for one second longer.

We turn in for the grand finale and I pivot too hard, bashing into Nifoal and feeling the stage slip out from under me in a prolonged scene of pure horror.

Time turns to molasses, the way it does when something insane is happening. If this was an HBO miniseries, this would be the part where the action goes slow motion while a stripped-down piano cover of a pop song plays. Let's say, for our purposes, that a hauntingly sparse retooling of "Wannabe" by the Spice Girls is playing distantly as the floor rushes up to meet me. Nifoal's arms slap against my stomach, which jiggles visibly, as she attempts to catch me.

She doesn't, and I finally hit the ground.

The music fades out, leaving complete silence. Bailey's borrowed dress is riding up and exposing my hairy legs. I'm lying on my hands, which saved my face from smacking on the floor. I can feel the rest of the girls freezing around me. I can feel the eyes of everyone on the tangle of gender-bent failure I've become. Worst of all, I can feel the glow of the cameras. I shut off entirely. Presented with all the options, I choose to feel absolutely nothing about this point of time. I'll get up, wipe the makeup from my face, take off this dress, and then I'll walk home. I'll continue to feel nothing about this until the day I die. The only other option is to acknowledge that the elevators from *The Shining* have popped up in my brain and are about to unleash a tidal wave of embarrassment. It will make what I said to Brison, all those weeks ago in the parking lot of the Dairy Freeze, seem like a quaint footnote in the epic tome of public shame that is my life.

But then someone starts clapping. The clapping turns to cheering, and the cheering turns to the kind of laughter that seems full of *with* and devoid of *at*.

"We love you, Anna Mossity!" someone bellows.

The elevator doors remain closed.

I roll over and dust myself off with measured flair, and the audience's roars only increase. As I pull myself back to standing, Rita grabs me by the hand. She's beaming her usual dark smirk and waving for the audience to keep it up. They cheer even harder, and Rita holds my arm skyward like a boxing champion. Bailey wipes away an exaggerated tear of pride for her drag daughter. Now Cora is hopping onstage, arm slung around Nifoal's shoulder. It sends our audience over the edge, everyone screaming for their iconic, clumsy queens. Cora's other arm finds my shoulder and we laugh with relief, sinking into a staggered and half-formed bow.

Aggie Culture watches reservedly, thin lipped and tactfully good natured.

The queens of Rural Realness step forward and join our busted duo, the group of us bowing solemnly while the hall continues to call out. I think I get why people like this. I think I might even like it. I may have made a fool of myself in front of a literal theater full of people, but damn if it didn't feel kind of good.

"You made your drag mother proud, bitch," Bailey quips while we bow again.

"Thank you," I say. "Dancing has always been my passion."

With my eyes adjusting to the light, I'm able to make out our audience. Brison and I lock eyes, and he claps pointedly in my direction.

"Yaas, Rural Realness!" he calls out.

The Goodes take to their feet for a standing ovation, and I wave as Jack wipes unironic tears from his own eyes. Michael and Frank are hollering. Gerald smiles somehow wider than usual. We begin to take our leave and then I catch sight of a couple standing next to him, the three of them squished together.

My parents and I see each other from across the hall. My dad grins as Gerald leans in closer to tell him something over the roar, and the two begin to laugh. My mother waves.

CHAPTER TWENTY-FOUR
A SET FANGS

"Am I a star now?" I ask the dressing room as I sag into Bailey's chair. "It's called a death drop, honey," Nifoal informs me as she lovingly brushes a strand of pink hair from my eye. "Not drop dead."

"You were supposed to cover for me," Cora says with a cackle, "not flash the entire audience."

"Don't listen to them, darling." Bailey's voice is soothing. "They could never serve the absolute *drama* you gave tonight." She revolves sharply and daintily lays the back of her hand upon her forehead before dropping to the ground. Rita screams and the room fills with clattering jabber and squeals of delight. Aggie, still mute, sits with a scrape of a chair before peeling off her wig.

"What are you doing, bitch?" Rita laughs. "We have to go meet our audience!" Rita watches as Aggie pulls her left set of eyelashes free and drops them to the table. As Alan's features begin to peek through Aggie Culture's, Rita's elation begins to deflate.

"They're going to want pictures, girl," Rita reminds Alan with a poke, her voice tentative as a pall settles over the dressing room.

"The show's over, Tilly," Alan says dryly. "I'm going home."

The audience clatter fills the dressing room as the queens' babble hits pause. Alan fishes around in his makeup bag and his eyes surreptitiously land on me, the space between us growing vast and prickly despite our close quarters.

"Ms. Aggie Culture," I try, smiling through my half-drag. "I know you're not getting out of drag before the masses have had their way with you."

"You don't have to keep putting on a show, Peter." Alan laughs wryly, peeling off the other lashes.

"Stop getting undressed," Rita pleads. The post-show cheer is melting from Rita by the second, replaced with a desperation trying to pass itself off as nonchalance.

"Yeah, girl," Cora agrees evenly. "Can we just cool down for a minute?"

"I don't know why you're all having such a great time," Alan says flatly. "Peter just ate shit in front of our first audience ever, and now he's just acting like it's some big joke. Which shouldn't shock me, I guess. He thinks we're all total jokes in the first place."

Silence follows and everyone avoids eye contact with everyone else. The party has left the building, and it seems to have no intention of returning. I blink through my own unnaturally extended eyelashes.

"What the fuck, Alan?" I demand. Alan placidly pops open a package of makeup wipes. When Rita plucks them from his hands, he only sighs and purses his lips stoically.

"We're a drag family," Rita tries, now entirely drained of celebration. "At least for tonight. So whatever is going on between you two can wait until tomorrow," she concludes, grabbing both our hands. "Please."

She gives our arms a shake and it dislodges just a little of my exasperation. The absence of Tilly's grandmother, easy enough for Tilly to ignore earlier tonight, is suddenly potent. It feels as if we're the only people Tilly has, and I clutch her hand just a little tighter as Alan slips his away. Shame gnaws at me while tears threaten Rita's eyes. She's spent the night of her drag debut playing buffer between two salty gays, which I'm beginning to see is a regular feature of this friendship. Embarrassed, and more than a little appalled by myself, I rally.

"Yeah," I say. "You're right. Let's just have fun tonight."

Alan's eyes finally land on mine, narrowing into a grimace of disbelief.

"We all know that Peter had one reason for doing this show," he says. "He only did it for himself."

With an almost audible click, that razored edge returns to me, pushing up from the dark, ugly chasm at the pit of my brain. The one that got me into this mess in the first place.

"You know what? Sure," I allow, throwing my hands up in defeat. "I did think that tonight might change the way people talk about me. But the only reason it went to shit in the first place is because I was protecting *you*," I point out, jabbing a finger at Alan. "You walk around with big cartoon hearts in your eyes and just expect everyone to do the same. You make a fool of yourself, and I'm the one who picks up the pieces every time you fall apart over the fact that the world isn't sunshine and rainbows."

"*You're* the one who made a fool of yourself," Alan levels back.

Bailey crosses to Alan, ready to console, but Alan brushes her off with a wave.

"You think you're cool because you're mean, Peter? You act like you want to fly under the radar, but what you really want is for people to notice how *cutting* and *clever* you are so they'll be too scared to come any closer," Alan continues coldly. "You act like what you said to Brison has been blown out of proportion, but it did exactly what you wanted it to. You *wanted* it to hurt, and you wanted everyone to take notice of how severe you are. You weren't protecting me; you were just taking the chance to lash out like you always do."

My headache, lost in the adrenaline thrill, emerges with a pounding thud. I pull the wig from my head and drop it on the table.

"Stop," demands Rita. "Both of you, stop."

"Can you even begin to register how self-obsessed you are?" I ask Alan. "I'm not going to sit back and let my life pass me by because Alan Goode prefers to keep me as his good little errand boy. If you thought you stood a chance with Lorne, you'd have made a move. But you didn't because you're terrified of living in reality like the rest of us."

I slip the dress over my head and drop it to the floor, anger numbing my natural aversion to displaying my stomach rolls and back pimples to the world.

"So I was right," Alan concludes sharply. "You think someone like me couldn't ever get with someone like Lorne."

I blink, straining for words. He's right, after all. I had thought that Alan stood no chance with Lorne. And I feel myself shrinking away from the floodlight that Alan has cast over my intentions. I feel as if I've been exposed for the callous little creature that I am.

"No," I reply, pulling on my shorts, eager to step over what Alan has just laid bare. "I just think you're jealous."

I brush past the queens as I pull my shirt back on, walking away with my face still made up. Gerald stands outside the backstage door clutching a bundle of six roses under his trademark grin.

"Fantastic work, Peter," he crows, pinching a rose and extending it my way. "I was going to toss these onstage at the end, but I had a feeling these thorns might put a damper on the curtain call."

I hold my rose and nod silently, taking in our audience as they bask in the outlandish triumph of the evening, blissfully unaware that it's all gone to shit. *The First Annual Mason County Drag Extravaganza* feels hollow. Even worse, it feels as if it always has been. It feels like a vanity project drawn out too far.

"Thanks, Gerald."

Gerald searches my face at the catch in my voice, but I'm already pushing through a wave of eager fans and making my way toward the stairs. I

barrel out the front doors and onto the sidewalk, nearly colliding with the
remaining protesters as I do. The storm has dried, and the air has cooled.
Mason's negligible downtown drips and drops with collected rainwater, the
closing of car doors punctuating the night as the unbothered mannequins
of the Salvation Army keep watch.

A toothless, white-haired skeleton of a man with a cigarette butt hanging from his mouth glares at me with a wordless warning. A sign reading
Not With My Tax Dollars rests against his shoulder.

"Jesus Christ." I laugh scornfully. "I'd tell you to get a hobby, but I'm
sure being a walking herpes sore is really time consuming."

I flash my middle fingers and turn to leave. Fuck Alan, fuck drag, and
fuck Jenna Wilbur's flying monkeys. This is what I get for breaking my rule
of invisibility. From now on I'll be imperceptible again. I will be entirely
unremarkable until I can graduate and get the hell out of Mason County.
I'll tolerate it only on major holidays and family tragedies. This place never
wanted me, and I certainly don't want it.

"Fucking faggot."

The guy with the sign says it plainly, noncommittally. Then, having performed his civic duty, he spits at my feet. I hear him gather his phlegm. I feel
it splatter across my heel.

That's when my steely edge cracks, breaking apart into something new.
Something I don't recognize.

I'm wrestling the sign from his hands before my brain can catch up with
my body. Then I'm ripping at it with a ferocity that is both foreign and
familiar. I get a corner chunk pulled off before he's all over me. He pushes
me against the brick of the building while screeching with a mouth full of
vowels about his freedom of speech through sour, smoke-stained breath. I
howl in return, shoving and digging at his crusty clothing and bony angles
while my rage dissolves my usual verbal gymnastics into a roiling mass of
guttural curses. I twist against his arms, and he tries to grate me into thin
slices against the course brick. Maybe if I push hard enough, he'll shatter

into tiny pieces along the sidewalk. Maybe if I just break him open across the pavement, they'll see that they can't fuck with us. Everyone in Mason County, in every place like this, will prickle as their lizard brains grasp instinctually that we cannot be whittled down under the pumice of a brick wall. They'll know that when the faggots bash back, we bash your fucking skull in. Every part of me is a set of fangs straining to close around this man's throat.

Anyhow, that's when Hot Alpaca Farmer shows up.

Michael, flannel akimbo, peels human ashtray off me before pinning him roughly against the wall. Another dusty protester joins the frenzy but is intercepted by Frank, who seizes him by the collar. A crowd is forming as our theatergoers take notice of the scuffle. A trio of jack-o'-lantern-faced men surge forward, pushing against Michael and raving into his face. Two bodies peel off from the audience and ward these three back, blocking me and Frank from the onslaught while holding their arms out in a focused defense. Brison and Chrissy stand next to Michael, Chrissy screaming back with formless vitriol before hurling out "You don't *touch* him, you got it? You don't fucking *look* at him again, you fucking twat!"

Lorne stands in the audience, his phone held aloft and recording.

Our security detail arrives and insists that Frank release his captive, who limps back to his friends while cursing in our direction. Blake, Kirk, and Andy form their buff-boy trinity and begin to disperse the crowd while voices continue to rise. My father, appearing out of nowhere for the second time tonight, is restrained by Andy as he screams in the face of Tax Dollars Man.

"What the fuck is wrong with you?" Dad rages. "You don't get to lay a finger on my kid, not a finger!"

My shock begins to subside as the security detail pulls the groups apart, Michael and Frank joining my father as they lay into the oatmeal-faced skeleton I'd been grappling with only a moment before. I exhale shakily before a gentle hand lands on my shoulder.

"Hey, are you all right?"

Brison Dallas, sweaty and disheveled, examines my face for signs of damage.

"Yeah," I mumble, rubbing my nose in an attempt to cover my face for a while. "That was kind of intense."

I search for Chrissy and find her about to throw herself at the walking anti-choice billboards, who cluck their tongues while recording the interaction on their phones. Lorne, still recording himself, has begun to narrate.

"You wanna get the hell out of here?" Brison asks over the tumult.

Despite myself, I laugh. This night is getting stranger by the minute. Brison Dallas driving my getaway vehicle makes a certain kind of sense, in that it makes no sense at all.

"Yeah," I say. "I do."

CHAPTER TWENTY-FIVE
SELLOUT HIT MAKER

Brison drives fast, Mason whipping past the open windows. The new car smell is cloying, but I don't mind it after the salty smell of bodies crashing into each other in the summer heat. We make our way through town without a word, passing Mason Tirecraft and zipping over the bridge leading to Lion's Park. We crunch across the gravel before Brison parks and turns the key. The hum of the car is gone, leaving a stiff silence that I begin to melt beneath. Any evidence of the Picnic Purge has been cleared from the place, the playset and gazebo lit faintly by gnat-swarmed streetlights before being swallowed by the dark of the forest and fields on the other side.

Maybe Brison drove us out here to kill me.

"Do you smoke?" he asks distantly.

"What?"

Brison retrieves a weathered tin from the armrest compartment and pops it open, revealing a dime bag of pot and a sleeve of rolling papers.

He fishes around and finds a circular grinder that is nearly as beaten-up as the tin. After pulling a glass pipe from his pocket, he grinds the bud and pinches it into the bowl with an air of routine. He offers it to me with ironic grandiosity.

"Oh, no thanks," I say evenly.

Brison nods before opening the car door and closing it behind him, waving for me to join him. We cross to a set of picnic tables, and the only sound is the soft fall of our feet on the grass. Brison's face sparks orange as he lights up and I sit across from him, careful of the smoke billowing from his lips. Is getting a contact high a real thing outside sitcoms and eighties movies?

"It really was a good show," Brison says after a while.

"Oh, you don't have to say that."

"No," he insists, fiddling with the end of the pipe. "For real, it was insane."

"Thanks. Yeah. If nothing else, it was interesting."

Brison laughs before choking mid-puff, coughing and wiggling his hands as he tries to shake it off. Soon we're both laughing, the space between us clearing of the smoke while Brison rubs at his nose. The strangeness of it isn't lost on either of us, I think. The thing building between us all summer has congealed and cooled, as if neither of us are entirely sure what the story was in the first place.

"That was your dad, right?" Brison asks as he sets the pipe aside.

"Yeah," I reply, fixing my eyes on the shifting dark of the forest. The subject of fathers hangs uneasily between us.

"That was really cool of him."

I squint, not sure I agree. Besides, is this really a topic he wants to get into right now?

"I guess. It's the one time my dad blowing up and screaming wasn't, like, the worst thing."

Brison laughs again, but I'm not sure if it's my comedic timing or the pot cloud creating his sense of humor.

"Thanks for getting me the fuck out of there," I try, grasping at a change in topic.

"Those guys should be arrested."

"Sure," I allow. "But getting their asses handed to them by a bunch of homos is pretty great, too."

"That is true," Brison agrees, and we're laughing uneasily again. "My dad would never have jumped in like that."

I nod. Maybe basic politeness will smooth over the sharp edges of the topic. Maybe the thing I'd said at the Dairy Freeze won't choke the life out of us both if I sit exceptionally still.

"Yeah, well. Maybe my dad just wanted an excuse to curse someone out in public."

"No," Brison says with a shake of his head. "He was just being your dad."

My phone buzzes in my pocket and I text my mother, assuring her that I'm both fine and alive. Brison plays with his lighter and I slide my phone into my pocket again.

"Do you remember David Johannes?" he asks, his eyes trained on the sky.

David's name rings a far-off bell, but it's one that feels like a trap.

"From elementary school?"

"Yeah. He goes to St. Beatrice now."

"Okay."

"Do you remember the thing that happened with the hand soap?"

Brison brushes the hair from his face and exhales sharply. I think for a moment, connecting David Johannes with some nebulous incident in the boy's bathroom of Mason Public School.

"I remember there was some . . . prank or fight or something that had to do with dish soap."

"Did you talk to David much?" Brison asks after a while.

I remember David's penchant for shiny anime shirts. I remember the graphic pictures drawn in the margins of his workbooks, usually featuring a spiky-haired cat-man killing another cat-man with a massive gun-sword.

"Not really," I reply, considering it for a moment. "He always gave me the creeps."

"Yeah," agrees Brison. "I didn't either. But in fifth grade, Conner Benson and Keegan Willard and that group of kids, they'd gotten some, like, beef with David about something. And they were convinced that David was gay."

"Wait. They thought he was gay as in *weird* or gay as in *currently wearing half a face of drag makeup*?" I wave a hand across my own face.

"I think in fifth grade it's kind of the same thing."

I give a hollow laugh. "Right."

"But I never said anything when other people would bully him because, you know, I didn't want it to seem like I was being defensive."

I nod and find myself leaning in. Everyone knows that the quickest way to be accused of being a homo is to defend someone else against the same accusations.

"So this one time, we sort of barricaded David in a bathroom stall at recess. And someone got the soap dispensers off the wall, and we poured that pink liquid soap all over his head. And he's cursing us out, which gets us going even more. I'd never heard David say so much at one time. He was a total loner, always writing or drawing something. But he was rattling around in there, trying to break the door down. And the guys are chanting, like, *clean the fag*, and *don't let him touch you, you'll get AIDS*."

Brison's fingers travel back to his pipe, and I remain silent. The memory of David being escorted to the principal's office dripping soap arrives fully formed in my mind's eye. I remember thinking that David brought it upon himself. That if he'd been smart, he'd have avoided those boys like I did.

"So we got into pretty deep shit for it, obviously," Brison continues. "Which is fine. They deserved it. *We* deserved it. I shouldn't have been there. Or I should have like . . . *not* done that."

"Yeah," I say. "And pink really didn't go with David's complexion."

"The point I'm making," Brison says through an uneasy smile, "is that my dad couldn't have been bothered. He thought it was funny."

Crickets invade the conversation as I fall quiet.

"Funny how?"

"*Funny* funny," says Brison. "*Clean the fag. Don't let him touch you,* the whole thing. You know, he thought it was just kids being kids."

My mouth curls in revulsion. "Jesus."

Brison lights up again, his face glowing and un-glowing in the flame. He exhales and I wonder if I should take him up on his offer before deciding that tonight has had enough firsts. The specter of David Johannes hovers ominously over the night's unexpected proceedings.

"Were things weird between you two, then? After you came out, I mean," I ask, the wall between us shrinking under the weight of Brison's inexplicable candor.

"I mean, yeah," Brison muses. "Or no. Probably. He wasn't gonna *shotgun wedding* the gay out of me. We mostly just made a point not to talk about anything around the topic."

"Oh, right. *That* I do know a thing or two about."

"Your parents came tonight, though," Brison says encouragingly.

"Yes," I laugh. "They did. Which is great."

Brison raises an eyebrow.

"It *is* great!" I protest. "I'm being sincere. For once."

He empties the ashes on the ground and sweeps away any residual bits from the picnic table. "It's kind of hard to tell with you," he says.

The videos and posts and calculations quite suddenly feel very small. The whole thing seems petty and misdirected. Brison, regardless of the image I've held of him as the sneering embodiment of gay villainy, is also just someone with parental issues. Someone who was ready to give me a ride and some pot when he thought I needed them.

"I shouldn't have said that," I say after some time. "About your dad. That was really fucked up." Brison's eyes get heavy, focusing on his fingers as they trace the lines in the picnic table below us. "And I'm sorry. It was really shitty."

The strange thing is that I mean it. Brison's pithy bullying of Alan's outlandish outfit choices doesn't hold the same weight it did twenty-four hours ago. The fact that hurt people hurt people is becoming increasingly evident the longer this conversation goes on.

A fruit bat flitters across the park, Brison dislodges a splinter from the table, and a wave of exhaustion settles over me. I could lay my head down on this picnic table and wake up next week.

"We could have been less shitty to you and Alan," Brison says after some time. "It was a mutual shittiness."

I laugh nervously while Brison continues to gouge away at the wood. With Chrissy gone and no camera in his face, Brison is unnervingly reserved. He's making it hard to hate him. It's not as if he's had an easy time of it lately. I guess money and good looks don't do much to make up for whatever was going on in the Dallas house before his father died. There's even a certain amount of shock at the thought of Brison being jealous of my parents and me. He's right. They had shown up, hadn't they?

"So are you in love with Lorne, or what's going on there?" Brison asks.

The shock continues.

"What?" I gasp.

Brison devolves into pot-laden giggles. "Did he take you pool-hopping?"

Oh my god. How does this night keep getting worse?

"Are you serious?" I scream. "He took you pool-hopping?"

Brison nods and crumples into hysterics.

"I hate literally everything right now."

"Oh, come on!" Brison howls. "You're a part of a long tradition of gays getting all hot and bothered for his dreamy straight boy routine."

"You too?" I squawk in disbelief.

Brison rolls his eyes. "Only for, like, a literal minute. It was obvious that he wasn't in the market after I'd made it very clear that *my* market was, you know..."

"Open for business?"

"Yup. And I've been in nothing but linen shirts and the shortest short-shorts all summer. Anyone passing this up is probably on the v-train."

There he is. There's the Brison Dallas I know.

"At any point did you plan on telling me?"

Brison cocks an eyebrow. "And ruin the fun? No."

He roars with laughter, and I bury my face in my hands.

"I'm never talking to another boy ever again," I grumble. "I'll just be one of those gay best friends in the romcom who has no love life of his own. They seem so happy."

"Yeah, maybe. Or maybe you'll be a super successful producer and the boys will be throwing themselves at you."

"Right," I say through my fingers. "Because tonight was such a success."

"You sold out, didn't you?"

"Yeah, but I might have ruined things with my best friend in the process."

Brison shrugs. "Chrissy and I have a blowout fight, like, once a month. You guys will be fine."

I ponder this while Brison stares at the stars for a while. Maybe things really are over with Alan. Or maybe this is just the first time either of us has been honest about something that matters. Sure, Alan is always putting on a show. But maybe so am I. It's kind of hard to open your arms to your best friend when they're so busy being folded all the time. The Peter Thompkin, Junior Curmudgeon act is entertaining enough, but it doesn't hold an audience for very long. There was an updated version of me tonight, and it might be one I like a lot more. Peter Thompkin, Sellout Hit Maker.

"So when's the next show?"

Brison's voice returns me to the picnic table.

"What?"

"Wasn't it called *The* First *Annual Mason County Drag Extravaganza*?"

"Uh-huh."

"Then there needs to be a second. Obviously."

A cool breeze tumbles across the park. It smells like the end of summer.

***

"But all in all, *this* reporter found the night to be anything *but* a drag. Reporting from Mason County, I'm Trey MacLachlan."

When the news returns to the reporting desk, my father lowers the volume. A dish soap commercial plays while I refill my water and Dad reaches for the pepper. Nobody has said a word about the way last night ended. Or how it started either. I could just take their attendance as a win and let the rest go. My sister is coming home next week. She'll have her new internship to talk about, and the house she shares with friends from school, and the drop-in hockey league she's joined. The dinner table will be as loud as a dressing room full of drag queens.

"You did a good show, Pete."

Dad says it with his eyes still on the TV. I wait for an addition, something that will kick the compliment out at the knees. But today there isn't one.

"Oh. Thanks. Yeah, it went okay."

Dad nods.

"And I liked all the costumes," says my mom. "Makes me wonder about getting the sewing machine out from the basement."

"If you need any sequins, I'm sure you could just give the town hall a quick sweep."

Mom laughs, and we fall back into silence for a while. I poke at the steamed carrots on my plate and consider leaving it at that. But leaving things unsaid hasn't gone well for me lately, all things considered.

"I didn't think you were going to come," I say cautiously.

Dad casts a glance toward my mom, and I catch her avoiding it.

"Well," she begins. "We had a nice time."

"We just didn't really think it was going to be our kind of thing," my father adds.

"Right," I say, searching their faces for the *something* currently being talked around.

"So why *did* you come?" I ask as lightly as I can manage.

A hose sputters to life across the street.

"Gerald Corres called," my mom says after a moment.

The spray splatters dully against wooden slats before landing on our neighbor's garden bed.

"He called the house," she continues. "It was nice."

I blank, not entirely sure where to go from here.

"He just . . . called you?"

"He told us how hard you kids had all been working on the show," Dad says with an almost auditory shrug.

The two avoid eye contact, making a point to show how nonplussed they are by the whole thing.

"It was good to see Gerald," Mom offers. "He seemed really in his element."

I watch the two of them as my father nods, wondering if they were planning on ever telling me this part of the story. Feeling like I need desperately to know what that conversation sounded like and also needing to never find out.

"He seems happy," my father says, and my mother hums in agreement. "Seems like he's doing well for himself."

My toes unclench. Maybe whatever happened between my father and Gerald is allowed to stay in the far-flung past. Maybe the three of them cheering for a gaggle of teenage drag queens at the back of the Mason Town Hall mended a little bit of whatever was between them. Even if it did take Gerald extending the olive branch. Even if I can still picture the high school version of my father as the kind of guy at the other end of Alan's baseball bat. The current version of him, the one doing the cheering, put himself between Jenna's protesters and a bunch of gays. That has to count for something.

"But those people out front, Pete," Dad says with a shake of his head. "Don't pay them any mind."

He leaves it at that. The subject of the fight has yet to arise, and I'm getting the feeling that it won't get much airtime in the Thompkin house. But I think Dad is almost proud of me for it.

Mom stares into the distance, a look of disdain crossing her face. "Apparently Jenna Wilbur is planning to throw a show of her own," she informs us. "Although I don't think the council should let her, given how her group conducted themselves."

"Jenna is throwing her own show?" I ask, stunned.

"It's something to do with *clean values*, or *family values*, or something like that." Mom rolls her eyes.

"I'd show up to protest," Dad says with a smirk, "but I'd hate to give her the impression that I give a shit."

Mom chuckles and swats at him. "I just don't know how she can walk around with hair like that," she says, cutting into a piece of cold chicken. "But it *does* take all kinds, doesn't it?"

I clear my plate and wash it off in the sink. My parents talk half-heartedly about the squirrels getting into the garden. *Shoes for the whole family at half the price, at The Shoe Barn!* the television proclaims.

CHAPTER TWENTY-SIX

MASON COUNTY'S MOST INTERESTING VIRGIN

"Well, students. It's that time of the year again," Bailey Hayes announces through my phone screen. "Back to school. But what the hell are you gonna do with your makeup? Let's dive into some back-to-school looks that are going to turn heads and maybe even up your grades."

Bailey Hayes makes no guarantee about your grades or their status in relation to the use of her makeup guide, adds a voice.

I click my phone off and slip my backpack on before walking out the front door. Children with backpacks larger than themselves amble up my street on their way to Mason Public School, while plaid-skirted teenagers in blue polo shirts make their way to St. Beatrice Catholic. I walk the four blocks to school while trying to focus on nothing but the leaves already collecting on the sidewalk.

In the clamor of the gym, I take a seat on the edge of a bleacher and tap my foot while waiting for the annual slog of the first day assembly. A stream of nervous and overly confident ninth-graders filter in and the place fills with the buzz of reunions. I scan for Alan, not entirely sure what I'll do when I find him. A twang of anxiety flicks through my chest as I find him on the other end of the bleachers, talking spritely with some girls that I recognize from the *Drag Extravaganza*. Alan is wearing a corduroy and floral ensemble, which he's actually pulling off. He looks good. The girls hang on his every word, tittering while he shrugs in a display of *what can I say?*

Alan glances toward the doors and I drop my eyes to the ground.

After the assembly I hang my bag in my first-floor locker. Next to me is Brie Kelland, draped in a witchy drawstring dress while pressing her face up against Luke Degraph's threadbare mustache. As they lock themselves together, it becomes official that everyone but Peter lost their virginity this summer. But the sting is cushioned by another realization, I may still be a virgin, but I'm willing to bet that none of the other virgins in this school successfully broke up a bigot blockade by firing a team of drag queens at them. I'm also willing to bet that none of the virgins in this school followed that up by pulling a reverse gay bashing.

So I think it's safe to say that I'm Mason County's most interesting virgin.

But I still hope that somewhere out there, Lorne the Soft-Serve Guy is slipping on the organic, fair trade linoleum of his alternative school. I catch Alan's eye as he closes his locker door just down the hall. I wave. Alan's face drops before he turns and walks off to class.

When lunch arrives I scope out the packed cafeteria, filled with microwave mung and the sweat-lined smell of conglomerated teenagers. Alan is missing.

"Congratulations, Peter."

I turn to find Chrissy standing behind me. She clutches a paper coffee cup, already leaning into the girl-who-loves-fall aesthetic.

"Your show was a success. A real hit, even," she observes from within the wrappings of her scarf.

"Yeah . . ." I reply, unsure how to proceed. "Thanks."

"Brison and I can't wait for the next one."

"Oh, I don't know if there's going to be a next one."

"We'd love to volunteer, you see," she explains, sipping her coffee pensively.

What is happening? Is she distracting me before her Poster fans descend to rip me apart in a cloud of infinity scarves and iced coffee?

"Right. Totally."

"And I should say . . ." she continues, words counted methodically, "that I'm quite sorry for what Brison and I said about you and Alan last spring. And online. It was unkind, and I am not that person anymore."

Chrissy concludes her proclamation. She tilts her head, as if listening back to her own words and finding them acceptable.

"I'm sorry, too, actually," I say.

Sure, Chrissy is the worst, but maybe she's making an effort.

"And thanks," I continue. "Really. Thank you for stepping in like that. After the show. You didn't have to do that."

Chrissy cocks an eyebrow.

"Of course I did. What's the point of taking kickboxing lessons if I don't get to, like, rupture a homophobe's spleen?"

Chrissy throws a viselike hug around my neck before sauntering off, coffee held pensively at her mouth. It seems that I owe her a second chance. She did try to punch someone into organ failure for me.

"Hey, Peter!"

Blake Roy waves with lapdog enthusiasm from a table, Andy and Kirk joining as they spot him. I slide onto the bench and greet everyone far more warmly than I would have a few months ago. At first it feels like fakery, like I'm playacting at being some calmer, kinder version of myself. As if an alarm is going to sound and make an announcement: *Peter Thompkin doesn't hang out with people like Blake Roy! Quick, everyone throw tater tots at his head until he drops the act!*

But as I take out my lunch, I find that no alarms are blaring. At first I'm amazed that they're even talking to someone as flabby as me, what with their gig as The Knights of Rural Realness wrapped up. But this trio does have a habit of proving that I can be a judgmental cretin. Andy, Blake, and Kirk are actually pretty nice. Supportive of each other, even. They listen when someone at the table speaks and are quick to point out their friends' achievements with a proud gleam in their eyes.

"Kirk has been killing this new routine he's got us on, Peter," Andy informs me. "It's pretty wild, but, like, Kirk is the king when it comes to yoga workouts."

Kirk shrugs modestly. "I'm just naturally flexible."

"No, dude," Blake maintains. "You've, like, really worked on your flow and it's honestly inspired me to incorporate yoga into my daily routine."

"Okay, man, sure," Kirk says, swatting away the praise and giving me a look. *Can you believe these guys?*

"So when's the next show?" Blake asks, suddenly all business.

I choke on my orange juice.

"Guys, really, I don't think—" I begin.

"Hey, when are you guys doing your next show?"

We all look to the head of the table to find Jamie Johannes standing there.

"Hey, Jamie!" greets Kirk.

"I don't . . . I don't really know," I answer skeptically. "Why?"

"Uh, because of my band," JJ sighs, clearly weighed down by the burden of his own musical genius. "They want to play your next show."

I nearly laugh at the joke until I notice the four faces of sincerity waiting for my response.

"Sure, yeah," I manage. "You should talk to Alan."

"Cool . . . cool cool cool . . ." Jamie says as he floats off. Kirk watches him go and waves placidly.

"Have you guys seen the new Vin Diesel movie?" Andy asks, rattling the sludge of his protein shake. He drives off a plane *into* another plane."

When the final bell rings, I step out of the front doors of the school.

Buses to Ridgley and Port Anders fill up while a mass exodus of students hits the sidewalk. At this point in the afternoon I'm usually meeting Alan to get the full rundown on whatever drama, crush, or hairstyle revelation has filled his day. But today Alan isn't anywhere to be seen. I wait for a minute, then two, before turning to walk home.

CHAPTER TWENTY-SEVEN
AN IDIOT WITH A PURPOSE

"He doesn't hate you, Peter," Tilly chides, disappearing behind the massive wheel of the antique tractor collecting rust beside the barn.

"Of course he hates me," I continue as I follow her, picking long grass from the lawn and tearing it into tiny pieces.

"Alan doesn't have a hateful bone in his body."

"The human body has, like, a trillion bones, Tilly."

"Talk to him!" she presses. "You're never going to squash this thing if you both keep coming to me as your middleman."

From the other side of the metal monster, Tilly turns her face to meet the wind coming over the field. Alan's ongoing silence has felt unnatural. Like watching Abbott without Costello, or seeing Bailey Hayes without a piece of jewelry that cost about as much as an SUV. It's become increasingly apparent just how much of my life used to be filled by Alan. Part of me is mad at him, but another part of me is mad at myself. The longer this plays out, the more useless it begins to feel. Best friends are supposed to put their differences aside and plot revenge against the boy who slighted them. We should be scheming to ruin Lorne's life, not pulling the silent treatment on each other. We should be finding a way to get him on the No Fly List or replacing his body wash with fire ants. You know, things that best friends do.

Since show night, time for contemplation has steered me into a new anxiety. One that my Top 100 Movies poster just doesn't have the power to counter-attack. The oncoming school year towers menacingly over me, and I feel as if I'm in ninth grade all over again. Who am I going to be if not the guy hiding behind the big gay quantum anomaly that is Alan Goode? Am I going to have to make new friends? Am I going to be totally alone for the rest of the year? Oh my god. Are Andy, Blake, and Kirk going to be my new friends? I don't have the upper body strength to survive that.

I may have lost my mind a little last month, but it did have a way of keeping me grounded in the present. Poking incessantly at my own thoughts hasn't just made me fear for my social future, it's also throwing Tilly's point into the harsh light of day. She's been caught in our cross fire long enough. She may default to keeping the peace, but maybe I've been taking advantage of that. And maybe I should do better by the friendships I haven't already torpedoed with my nuclear weapons of social incompetence.

"So how did things land with you and your grandmother?" I ask.

Tilly exhales and shakes her head. "Your guess is as good as mine at this point. She doesn't want to talk about it. And that's kind of all there is to say."

I nod, searching for something to say. A quick joke to water down the moment, or even some jab at Tilly's grandmother. But sometimes there isn't anything to say. Maybe sometimes our families just drop us hard enough to break a little. Tilly slides an arm over my shoulder as she guides me back toward the barbecue, the noise of which is drifting across the yard. "Let's have some fun tonight," she suggests. "We've earned it."

We round the corner of the barn and find the mini-giant that is Blake Roy.

"Have you guys seen Alan anywhere?" he asks.

I get the feeling that he wants us to think that he doesn't care one way or the other. Tilly raises an eyebrow before turning to Blake and placing a hand on his sizable forearm.

"He's not able to make it tonight, babe."

"Okay, cool," Blake quips, smiling thinly and looking back as if someone called his name. "No worries."

An errant Frisbee whizzes past. Blake runs to catch it with the snapped focus of an oversized Labrador. The real dogs, who recently hunted me like a prized quail, zip eagerly after him. Blake catches it and they collapse into a literal doggy pile.

"What's going on there?" asks Tilly, watching him go.

Blake leaps back up, full *Call of The Wild*–style, and bounds off toward the alpaca enclosure with the dogs in his wake.

"I'm starting to wonder if the only reason he wants to do another show is so he'll have an excuse to guard Ms. Culture's body," I whisper conspiratorially.

"Among other things he might do to her body," Tilly gasps as she pulls me back toward the party.

I push her back as she continues to describe their dragged-up love affair with a sweaty fan-fictional passion.

"Who wanted the veggie burgers?" Frank calls over the barbecue.

Nifoal and Cora raise their hands along with a few of Frank and Michael's friends. There are eight of them, and Michael took extra care to introduce us upon arrival. They're a smorgasbord of neon colored buzz cuts, piercings, tattoos, and a swirl of patches and pins. Peppered throughout is the rainbow of the Pride flag, the pastels of the trans flag, buttons reading *dykes on bikes* and *too queer to care*. It's easy to see why Michael was so insistent on THORR attending tonight's festivities. Tilly joins the picnic table in the yard and sits beside someone with Elvira, Mistress of the Dark emblazoned across the back of their arm.

"This tattoo, though!" Tilly marvels.

The two gab with delight while Nifoal and Cora delve deeper into whatever gossip they're spilling with Gerald, who is now dishing out further helpings of his potato salad to the twiggiest members of Rural Realness. Gerald hasn't said anything about his opening night phone call to my parents, and I'm happy to leave it that way. It's been a week since the show, but the whole thing feels like a memorable dream. Still fresh in my mind but with a silvery film hanging over it. My instinct tells me to leave it that way.

"Should the alpacas expect an encore this evening?"

Michael trots down the steps of his back porch and passes a Coke to his husband.

"They should not," I say with a laugh. "I left my running shoes at home."

He ambles back up to the porch and adjusts the sheet he's fashioned into a projector screen, tightening it against the breeze. I follow him up and watch as Tilly points out the spots on her arms and legs she will fill with ink the minute she's out of her grandmother's house.

"Aggie Culture was the real queen of the alpacas, anyway."

Michael, it seems, hasn't let Alan's absence go unnoticed. "It's too bad he couldn't make it," he says diplomatically.

"Yeah," I concede. "Things are just kind of weird with us right now."

"Drama? With drag queens?" Michael gasps. "I'd never have imagined."

"Okay, yes," I admit. "But I don't know. I think I might have messed that one up for good."

Michael considers this for a second. He nods to the burly guy next to Gerald, who is wearing a *Trans Rights Are Human Rights* T-shirt and has giant spacers in his ears.

"See Jeff?"

"Yeah."

"When we went to Mason Central, we both had a crush on the same boy."

I watch his face for the joke.

"You do know that your generation didn't *invent* the concept of being queer, right?"

"Yes!" I retort, clutching my heart. "But I like to think that we perfected it."

"So I tell Jeff, and he's all *that's great, babe! You should go for it!* But the next weekend I find Jeff and said boy just *attacking* each other's mouths behind the woodpile at Zack Wilson's bush party."

"I guess I'm the Jeff in this situation?"

"If Alan is the Michael, he's probably not feeling very good about himself right now."

"I know," I say, taking a sudden interest in the garden beds. "You two are still friends, though."

"We are," says Michael. "I never thought I'd be the type to hold on to high school friends." He watches Frank at the grill, who is now debating the results of last week's *Dragathon* with Nifoal Dressage. "Frank doesn't get it either, but he's not from around here. I think Jeff and I understood each other in a way that no one else did. It's hard to let go of that."

The food on the barbecue becomes little more than table dressing as I begin to lose my appetite.

"What did you do after it happened?"

Michael thinks on it for a moment. "I acted like it didn't bother me," he explains. "In high school it was like I had no real sexuality in the first place, since it's not like I was acting on it. So I had no right to be mad about it, you know?"

"Yeah," I agree. "I do know."

"But then I really *was* mad about it. And it made me feel like I was nothing. So I told him that."

My neck sweats return with a sticky vengeance. "What happened?"

Michael pulls himself to his feet as Frank waves him over to the grill.

"He covered my locker in cellophane and streamers and glitter and stuff. And when I opened it up, all these little bits of paper fell out, and he'd written *I'm sorry* like a million times." He regards Jeff fondly, who now seems to be regaling the table with a story about getting attacked by a giant mammal of some kind. "He knew I'm a sucker for big gestures."

Michael descends the steps to join Frank, who smiles and kisses his cheek. The barbecue sizzles and the table erupts into screams of disbelief at Jeff's daring escape. Andy and Kirk give solemn gym advice to Gerald. Cora gives a concealer tutorial to a trio of Michael's friends. The pink sky darkens over Mason as night begins to fall.

"I heard there was some kind of viewing party going on tonight?"

Bailey Hayes emerges from the sliding doors, adorned in an autumnal palette and wearing what might be the highest stacked wig I've seen yet. Her blonde curls have morphed into a beehive nearly half her height. The party cheers and pounds the table as she clops over to strike a dramatic pose at the railing, taking her audience in with mild interest. Bailey presses play on a nearby laptop, and the projector flickers to life. The glitzy opening riff to *Dragathon* starts playing while the party gathers closer in anticipation. As the sun sinks into the cornfields, the show begins.

***

The lights of Mason form a halo around the town, and I watch them glow from the back seat of Blake Roy's silver pickup truck. The sky is clear, and the stars gleam in perfect visibility through the open window. Tilly reaches over and turns up the volume on Blake's jangling folk music.

"What exactly does *snatched* mean, anyway?" Blake asks from the driver's seat.

Tilly clasps his arm and howls, all too happy to provide an answer.

The wind is cold against my face, and I close my eyes, trying to focus on nothing but the rushing over my ears. Trying to hold still in this moment. The future is glowing on the horizon, but right now I'm in a truck, in the wind, in a night that remains in the present tense. Trees whip by in the distance and an idea reveals itself to me. A big gesture.

"Hey, Blake," I say, poking my head between the front seats. "I have a proposition for you."

***

The Apartment was directed by Billy Wilder. *Goodfellas* was directed by Martin Scorsese. *Pulp Fiction* was directed by Quentin Tarantino.

I adjust the camera on my computer. It blinks green. I clear my throat.

"My name is Peter Thompkin," I begin. "Some of you might know me as the producer of *The First Annual Mason County Drag Extravaganza*. And some of you might know me as the guy in that video saying that thing about Brison Dallas. It's not a very flattering video. But then again, there are two videos of me falling on my ass from last month alone, so maybe that's my thing."

My eyes search past the screen, as if an answer might be written there. One that will tell me how to do this without looking like a very bad actor in a very bad movie.

"There's been a lot of stuff posted about me online. That I'm toxic, that I'm a total piece of shit, that my fivehead would be my only sellable feature if I could rent it out as a landing strip to small aircraft. I kind of liked that one. Sometimes it's just nice to see that people are putting in the effort, you know?"

My smile fades quickly, the attempt at a joke breaking apart on impact.

"If you came to our show, you'd know that I'm also a pretty decent producer when I put my mind to it. And that I'm a terrible dancer. Some people might even know that there has been some tension between me and my best friend, Alan Goode. Also known as Aggie Culture.

My eyes fall to the table as I search for words that land somewhere between *honest* and *horribly saccharine*.

"I've been thinking about it, and I can see that there's been a lot of performing going on. Drag, and videos, and everyone posting their hot takes about drag and the videos and me and Brison. It gets tiring. Putting on a show all the time, I mean. Performing the person you want to be. It's been brought to my attention that I can be a bit cutting. That I tend to go for the jugular instead of letting people get close. I have a habit of judging people before I give them a chance. It's easier to put people in a box, I guess. Because a box is going to, you know, put a nice set of walls between the two of you. But the only reason I'm making this video in the first place is because people keep proving me wrong. A prime example being that a month ago I wouldn't have been caught dead making one of these things. I've been surprising myself a lot lately, and everyone who saw me upside down on the stage of the town hall can tell you as much. I told myself I was doing it to try and save the show, but the show would have been fine without me. I did it because it looked like a fun time with my friends. Which it was. I produced the *Drag Extravaganza* because I thought it would make you all forget about the video with Brison. But I don't think I care anymore. I don't think I have anything left to prove. Brison isn't the person that I thought he was. And I'm probably not the person you think I am. I think I'm starting to care more about what I think of me than what you do."

I run out of steam and begin to pick at the cuticle that I'd eviscerated backstage during the show.

"Not that this has all been some grand moment of self-discovery. If anything, I have more questions than I did before. I just don't feel like performing that version of myself for you anymore."

I wipe sweat from my face. The heft of the summer heat has dropped, but the effort of keeping this video going is somewhere close to Herculean.

"I want Alan to know that when I was onstage with him, I liked that version of myself. I was an idiot, but at least I was an idiot with a purpose. When I get out of my own way, I actually have a pretty good time. And most of the time, the person getting me out of my own way is Alan Goode."

I think for a moment before plunging into the grand finale.

"If you liked *The First Annual Mason County Drag Extravaganza*, thank you for coming. And if you protested the show, thank you for coming. It felt good to tell you where to shove those signs. To both camps, I'll say this:

If you're a student at Mason Central Secondary, you might want to pay attention to the announcements tomorrow. I'm sure it'll give you a lot to post about."

I reach out and turn the camera off. Then I post the video to *@ptkns1358.*

CHAPTER TWENTY-EIGHT

PETER THOMPKIN, ARTISTIC PRODUCER

"Will all members of The House of Rural Realness please report to the art room at the beginning of the lunch period?" a voice booms over the school's PA system.

The art room is bustling with the chatter of our newly assembled team. There's Abbie Lillard, who told me that she's always been interested in costume design. There's Scarlett Tillerman, who informed me in no uncertain terms that she will be doing my makeup for the next show. Beside her is Sam Watts, a tenth-grader who let me know that I'll be needing their services as a choreographer. There's Julian Kemp, a twinky ninth-grader on a warpath to be King Gay of Mason Central. Clearly he hasn't heard that the title belongs to Brison Dallas. Then there's Blake Roy, our head of security. We're seated around the art room eating our lunch and talking about the latest episode of *Dragathon* when Alan bursts through the door. He takes us in with alarmed confusion.

"Personally," I say, "I think Lucy Fur's nine circles outfit should get Best Look of the Season, but I do wonder if Bella DaBall's ball gown is going to win. That being said I wouldn't mind if Myah Tourney's powdered wig piece beat them all out."

I turn and beckon to Alan.

"Oh, hello, Alan. Won't you join us?"

Alan closes the door behind him before cautiously stepping inside.

"What's . . . what is this, Peter?"

Alan pulls at his Peter Pan collar, his Masc Wednesday Addams ensemble turning the heads of my drag-enthused assemblage. In response I hold my arms wide, a mad scientist displaying his unholy creation.

"It's the first meeting of the Mason Central chapter of The House of Rural Realness. Clearly."

Alan watches with unwavering skepticism as I cross the room and introduce everyone with their official position. "And then there's me," I say. "Peter Thompkin, Artistic Producer. Title pending the cosigning of our Artistic Director, obviously."

I nod to Alan, waiting for him to take the linguistic catnip of his new official title. He doesn't move and I begin to feel my grand gesture crumbling in my hands.

"What are you doing?" Alan asks, head tilted high, ready to flee.

"People keep asking when our next show will be. I figure we'll have to go bigger and better this time. More tech, more music, more queens."

Alan holds his silence. For a second I wonder if he's going to grab a nearby clay pot, fresh from the kiln, and hurl it at my face. Maybe that's what I deserve for thinking I could pull off a gesture as grand as this one. I'm not a grand gesture kind of person. The only gesture I'm any good at involves my middle finger.

"The people are demanding a second show," I try, confidence warbling beneath my feet. "Who am I to deprive them of one?"

Alan appraises us, scrutinizing these fresh additions with implacable calculation. His face, which I can normally read easier than a book of ABCs, remains closed to me as he impassively crunches some numbers.

Then he turns to leave.

"Listen," I try, making to follow him. "Alan."

Alan pulls the door open to reveal Chrissy McPhee, her iced coffee clinking as she slips past Alan into the room.

"Okay, sorry I'm late! But it is *not* easy to get iced coffee when the nearest Starbucks is an hour away. My name is Chrissy," she continues breathlessly, "and my dear friend Peter has brought me on to be your social media manager. I cannot tell you how excited I am to be representing this amazing group because representing underrepresented groups is really—"

"Thanks, Chrissy," I say as I rush past her. "Why don't you tell them about your campaign design? I'll be right back."

"Hey, Peter," someone calls as I bolt through the door. Monica Whitehead and friends wave from a wall of lockers.

"When's the next Extravaganza?" one of them asks.

"Let me get back to you on that!" I shout over my shoulder.

Alan is wrestling open his locker when I finally catch up to him. He doesn't acknowledge my presence and instead begins to root around the already overflowing locker contents. A stack of notebooks clatter to the floor and I stoop to gather them.

"That really fucking hurt," Alan says.

I don't have to ask him to clarify. He doesn't elaborate, and we sit in the filth of the moment for a bit. A locker slams down the hall, followed by the broken-voiced jeering of some baby ninth-graders.

"Yeah," I nod.

"Because I am jealous of you a lot of the time, you know."

Alan continues to gather things from the back of his locker, already filled only a few days into the school year. A lime green wig falls on his face, followed by a single clown shoe. The shoe barely registers next to the thing he just said.

"What?"

"Backstage at the show. You said I'm jealous," Alan says, producing a hairbrush. He sets it aside and keeps digging. "And I am. You're not scared of telling people what you really think." His daily-use makeup bag slips out, and I catch it before adding it to the growing pile of locker droppings. "And sometimes I should just tell a boy what I think instead of hating myself when he doesn't pick up my signals."

"Well . . ." I begin, finding my words as I go. "I'm jealous of you. A lot of the time."

A black corset flops to my feet, falling from the top cubby. "You let yourself be, you know, open and vulnerable with people, or whatever."

I resist the urge to try and cram the words back into my mouth. "And maybe sometimes I need to be honest with people about how I feel instead of just what I think."

Alan shoves a pile of Aggie Culture back into his locker and I pass him another teetering mass of drag. He drops it inside and I breathe again, grateful to break from our navel-gazing.

Alan clucks his tongue and evaluates my hair.

"You look like shit," he assesses, already taking the brush to my scalp. "Two weeks without me and you look like your parents have been keeping you chained to a radiator for seventeen years."

"I look fine," I protest, slapping at his hands.

"*I* look fine," Alan corrects.

He wipes away the tears in his eyes before picking at my hair again. And because I'm such a good friend, I let him.

"You look like you're named Greggory," he says tersely. "Not *Greg.* Greggory."

"My parents said they almost named me Christopher."

"Ew." Alan sneers.

"I know. I'd probably have, like, a rattail and a boa constrictor."

"You'd probably wear a necktie over a polo shirt."

Alan tosses the brush back into his locker, where it lands with a clunk, before pulling out the dented form of Helen Bunt.

"I know you're mad," I say, laughing. "But I didn't think you'd resort to violence."

Alan presents me with the baseball bat. When I don't take it, he just nods like an impatient swan until I do.

"What are you doing?" I ask incredulously.

"I'm giving you Helen Bunt," he announces with drawn-out reverence, singing her name just a little.

I take it.

"Why?"

"It's come to my attention," Alan continues with reserve, "that I could stand to give you a touch more credit. About all you do for the queens of Rural Realness, and whatnot."

He waits expectantly.

"What does that have to do with Helen Bunt?"

"Consider it a knighting," Alan says with a sarcastic flourish. "Helen should be in the hands of the scariest member of Rural Realness. You know, for our own safety. And by all reports of what happened outside the town hall, that would be you."

"I got thrown on my ass for the second time in one night, Alan," I point out, pressing the bat back toward him.

"And next time, you'll be ready," Alan persists, pushing it back to me.

I nod and squeeze the rubbery grip. It may be silly, but I don't mind the weight of the bat in my hands. I might even feel a little of Helen Bunt's power flowing into my dainty little digits. *Scariest Member of Rural Realness* does have a glittery little ring to it. Maybe my barely contained rage issues aren't always such a terrible thing. Especially if they're the thing coming between my friends and the next person to pick up a protest sign.

I give the bat a twirl and immediately drop it on the floor with a tinny *clonk*.

"I shouldn't have lied to you," I tell Alan as I bend to pick it back up.

Alan shrugs.

"Really," I say. "I'm sorry."

"Well," Alan replies, exhaling and quietly restacking a pile of papers. "I'm sorry too. I might have been a bit harsh backstage, all things considered." He puts his palm under my manboob and flips it with a little sizzle, smiling like a child reunited with a lost dog. "Besides. I missed your *li'l tiddies.*"

"Gross."

Alan clicks his lock back into place before pulling me into a standard Goode Bear Hug. It smells like sweat, face cream, and lilac, as it always has. Alan retrieves his makeup bag with a grin. It pairs nicely with the hate-crime deterrent in my own hand, and altogether I think we make a nice pairing. He leads me back toward the art room, Helen Bunt swinging by my side.

That's it. I've made up my mind. I'm joining a baseball team. They probably shower together, right?

Through the art room window, I catch a glimpse of someone tall, with a warm face and the keen demeanor of a herding dog. My hand lands on Alan's arm as I remember the second part of today's plan.

"What?" Alan asks, fixing my shirt. "Flannel is cute, Peter, but we really need to talk about what all this red does for your complexion."

"Blake Roy," I tell him.

"What about him?"

"You thought he was cute."

"Of course I think he's cute. Look at that face."

"So maybe he thinks you're cute."

Alan jerks his head back and waits for a joke to arrive. When it doesn't, he simply unzips his makeup bag and pulls out a glue stick before throwing open the door and waltzing through it.

"Who knows how to block an eyebrow?" Alan asks his new charges.

Nobody raises their hand.

"We'll begin with a tutorial then," he proclaims, daintily stepping into professorial mode and striding into the center of the room. "I'll need a volunteer."

Several hands go up, but Alan points to Blake.

"You don't mind, do you?"

Blake grins and shakes his head. "Nope."

"All right," Alan says quietly. "I don't either."

They smile at one another, and for some reason it kind of hurts. For a second, Alan is sharing something with Blake that is a little world of their own. It's a world that is entirely separate from the one we share and the bruised feelings that are still filling it. But maybe that's just how it works. Maybe it always feels like this when you watch someone need you a little less.

Alan begins to apply the glue stick to Blake's eyebrows, and the Mason Central Secondary chapter of The House of Rural Realness huddles closer to take in their inaugural lesson.

Alan has the first layer of glue smeared into Blake's eyebrows when the classroom door opens again. Brison Dallas steps through and waves.

"Are you still taking new members?" he asks.

Alan looks at me. For the first time in a while, an entire conversation passes between us without a word.

"Totally," I call back. "Come on in."

ACKNOWLEDGMENTS

THANK YOU first and foremost to Khary Mathurin for saying yes, and for creating this book with me. I am so proud of what we made together.

Thank you to my many, many early readers for seeing what this book wanted to be and helping me get out of its way.

Thank you to Eric Coates for giving me a place to be and teaching me how to speak over a Shop-Vac.

Thank you to Scott Middleton for knowing that there was a book in me somewhere.

Thank you to Judith Rudakoff for telling me when I was writing dishonestly, and showing me how to do otherwise.

Thank you to Kevin Connery for taking the first red pen to Peter's inner monologue, and for too many other things to count.

Thank you to my parents and my brother, who have no idea where I came from but who keep me around nonetheless.

Thank you to Merlola Bordeaux. Alanis Percocet wouldn't exist without you, and neither would this book. When we get together it is like total, total and utter insanity. It's like two of the most gorgeous girls raising hell.

CURTIS CAMPBELL is a writer, comedian, and theater artist. His plays are mainstays of the Toronto indie theater scene, and he is the winner of the inaugural Second City Award for Outstanding Comedy. *NOW Magazine* has described Curtis's work as "razor sharp," the *Toronto Star* called it "pitch perfect satire," and Curtis's mother described it as "just not my cup of tea." Curtis grew up in rural Ontario and now lives in Toronto with an artist named Kevin and their dog, Pip. *Dragging Mason County* is his debut novel.